I looked across
mind could stop me, began running toward the light, staying at the edge of the woods that surrounded the church. Probably no one was there, since the Klan seemed to be congregated across the road, and I could get to the phone and call the sheriff or Daddy, anyone who might help Elizabeth and Quincy.

As I rounded the corner, making my way behind the gin to look for an entrance, terror seized me. There sat the brown Buick. I could only hope the phantom riders were across the street with their brood of murderers. Just as I got to the back door, I heard the pickups at the church start up. One of them tore from the scene, with the KKK crazies, as Mama referred to them, whooping like a bunch of school boys out vandalizing mailboxes or tipping cows. I had to hurry!

The blast that came next took the life right out of my body, and I fell to my knees. Flames shot so high in the air I could see them over the tall cotton gin as I jumped to my feet to run back toward the church.

"Liz Bess!" I screamed as I charged in the direction of the flames.

The Gully Path

by

Dr. Sue Clifton

Daughters of Parrish Oaks, Book 1

The Gully Path

Cover Art by *Tina Lynn Stout*

The Wild Rose Press, Inc.
PO Box 708
Adams Basin, NY 14410-0708
Visit us at www.thewildrosepress.com

Publishing History
First Mainstream Historical Rose Edition, 2014
Print ISBN 978-1-62830-611-8
Digital ISBN 978-1-62830-612-5

Daughters of Parrish Oaks, Book 1
Published in the United States of America

Dedication

With all my love, I dedicate this book to my children:
Tracy Clifton
Jeff Gentry
Niki Clifton Burchfield

Acknowledgements

With special thanks to my son Jeff,
who wrote a scene in the last chapter,
"The Promise"

Wormwood

Steeples catapulting to oceans of flames below!
Bodies ablaze, running, flailing!
Screams of agony!
Pleas for help and salvation!
Hopeless pleas.
Running, tackling, rolling, smoldering!
Pulsating blue lights!
Sirens!

.

Silence!
Surreal tranquility.
Desecrated crosses.
Sacred ashes.
Bodies and minds drained of tears.
Hope of heaven, eternal utopia.
Brotherly love.

(August 26, 1964)

.

It was 1964, and "Small Town," Mississippi was on fire. The blast could be heard for miles away. Flames illuminated the sky like the Seven Trumpet Judgments of the Apocalypse. Satan's meteor shower of racial bitterness drenched Bartonville, and Jim Crow and the floodwaters of hatred drowned the last vestiges of southern purity and peace and changed the town's name, or at least its meaning, to Wormwood. Then, as quickly as it had festered, it ended, and the long process

1

of healing began.

Cars stretched for miles, the longest funeral procession ever remembered in the county, behind two black hearses carrying the earthly remains of two unlikely heroes, one black, the other white. Even more unlikely was the procession of mourners with blacks and whites, and no racially designated order for the convoy as both proceeded to the same church, the same cemetery, the same eulogy. Centuries of hatred were buried for a day while mourners, like the fallen heroes, embraced each other (though some from a distance) not in the forever act of caring but in the temporary, guilt-driven moment of compassion and forgiving.

Book I

Where the Gully Path Begins

Chapter One
A Betterin'

I was born in the middle of Interstate Highway 55, northbound, in the fast lane. My life began in the fast lane, and I've been speeding in everything I've thought and done since. And I know it was northbound, because every thought that ever entered this not-so-gentle southern mind has by some fluke been tainted with what is deemed as northern liberalism, modern idealism, southern extremism, or, as my Confederate neighbors and kinfolk would call it, "nigga' lovin'," an abominable term…but the "lovin'" part was a term of endearment to me who has always judged those I love by their soul, not by the color of their skin.

Maybe it's all coincidence. Maybe I'm carrying the symbolism too far, reading too much into my birthplace. After all, in 1945, it was nothing more than a ramshackle, board-and-batten house on a gravel road in Mississippi. A four-lane highway wasn't thought of in that part of the country then and wasn't wanted, either. "Too much like Memphis," it would have been. "Might bring too many outsiders, no-gooders, especially Yankees—heaven forbid—into the state." Country folks needed nothing more than gravel roads. Two-lane-wide paved roads, preferably with no center stripe, would suffice. Progress in Mississippi was not digestible more than a tad at a time.

More than the road, the real symbol of the times was a brick-siding house, a symbol of temporary poverty. Brick siding was faking being something better than you were without totally leaving reality. But if you wanted "better" enough to fake it, then eventually you would attain better, maybe not to the point of real brick, but definitely better than board-and-batten or black tarpaper. Tarpaper and unpainted, weathered wood usually meant hopeless poverty with not much chance of bettering yourself and were mostly for po' white trash or for somebody's grandfather who lived before brick siding and didn't know its true meaning.

I was born a "betterin'," not in a hospital but at home in an unpainted board-and-batten house, delivered by the local doctor from Shadywood, Dr. Martin. Entering the world on the cotton-filled mattress of my parents' bed, I was protected from the could-have-been grime of a poor family's environment by boiled cistern water and the every day's scrubbing by an immaculate mother driven by a vision of bettering, regardless of the house she was forced to live in and raise her daughters.

Because I was the youngest of three, my birth seemed easy, but Mama said it was because of the exercise she got picking cotton that fall while she was pregnant with me. She picked cotton so she could buy a stylish long red cashmere coat from Goldsmith's in Memphis, so she would look like somebody who perhaps was a receptionist in a doctor's office or maybe a cotton-buyer's secretary, or a beautician. No one would suspect her of being a cotton-picker.

As betterin's do, we only lived a short time in the board-and-batten house, moving down the road to a better house, even better than brick siding. It was a new one that Daddy built from lumber salvaged from a Japanese prisoner-of-war camp. With indoor plumbing still not considered a necessity, the house maintained better status due to white asbestos shingles on the outside and one bedroom enhanced with elegant red Chinese wallpaper.

Chinese wallpaper must surely have been another symbol for betterin'. My mother didn't care that it seemed pretentious. Knowing what her station in life was to be, her nose was pointed toward middle class, and an outhouse hidden by mimosas and honeysuckle a hundred feet behind the house was not going to stop her.

My life had started at the board-and-batten stage, but I still didn't have quite as far to go to reach a level of being socially tolerated. Not accepted, but tolerated. My oldest sister Mattie Lynn had to start at the real bottom—the unpainted wood and black tarpaper stage—at the time when Daddy was a drunkard.

Even though Daddy was a drunkard, he had some prestige by owning the Waterin' Hole, a tarpapered shack of a juke joint, good economics since he could soak up his pleasures at wholesale price. Mama didn't like the drinking, but the aftereffects sent her into mad-dog seizures; Daddy's clientele always relieved themselves out back of the juke joint, which just happened to be in the front yard of the unpainted and tarpapered house.

The camel-breaker came one day when an old man peed in front of Mattie Lynn, who was only eight years old. Mama swore that would be "the last limp faucet her baby girl'd ever have to see."

That night after Daddy passed out from a rough day at the office, Mama sneaked down to the juke armed with matches and gasoline and relieved herself of the Waterin' Hole. She never told Daddy the truth about it, but he never rebuilt it. Soon after, Daddy quit drinking. He said his permanently crooked finger was broken in a fight and it cured him of his drinking desires, but I always wondered if that was more of Mama's wrath.

The betterin' got better and, when I was eight years old, after my grandfather died, we moved up the road again into Old Pa's older but much bigger house with a porch all the way across the front. It was a palace compared to the board-and-batten house, and to make it even better, Daddy put in indoor plumbing.

It didn't bother me that Old Pa had to die for us to get there, since I never liked the old goat anyway. As surely as Old Ma was an angel sent from the Southern Baptist Convention, Old Pa was a devil straight from the depths of hell. I was terrified of him. The only time I ever heard him laugh was when he accidentally locked little George Williford in our family's country store that was just a few yards from my grandparents' house. Old Pa found him two hours later with chocolate tears dripping over cheeks stuffed full of bubble gum.

After Old Pa died, Old Ma wanted us to move into the big house to be near her. Daddy turned Old Pa's store into a little two-room house for Old Ma. It never seemed quite fair to me, but it was what she wanted. I loved life in the big house, and I loved being close to Old Ma without Old Pa there to scare me. Old Ma was my best friend—my only friend, most of the time; we lived a long way from town and from anyone with little

8

girls my age.

It was in the big house that the real me, the real Sue Ann, began to surface: not a poor, or a betterin', or even a middle. I was something different, at least from what was expected in a sometimes poor but always pure southern family. I was considered distastefully unique by most, not misunderstood but just not understood at all. I was considered controversial: scorned and adored, abused and confused, hailed and helled.

Through my entire life I would battle, not only with my hometown but also with my own conscience, just to be me: not the façade of the gentle, weak southern belle, but a free spirit. Where did this spirit come from? What caused such a mutation of mint julep-ism? The only thing I could ever figure out was…

I was born in the middle of Interstate Highway 55, northbound, in the fast lane.

Chapter Two
Queen for a Day

"Rita Jean, run out to the hen house and get me some eggs. I'm gonna make boiled custard this morning, and Daddy will freeze it for us tomorrow afternoon. Uncle Marshall and Aunt Rose are gonna eat Sunday dinner with us, and we can sit under the pecan trees and eat frozen custard tomorrow afternoon."

"Mama, I can't right now. I just painted my nails and they ain't quite dry yet. Let Sue Ann get 'em."

"I'm busy. I've gotta find my old binoculars from the war that Cousin Adelle gave me, and then I'm going to the hideout," I yelled from the closet in the front bedroom where I was upside down, digging in a metal trunk.

I knew what was coming next without waiting for the reply. Mama always gave in to Rita Jean, especially when she was playing movie star. Rita Jean had her hair all up in big metal rollers that made her look like she had been tossed down from outer space. Sitting there with her legs crossed, swinging one foot with Mama's high-heeled house shoes on, she waved her long red fingernails in the air like she was at least eighteen years old.

"Put 'em in cold water like Mattie Lynn does and it won't take so long for 'em to dry." I offered this as if I were an expert at fingernail painting.

"Shows how much you know about girl things, Sue Ann. Cold water don't work. It just messes them up. I've worked too hard to mess these gorgeous nails up now. You could take a lesson or two in beauty yourself." Rita Jean waved her nails in the air again after blowing on them. She gave me a smile that was more of a smirk, because she knew what Mama's reaction would be.

"Sue Ann, go on out and get the eggs. Your sister is right. I swear, just look at you, cowboy boots and shorts. You're almost eleven years old and you still don't ever brush your hair. And such nice hair you've got, too. Lord, how I wish Rita Jean had gotten those pretty blonde curls instead of you. She'd know how to put them to work for her."

My blonde, curly hair was a constant source of displeasure and envy to both Mama and Rita Jean. Rita Jean was cursed, as Mama said, with plain old dull brown hair, and it was straight, at that. Even so, Mama kept a Toni at the house so that when one permanent wave wore off, she could give Rita Jean another one right away.

Mama lied to everyone, saying we both had naturally curly hair. She said we got it from her side of the family. The truth was Rita Jean got hers from Mama and I got my blonde curls from Daddy's side. Every time Mama made the statement, Daddy and I would look at each other and grin. I looked forward to the remark just so Daddy and I could talk silently to each other.

When I was coming out of the hen house, I noticed a tall, lean, light-brown figure approaching from the gully path, the new Saturday help for Mama. Daddy had rented the board-and-batten house to a colored family from the Delta and was only charging them ten dollars a month, plus the old lady in the family had agreed to help Mama on Saturdays.

I wondered how long this one would last, since Mama could never find help she could keep. Either they couldn't stand her demands or she couldn't stand their slow pace. Somehow, I sensed from the countenance of this person on the path that she might be different.

She walked deliberately, each step instinctively measured, her head held high and proud with just the slightest stoop to show her age, or her life, in miles. Her gray hair only hinted at the kinkiness common to her race as it lay close to her head, pulled back in a tight ball.

It wasn't until she came through the gap by the barn and entered the pecan grove that I realized there was a shadowy presence behind her. Announcing to Mama that her help had arrived, I hurried to the back yard with the curiosity and manners of a ten-year-old to welcome the new help and the shadow.

"I'm Nagalee, ma'am. I hears you all needs some Sa'day help."

"Yes, Nagalee, but I can tell you up front I can't abide no laziness. I expect six hours of work and I'll pay three dollars a day if you work good." Mama was not known for tact or "beating around the bush" as she called it.

Posing by Mama in the kitchen door, Rita Jean gawked at the tall, proud Negro lady as Nagalee returned the interest.

"Yo' girl 'bout thirteen, fourteen year old?"

"She's not quite thirteen yet, but she acts like a

teenager. She loves pretty clothes and takes a lot of pride in herself."

"She a fine-looking girl, 'bout the size of my Leonia. I ruther work for yo' daughter's ole clothes, if it be all right with you, Miz Taylor. I has a hard time keepin' my chillun in clothes for school. I got three at home still; one of my own, my son's boy, and this one here that 'longs to my daughter, Lucille."

Nagalee reached behind her and pulled the shadow to her side. Rita Jean's mouth flew open, Mama opened the screen door to get a better look, and I flopped down on the bottom step just to be closer to the most beautiful child I had ever seen.

Her skin was not light brown like her grandmother's, but taupe, the color of Rita Jean's stockings she wore on Sunday morning. Her hair hung in thick, black crinkles over her shoulders and cupped around her waist. Looking down not in shyness but in purposeful distance, the girl sensed her difference from both her grandmother and the strangers she was forced to confront.

"My name is Sue Ann. What's yours?" I was determined to get to know this magnificent creature.

The child looked up and, with eyes the color of a summer fern, smiled. "I am Liz Bess. Pleased to meet you."

"My word, what a beautiful child! Are you positive she's your granddaughter?"

Even if my mother had possessed tact, she would never have thought it necessary to use it in talking to a Negro.

"As sure as these two hands are that pulled her from my daughter's pain into this mean ole world."

Nagalee stiffened her shoulders as she spoke. Mama had met her match.

"Well, she's a little shorter than Sue Ann, so you can work for hand-me-downs for her, too."

"Not needed, ma'am. Her mama take care of her clothes. She don't need none, but Leonia do. Leonia just got me, no rich city mama to take care of her. If y'all give me my orders, I be 'bout my work. I don't likes to talk, jes work 'til the job be done. Liz Bess, you jes sit here on de step and wait for me. Here's yo lunch. Don't get in nobody's way." With her head held high, Nagalee followed Mama into the kitchen.

"Yes, Mama. I'll just read my book and wait."

Liz Bess removed her book from her pocket and began reading. It was obvious this was a routine procedure for her.

"Why didn't you stay home with your sister Leonia?" I was both curious and trying to find a way to become friends with Liz Bess.

"Mother told Mama not to ever leave me alone, not even with Leonia. She's afraid someone might hurt me or kidnap me. She pays Mama to keep me so Mama minds what she says."

"Why don't your real mama keep you?"

"You should say 'doesn't,' not 'don't.' Mother works in Memphis. She's a model there and works a lot. She doesn't want me to be brought up in the city where there's too much crime."

"Why don't you talk like other colored folks? You talk better than most white folks."

"Mother paid a tutor to teach me when we lived in Beeville. She wants me to be smart. She says I'm going to be somebody important some day."

"You can keep correcting my talking like my teacher at school does, if you want to, Liz Bess. I want to be somebody important, too."

The distance between the goddess child and myself had closed, and I knew I had found a friend. Her beauty would not be an obstacle to our friendship. I could thank Rita Jean and Mama for that.

Nagalee ironed a basket of clothes in half the time it took Mama's last help. Every piece looked as if it had been laundered by Delta Chinese. In fact, Nagalee worked so hard and so fast that Mama was running out of work for her to do.

Liz Bess's imagination was as big as mine, and we never lacked for things to play. In a short time, two playhouses stood ready for occupancy, constructed out of boards and tin cans from our garbage dump. We were on our way to the barn hideout when I looked up and saw Old Ma coming down the path to the house.

"Uh, oh," I said. "I bet it's ten o'clock. There comes Old Ma to watch *Fury* with me. We watch it together every Saturday morning."

"What do you mean, you watch *Fury*?" asked Liz Bess, drawing her brows together in puzzlement. Liz Bess stared at me, waiting for my explanation. I realized then that she didn't know what a TV was.

"Come on, Liz Bess. I'll show you."

"Hey, Old Ma. This is Liz Bess, my new friend. She lives in the board-and-batten house. Ain't she pretty?"

"Don't say 'ain't,' Sue Ann. Pleased to meet you, ma'am."

Old Ma scrutinized Liz Bess with kind wonderment. "You got some pretty cat eyes, don't you?

Must have Injun blood in you. That right?" Old Ma wasn't being rude, just honest, as always.

"Maybe. Mama says we have Indian blood in our family."

Liz Bess did not seem offended, having a good head for distinguishing sincere interest from cruel curiosity.

"*Fury* on yet, Sudi?"

"Should be. Liz Bess ain't, I mean hasn't, ever watched television before. I want her to watch *Fury* with us."

"It's okay with me, but you better ask your mama, Sudi girl."

I didn't have a clue why I'd have to ask Mama if Liz Bess could watch television, so I did not ask. I wished later that I had.

Right at the end of the show where Fury was trampling a rattlesnake in order to save Joey, Mama walked through the living room and pitched one gigantic fit.

"Sue Ann Taylor, what do you think you're doing? Get that colored child out of my living room right this instant! You know whites and colored don't mix!"

"We ain't, I mean aren't, mixing nothing, Mama. We're just watching *Fury*."

"Get her out of here now, Sue Ann, or I'll wear your butt out with my butter paddle!"

Nagalee never looked up from the ironing board, but I could see her veins tense in her thin neck and she began ironing faster, pounding the iron into the padded wooden board.

"Come on, Liz Bess. We can have more fun outside. I'll show you how to play Queen for a Day."

Embarrassed and confused by Mama's actions, I was determined to make it up to my new friend by letting her be queen first. She could give out the orders and I'd be her servant, whether Mama liked it or not.

"I like being queen. I was supposed to have a queen's name, Elizabeth. Mother left when I was just a few days old, and Daddy Bay had to fill out papers to name me. Mother said my name was to be Elizabeth like the queen, but Daddy Bay didn't know how to spell it. He named me Liz Bess."

"Why didn't your grandmother spell it for him?"

"Mama can't read or write. I try to get her to let me teach her, but she's too proud. I think Mama's name was supposed to be Natalie, but it ended up Nagalee."

Queen for a Day became our favorite game. In the barn hideout, I built Queen Liz Bess a throne out of hay and made her a crown out of cardboard. When she walked through the pecan grove, I carried her pecan-sack train and yelled, "Hail to the Queen," which later turned out to be "hell to the queen." How something so innocent could turn into such a source of displeasure for Mama made no sense, but it did.

During supper, Mama asked me if she saw me actually bowing down to "that green-eyed Nigra girl." I tried to explain that it was just a game, but Mama wouldn't listen. Old Ma tried to take up for me by telling how Daddy always played with the children of the tenants, but nothing mattered to Mama. I was never to play with Liz Bess again unless she was going to let me be queen and her be my servant, and that was only when she came to work with her grandmother. While she was at it, she told Daddy how I had the audacity to bring Liz Bess into the living room and sit alongside her to watch television.

"If we allow this kind of socializing, next thing you know they'll be wanting to go to school with our children and eat alongside us in restaurants, like I've heard they do up north in some places."

Even Mama could not have predicted the wisdom she was speaking at that moment. Mama's warning would later become the crusade of the '60s, and the games we played as children would turn into a reality referred to as "equal rights."

Chapter Three
A Run-in with a Booger-Bear

"Sue Ann, I'm going to town. Did you say you wanted to go with me?"

"Yeah, Daddy. Give me a minute to get my boots on. I need a new notebook. I've 'bout filled up my old one, and if I have enough money left, I want to buy a new Nancy Drew mystery."

I had more passions—not hobbies but passions—as an eleven-year-old girl than most adults have in a lifetime. My heroes were Nancy Drew, Roy Rogers, the Lone Ranger, and an imaginary Indian girl I made up named Sacahonta.

I pictured myself as her, smart like Sacagawea and brave like Pocahontas, both running with wild ponies and following their own set of rules, more brave than squaw, more bear than deer. Contradictory to my image of Sacahonta was my insistence on wearing cowboy boots rather than moccasins, although I would have preferred moccasins to the pointy-toed flats Rita Jean wore.

And of course there was my desire and ability to write my own series of mysteries starring the genius girl sleuth Susan Taylor. I considered my writing talent to be a fluke of heredity since no one else in my family wrote—or read much, for that matter, with the exception of Old Ma, who read her Bible for hours daily. But then, my parents were never exposed to such literary geniuses as Carolyn Keene, as I had been privileged to since discovering *The Hidden Staircase* in the school library at the ripe old age of eight. I had read every Nancy Drew mystery in the Shadywood School library at least twice and had checked out a few from the Bookmobile that came around once a month.

"You mean you've wrote a whole notebook full, Sue Ann? Lordy be!"

"No big deal, Daddy. I wrote one story that was thirty-four pages long when I was just in fourth grade."

Only Daddy and Old Ma were impressed with my writing abilities. Of course, no one in my family had read any of my literary endeavors, but Old Ma had listened attentively while I read her chapters I thought were particularly brilliant. Old Ma also listened to me read the love letters I got from Sid Moore in school.

I would have never trusted Rita Jean with this information, knowing she'd never believe me capable of having a boyfriend anyway. Practically on a daily basis I heard, "Cowboy boots and dresses to school! You ought to get an A-plus for tacky, Sue Ann."

I did have one literary critic, and her encouragement and praise was motivation enough. Liz Bess was my best friend in the whole wide world, which was actually not very wide in sixth grade. We met as often as possible in the big gully. Mama pitched such a fit about us playing together ever since Queen for a Day that we had become secret pals, making the friendship more beguiling.

The gully was a utopia for the two of us, a place where we refused to acknowledge that we were racially different. In fact, we preferred to think of ourselves as

Indian and one, I being Saca and Liz Bess being Honta. Our salutation and our farewell were always the same. Liz Bess would speak first, holding her hand up in front of her face with fist turned outward facing me stoically and say "Saca!" I would follow suit, fist out, expressionless, answering "Honta!" Giggling, we'd become ourselves, totally oblivious to the southern taboos of our elders.

We had a secret sign to let each other know when we would meet in the gully hideout. I'd hang a red coffee can on the fence post at the end of the pecan grove. When Liz Bess got home from school, she would see it. Since there was only one colored school in the area and the kids had to be transported from a long ways, Liz Bess always got home later than I did.

Nagalee, proud for her granddaughter to have me as a friend since her real mother would not allow her to have Negro children for friends, always let Liz Bess come when I signaled. She also never mentioned anything about our meetings to Mama when she came to work two Saturdays a month. I didn't understand Liz Bess not having friends, but she said it was okay. The kids made fun of her light skin and green eyes, so she never went outside for recess, choosing to stay in the classroom and help the teacher, or read what few books her school had.

Daddy let me out at Sterling's Five and Dime while he went around to the hardware store. I was just about to go inside when I heard the high-pitched girlish taunting of the local redneck bully, Booger Melton, nicknamed at school for his favorite snack. Booger sounded like a girl, but he was mean as a yard dog and had two poor children cornered by the colored service window of Nelly's Ice Cream Shack, trying to take their ice cream cones away from them.

"Where'd you niggas get money fer ice cream? Betcha stole it!"

Booger grabbed the ice cream from the little boy, who looked to be about six years old. The little boy began to cry, and the girl with him stood up and demanded that Booger give it back.

"You green-eyed nigga! Who you thank you talking to?"

Booger pushed the girl to the ground and began kicking her. It was then I realized this was Liz Bess on the ground and the young boy with her was, in fact, her first cousin, Ben, Jr., who also lived with his grandparents.

Without thinking of how my actions would be judged, I yelled for Booger to stop, ran across the street, and tackled him, pulling him off of Liz Bess. Booger retaliated by knocking me to the ground, straddling me, and locking my arm behind my back as he pushed my face into the dirt.

Several adults, both black and white, viewed this scene from a distance but offered no help. Mr. J.T. Harvey, local rich man who pretty much owned the town, witnessed the whole thing, passing within a few feet of Booger's assault, and never even turned his sunglasses-covered eyes in my direction to acknowledge any sympathy or thought of saving me from this redneck pulverization as he walked into his office building without so much as a glance back.

It seemed hours before someone finally rescued me from Booger's headlock, but I guess it was just minutes; otherwise, I'd be dead and unable to finish this narrative. A nice-looking young man who I did not know came out of the Harvey Building, probably from one of the law offices, and did not seem to mind one bit getting his white shirt all dirty by picking Booger up by the overalls straps and holding onto him until I could get my footing.

"You all right, Liz Bess?" I helped her up off the ground.

"You ain't nothin' but a nigga-lover, Sue Ann Taylor! You better watch yore back at school when I get there." Booger sounded like a female panther about to pounce on her supper.

Liz Bess brushed off her dress and herded Ben in the direction of the Piggly Wiggly where Nagalee was.

"Thank you, Sue Ann," she whispered, as if afraid she would cause more harm to me by acknowledging my help.

"That's what friends are for, Liz Bess."

"You best find your daddy, Little Lady, before I let this wildcat loose." The young man held tight to Booger's straps as he flailed and kicked trying to get free. "That was a brave thing you did, taking up for those colored children. You needn't be ashamed. In fact, you should be proud of yourself."

"Thank you, sir. I'm not ashamed." Spitting dirt, I headed down the street.

You can always judge a person by their foot attire, and my rescuer was a perfect example of this. He had on the most beautiful snakeskin cowboy boots I had ever seen. (I got a really good look since I was eye level with them just prior to his removal of Booger from my back.) I think they were python, like the snake I saw on "Nyoka the Jungle Girl," a serial short that came on before the main feature on Saturday nights at the Palace Theatre.

The stranger's boots had black-and-white irregular patterns, with bits of snakeskin overlapping to show authenticity. Only a lawyer could afford such elegance. I knew they cost over a hundred dollars because I had seen them in a western catalog that was delivered to our house by mistake one time. It should have been delivered to Barney, Daddy's cousin and a real cowboy from Shadywood who I admired greatly. Before Daddy took it to Barney, I digested and memorized every page of it.

Running in the direction of the hardware store, I decided the notebook and Nancy Drew could wait until the next trip to town. Daddy was coming out as I ran through the door.

"Whoa, girl! What in the world happened to you?" Daddy was eyeing me up and down and started brushing dust from my blue jeans.

"You might say I ran into a booger-bear, Daddy."

I was quiet on the ride home from town. Daddy could sense I had a lot on my mind and finally broke the silence.

"You want to talk about it, Sudi?"

"I don't get it, Daddy. Why do white people hate colored people so much? Mama don't want me to play with Liz Bess, and Booger jumped on her and Ben just 'cause they had ice cream and he didn't."

"Not everybody is like Booger, Sue Ann. Booger's family is dirt-poor. He won't even go to school 'til cotton-pickin' is over, probably late October. His daddy is a sharecropper, and Booger's got to help the family or they'll starve to death, all eight of them. Seeing those colored children having something he couldn't have just set him off, I guess.

"Truth is, Liz Bess and Ben Jr. are probably higher class than he is. A lot of time it's the poor whites that pick on the colored. They're the only ones folks like Booger think they might be better than. It really tears them up when they think a colored person might actually have more." He shook his head. "It's a crazy world, Sue Ann. You just have to follow your heart as to how you react to these things, but try not to get hurt in the process, ya hear? Now smooth that hair down and try to look like you went to town with your daddy and didn't get in no town brawl, and don't you fret about your Mama not wanting you to play with Liz Bess. I'll have a talk with her when the time is right."

I brushed my hair down with my hands and ran my fingers through my curls, trying to get the tangles out. What I really didn't understand was how a big, important man like Mr. Harvey could just pass right by children being hurt, hiding under his sunglasses like he didn't see it or, worse still, didn't care. Daddy would have helped Liz Bess if he had been there. I don't know about Mama, but Daddy would have.

When I got home, I ran to the edge of the pecan grove and hung up the coffee can, needing to know that Liz Bess was all right. I waited impatiently by the post until I saw Liz Bess crossing her yard heading to the gully hideout.

The hideout was a rusty, tin-covered washout between two giant, red-clay peaks we loosely referred to as mountains. Inside, wooden apple crates filled the clay floor as makeshift cabin furniture.

I almost hugged Liz Bess when she entered the

hideout, I was so glad to see she and Ben were all right, but showing affection was something the Taylor family never did, not that I wouldn't want to. Liz Bess came in with a look of terror in her eyes and completely forgot about the Saca/Honta salutation as she dove right into the dissertation she had obviously been planning since the Booger attack.

"Sue Ann, you must never take up for me like that again in public. Mama said it is too dangerous. You might get those men in white sheets after you."

"White sheets? What are you talking about, Liz Bess?" I sat and watched Liz Bess pace back and forth on the red clay floor of the hideout.

"I don't really know. That's what Mama and Daddy Bay talked about when they didn't know I was listening. They called them 'night riders' and said they're white men who dress up in sheets and hoods and hurt Negro people who they think are getting too uppity. They hurt white people, too, who try to help Negroes. It was very scary, what they were saying." Liz Bess stopped pacing and crossed her arms as she stared down into my eyes.

"There was a young Negro boy about Leonia's age, named Emmett Till, who was murdered over in Tallahatchie County last year. Daddy Bay said the boy was from Chicago and didn't know any better and flirted with a white lady in a grocery store. That lady's husband and another man dragged that boy out of his uncle's house one night, beat him, shot him, and then threw his body in the Tallahatchie River."

"That's terrible!" I stood, facing my friend, certain my eyes reflected the outrage I saw in hers. "What happened to the white men? Did they get sent to the electric chair?" Naively, I assumed that such a hideous crime would certainly demand an equally hideous punishment.

"Nothing happened. They were found not guilty. Mama said that I am never to stand up to a white child again no matter what is happening to Ben, Jr. or me. I am to run to her or Daddy Bay for help."

"That's crazy! I'm not going to stand by and watch people get hurt like old Mr. Harvey did or those other grownups who were standing across the street. Daddy said 'follow my heart' and that is what I did and what I'll always do. No bed sheets are gonna stop me from doing it again, either." We both sat at the same time on the apple crate. I stared at Liz Bess, who stared quietly straight ahead for a few seconds before turning to face me.

"Sue Ann, you are my best friend, my only friend. Please be careful. Mama says big things are about to happen in the South. They talk about it in church. There's a man named Martin Luther King who wants Negroes to have the same rights as whites. Daddy Bay says if you could snap your fingers and all this would happen it would be great, but white folks won't stand for it. If Mr. King gets his way, whites and Negroes will go to school together and eat in the same restaurants. Signs that say 'colored' and 'white' will be a thing of the past. Daddy Bay says Negro young people will pay a big price for all of this with their blood. I am so scared, Sue Ann." At the same time, side by side, we propped our elbows on our knees and put our chins in our hands, both of us in deep thought.

We sat in fearful silence, wondering what Bay had meant by all of this. My thoughts were so torn. Being able to walk into Nelly's Ice Cream Shack with Liz Bess, sit down, and have a double dip of black walnut sounded wonderful, but Liz Bess was very different from the other Negroes I knew. But then, I really didn't know any other Negroes personally.

I needed to be honest with myself. Would I have taken such a liking to Liz Bess had she not been light-skinned and beautiful? What if she looked like Sadie Pugh's little girl, Roweena? Mama bought peas from Sadie every summer, and Roweena was always with her mother when they came peddling their produce. Roweena's hair stuck up all over her head like fuzzy worms and attracted lint like a magnet. Her teeth were bucked, and she was extremely dark-skinned, what Liz Bess called "blue." Roweena was also my age, but I never had any fascination with her like I did Liz Bess, nor did I make any effort to play with her.

Would Liz Bess and I be like Daddy and the children of the field hands on the farm where he grew up? Daddy played with them, all of them, when they were boys, but where were they now? They never visited on a Sunday afternoon. I could not bear the thought of growing up and never seeing Liz Bess. Surely the world would change for the better and would allow Liz Bess and me to be best friends for the rest of our lives. Hopefully, our kids would some day be friends, too.

"Sue Ann...Sue Ann! Supper's ready!" yelled Rita Jean from the back door of the house.

We departed from the gully as Saca and Honta, remembering our farewell sign as we did every day, but it did not seem like "every day" to me. The sun was going down like always, but would it rise again in the same way it had before this day? I had too much to think about and not enough information to make sense out of any of it. Worse still, I didn't know how long the darkness and ambiguity would last before it would be over, if it ever would.

Chapter Four
The Sunday Quilt

"Sue Ann, go down to Nagalee's house and tell her I won't be needing her on Saturday. I've got some business to attend to in Memphis and will be staying at Annie Bell's this weekend."

"Oh, boy, will Tommy be there? I haven't seen him in so long." I jumped up and down and clapped my hands, excited at the thought of seeing my cousin Tommy.

"You're not going. You and Rita Jean will stay with your daddy and Old Ma." Mama kept on putting groceries away, oblivious to the fact that she had burst my bubble.

"Dadgum it! I never get to go to Memphis," I mumbled as I stomped through the pecan grove.

Tommy was my favorite cousin, even though he was a city boy. There was so much to do when I visited him, like walk to the little store on the corner and buy popsicles, or ride the bus to the movie theatre, not to mention pouring out his daddy's whiskey that we found hidden in corners of the garage.

My Uncle Bud had at one time been a business partner in the Waterin' Hole. Once the business was "dissolved," he and his family moved to Memphis and sought out other means of employment, but my uncle had never given up the family pastime, much to the disappointment of his wife and children.

Tommy and I felt it was our duty to lessen the amount of drinking his daddy did and made finding his stashes a major goal of the Taylor Detective Agency that provided many cases for my Susan Taylor series.

I even learned how to ride a bike when I was at Tommy's. I didn't have a bike but hoped some day I'd get one for Christmas instead of the cheap, boring presents I usually got. Fat chance! I never got anything for Christmas that I really wanted.

Nagalee sat on the front porch, patching and adding to a beautiful quilt that looked to be several years old. Her experienced eye meticulously measured each stitch as her deformed fingers worked their magic.

"Mama says she won't be needing you this Saturday, Nagalee. She's going to Memphis." I looked around the porch and peeked through the screen door to the house. "Where's Liz Bess?"

"Her mama down from the city. She took her to town to spoil her some more, like she need it. She oughta be back d'rectly. You doin' all right, Miss Sue Ann?"

"Yes, ma'am." It irritated Mama that I said "ma'am" to Nagalee. I explained to Mama that she had taught me to say "ma'am" and "sir" to my elders and Nagalee was my elder. Mama gave up, and Nagalee and I continued to say "ma'am" to each other.

I had never seen Liz Bess's mother, except in a picture that Liz Bess had shown me, and I hoped she might drive up while I was there. I started a conversation both out of interest in what Nagalee was doing and also to delay leaving in case Liz Bess came back.

"Is it hard to quilt? It sure looks like it is." I sat in the chair beside Nagalee.

"It take practice, like anythin' worth doin' right, but is a real joy when it be finished. I made this 'un long time ago but keep addin' squares so's I can 'member all de 'portant stuff dat happen in de fam'ly. It be wearin' out, but I jes keeps patchin' it cause it so special. This here a Sunday quilt, only get put on de bed on Sundays."

"You sound like Mama, saving the good stuff for Sunday or some special occasion. Mama uncovers the living room furniture on Sunday, and we can turn on the air conditioner on Sunday afternoons if it's really hot. Why don't you keep it out so you can enjoy it every day?"

"'Twouldn't be as big a joy if'n it was out ever' day. Sunday is the Lord's day and is special all on its own; it a day to put your best forward. I wears my best clothes to church; I puts my Sunday quilts out. The best on de best for the best."

"Wow, these squares are beautiful!" I moved my chair closer to Nagalee to get a closer look.

One square sat in the middle of the quilt, dominated by a bright yellow sun with triangular rays emanating in three directions from its corner position, with the rest of the square consisting of dozens of tiny squares, each a different fabric—flannels, wool, even satin.

"They not just cloth. Each piece a special meanin'. See dat sun in dat piece? Dat Bay. Ever little piece of cloth unda dem rays has a story 'hind it."

"Nagalee, you should tell me the stories behind each piece and let me write it down for you. It would be like your autobiography."

"What dat mean, auto…?"

"That's the story of your life. You tell it, and Liz Bess and I can write it."

"No. Dis quilt tell de story by itself. My fam'ly will have de quilt. Dat all dat matter."

A long black car drove up in the yard, and a young black man in a plaid chauffeur's cap and fancy suit and tie got out and opened the back door. I walked to the edge of the porch in curious anticipation to meet Miss Lucille, Liz Bess's mother.

"Mother, this is my best friend, Sue Ann. Sue Ann, this is my mother, Miss Lucille Donnelly." Liz Bess stared adoringly at her mother and held tightly to her hand as they came up the porch steps.

"Pleased to meet you, ma'am." I walked over to Miss Lucille and offered her my hand like Liz Bess had taught me, explaining for our Queen for a Day scripts how it was the twentieth-century version of the curtsy.

"What a well-mannered young lady!" She took my hand and placed her other hand over it, giving it a little pat before turning it loose. "I've heard a lot about you, Sue Ann."

Mesmerized by the beauty of this city lady, I envisioned her as a fashion model. Light-skinned, though not as light as Liz Bess and not as brown as Nagalee, she looked like the Goldsmith's ads I had seen in the Sunday edition of the *Commercial Appeal* when I was visiting Tommy in Memphis. The elegant lady's high-heeled shoes must have added another three inches to her already stately frame as she floated rather than walked to sit majestically beside her mother on the porch.

"Mama, why do you insist on patching these old raggedy quilts? Look at your poor crippled hands. I told you I'd buy plenty of nice new thick blankets for you."

Nagalee stared at her daughter as if not believing her lack of understanding.

"A city blanket don't tell no stories, Lucille. Dey jes cover up thangs ought not be 'membered. Some day you gonna be proud yo mama set in de shade and sewed togetha these mem'ries. Least I hopes you live so long."

"Don't start with me, Mama! I've got to get back to the city now. Take care of my precious. Daddy, promise me you'll keep my little girl out of harm's way?" The grand lady stood, directing her orders through the screen door of the board-and-batten house.

Remembering the fight Liz Bess and Little Ben had in town with Booger, I wondered if Miss Lucille knew. As if reading my mind, Liz Bess gave me a quick warning glance that told me not to mention the incident, and I knew that her mother did not.

Bay walked out on the porch when he heard his daughter was leaving.

"Take care of yo'self, girl. You mighty precious to Mama and me." Bay emphasized the word "you" to remind Lucille that she was still their little girl.

Liz Bess followed her mother to the car, holding on to her like she would never see her again.

"You'll come again soon, won't you, Mother?" Liz Bess looked dejectedly through the car's dark window that had been rolled down for parting dialogue.

"Yes, girl. Don't you worry. Mind Mama and Daddy Bay, now. Watch the mail for some surprises. Remember your manners and your learning, and don't forget you are Elizabeth."

She spoke the name with dignity and superiority, the name conjuring up in my mind images of ornate robes and jeweled crowns over shoulders, and a head held elevated over lowly-postured subjects.

Miss Lucille reached through the window and pulled Liz Bess halfway in, giving her the biggest kiss and hug I had ever witnessed outside of television. The moment gave me cold chills. I dreamed of my parents showing me that kind of affection, but it was just that—a dream.

One night when I was little, I had called Daddy in before going to bed and said, "Let me tell you a secret, Daddy." When he leaned down, I gave him a kiss just like I had seen on television when David and Ricky kissed Ozzie and Harriet before going to bed. Daddy smiled and hugged me like he really liked it.

Then I called Mama in to repeat the performance, expecting the same result. I said, "Let me tell you a secret, Mama." She leaned down and said, "Okay, but don't kiss me. I've got cold cream on my face."

I don't remember what secret I made up at the last minute to cover up my disappointment, but I did not kiss her. Open affection with my parents would be an accolade saved for the Taylor sisters' adulthoods, a delay much regretted by my parents in their later years.

Liz Bess gazed pensively as the elongated car disappeared around the curve of the gravel road. Her mood changed quickly to melancholy, and I found myself unable to remove her from it. My suggestion to go to the gully hideout as an escape for Liz Bess's despair was rejected as she excused herself to the dismal depths of the board-and-batten house. Bidding my goodbyes, I took refuge from this scene in the hideout to contemplate what had just transpired.

What did Nagalee mean by her remarks about the blanket? How could a mother visit her perfect, beautiful child so seldom and for such short periods of time?

I decided that even though Miss Lucille openly displayed her love and affection to her daughter, Liz Bess was to her only a Sunday quilt, cherished for how she looked or what she could be rather than what she was. Persons, like special things, were to be treasured every day and not wrapped in brown paper or flour sacks, tucked away, brought out in their perfect states only on special occasions for a privileged few.

"Liz Bess Donnelly and Sue Ann Taylor are both unique treasures and will be cherished and reckoned with every day. I'll see to that." I made the statement aloud, standing and putting my hands on my hips to show my conviction. Liz Bess was my best friend, and together we would be seen and heard.

Chapter Five
Silas Metcalf Play De Boogie

When Silas Metcalf play de boogie,
Cotton rows jump, pound turn to bale
Train jump track, rail dun snap
All Taylor Spur unda Silas's spell.

.

When Silas Metcalf play de boogie,
Dish' rattle and fruit jar brokes
Old mens keep sittin', but stop der spittin'
Den gots plumb tobacco choke.

.

When Silas Metcalf play de boogie,
Time run away on all dem clocks
Milk dun clabber, egg dun scrumbles
And dem sittin' in de ice box!

.

When Silas Metcalf play de boogie,
Preacher thought de worl' cum to a end
De erth it quake, de church it shake
Old folks beg "Little longer, please, Jesus,
Friend!"

.

Now Silas Metcalf don't play no boogie,
Good Lawd dun calls him to his fate
But when us hear dat thunda, can't help but wonda
Is dat Silas banging past dem perly gates?

(November 28, 1956)

One Sunday afternoon, there was a knock on the back door. Standing there was a tall, blue-black man with his back pressed tightly to the screen door, looking like he was trying to blend in with the white outside wall of the house—an unlikely scenario.

"Is yo daddy home?" he asked with darting glances right and left like he was trying to ward off an attack.

"Daddy!" I yelled loudly, causing the stranger to teeter on the narrow top step where he had precariously perched his oversized frame in his unwieldy camouflage attempt.

"Well, Silas Metcalf, when did you get back in these parts?"

Daddy pumped Silas's hand and affectionately slapped him on the back while pulling him into the kitchen. I honestly think Daddy wanted to hug him, but could not or would not due to the color barrier, or perhaps the manly barrier, of the times.

"Silas the Boogie Man Metcalf! It must be ten years since I saw you."

Daddy then dove right into the "remember whens" while Silas widened his grin. He looked more secure as Daddy motioned for him to sit down at the kitchen table.

Finally, I would meet one of Daddy's childhood soul mates. Intrigued, I sat on the floor to listen to the reminiscing. Daddy hardly gave Silas a chance to talk as he rambled on and on about grabbling for catfish in the Yocona River, stealing watermelons from Mr. Charlie Dee's prize patch, and breaking Old Pa's young mule Gussy by riding her into Shadywood one night with her bucking all the way. Daddy and his friend guffawed as they talked about Gussy.

"Sue Ann, this here is Silas, the best piano player in north Mississippi, and he ain't never had a lesson in his life."

"Really?" I asked.

That was hard for me to imagine, me, the nonmusical daughter in the Taylor family. Rita Jean and I had been forced to take piano lessons every Saturday morning for the last three years from Miss Johnnie, a retired school teacher and wife of Mr. Todd of Todd's Drug Store. Rita Jean had taken right to it and could already play "What a Friend We Have in Jesus" from the *Baptist Hymnal*. Piano lessons took up valuable gully-climbing time, and I loathed them. Sure I would be a mountain climber some day rather than a concert pianist, I believed the gully was more practical than the piano. It was career planning.

I made sure I learned very slowly, hating every minute of the lessons. I much preferred "Chopsticks" to Chopin. My thinking was that eventually Mama would think it was a waste of money and would let me quit.

"I wish *I* could play by ear so I wouldn't have to waste any more time on lessons." I emphasized the word "I."

Daddy laughed at my remark, knowing how I hated having my Saturday mornings taken by such a trite undertaking.

Rita Jean, on the other hand, picked out songs on the piano without any sheet music to go by. She sounded just like a music star when she played and sang the popular songs we heard on the radio.

"Would you play something for us, Mr. Silas?" I asked.

"Mr. Silas…Did ya hear that, Zeke? I don't thank I's ever been called Mr. Silas. Sho' I will, little girl."

"Play a boogie, Silas," requested Daddy, and play Silas did.

I thought the house would fall off its foundation as Rita Jean was drawn in trying to jitterbug to it. Then Old Ma came bouncing, almost running, down the path as the sound brought back memories of Daddy and Uncle Bud's childhood.

Mama was at the church giving it a good cleaning after being embarrassed that morning that a visiting family had seen it "looking like Old Ma's house." Thank goodness she was gone; I didn't know how boogie-woogie fit with Baptist doctrine, although Mama had proved to be a good dancer by teaching us to jitterbug and Charleston. I knew she had a flair for singing, too, because we could hear her over the rest of the choir at church always holding the last note longer than anyone else so it was like a five-second solo.

The boogie ended all too soon for Rita Jean and me, and Mr. Silas requested to speak to Daddy in private. Daddy walked out the back door, across the yard, and turned toward the barn with Mr. Silas, and at one point I saw Daddy shake his head as he pulled out his wallet. After handing Mr. Silas something, Daddy gave him one more pat on the back and began walking back toward the house.

Mr. Silas walked toward the woods instead of the gravel road, which made no sense at all to me. When Daddy came in, he was quiet, a little uncanny for someone who only a few minutes before was boogieing with the rest of us.

"That was really something, Daddy," remarked

Rita Jean. "I wish he could teach me how to play that boogie-woogie. You think he might do that some time?"

"No. Silas is heading back up north. That's where he's been for a long time. That man does have a gift, don't he?" Daddy managed a little smile, but I could sense there was some concern behind it.

It wasn't long before Mama came in. Mama had an abundance of energy and never took a day off, even on weekends. She also couldn't understand why Daddy and the rest of us couldn't find something "productive" to do on weekends. Daddy argued he was being productive by resting up so he could sit on a bulldozer all week.

"I'm glad I had to clean the church today. There is no better place to really think than in the Lord's House, especially when you're there all by yourself with Him. I've made a big decision, one I've been pondering over for a while, and one that will affect all of us."

We all stopped what we were doing, interested in hearing Mama's big decision. Mama was so routine-oriented that it was surprising to think she had made some earth-shattering decision that was going to change things in the Taylor house.

"I'm going to beautician's school in Memphis starting in June. I talked to the admissions person at Moler's Beauty College when I was in Memphis a couple of weeks ago. I've had my application all ready to send in, but just couldn't decide if it was the right thing to do or not. It means I have to quit work for the eight months it will take me to complete my training and get my license, and that is where it affects all of you."

Mama had the attention of all of us. Daddy didn't seem too surprised, so he must have known she was thinking about this.

"We have to save money for the next six months so we can make it without my salary next year while I'm in school. I can live in the little apartment that Annie Belle rents out next to her house, but that'll cost extra. Rita Jean and Sue Ann, you will have to stay with Old Ma and go to school, without me here to cook for you and make you do your homework. Do you think you can manage?"

"You a beautician...wow! That means I'll be able to keep up with all the new hairdos, makeup, and everything!" Rita Jean was way ahead of what Mama was saying.

"Yes, that's true, but you will have to make some sacrifices in the process. You won't be getting as many new clothes, and you won't be going to as many movies as you're used to. Sue Ann, no talking your daddy into buying you frivolous things like new cowboy boots or .22 cartridges for that rifle I know you've been sneaking out to shoot rats in the garden. And both of you will have to take on more chores, like cooking for your daddy and doing laundry. Christmas will probably be pretty slim this year, too. We'll have to tuck every dime we can away in the savings account. Do you think you can handle all of this?"

For the life of me, I couldn't imagine how Christmas could get any slimmer, but it didn't matter to me. I always lied to my friends about what I got, anyway. Once I asked for a Tiny Tears doll that wet and cried real tears that I saw advertised on television, but all I got was a do-nothing cheap doll like I saw at

Sterling's. Evidently, Santa shopped at different stores for different little girls, because my friends all got Tiny Tears.

I stopped asking for dolls when I was about eight, just to keep from having to tell everyone that my doll didn't have a stamp on the back of her neck. In fact, my dolls never had necks; they just went right from rubber heads into flimsy, cloth bodies.

Then there was the BB gun I asked for when I was ten, which was really a long shot since "girls don't have need of such things." I got a sewing box, a View Master, and a Bible. Imagine that…Sue Ann Taylor with a sewing box! That Christmas, I spent the day in the barn hideout crying and cussin' Santa Claus. I guess I really needed the Bible.

Rita Jean, on the other hand, might really suffer. She always got clothes and was quick to point out to her friends what she got for Christmas when she wore the new outfits to school. She looked worried about the prospect.

"Don't worry, girls. Christmas won't be that slim. I've got a trick or two up my sleeve." Daddy had noticed Rita Jean's face drop and rushed to reassure us.

Christmas was only a month away. Whatever trick Daddy had would have to happen pretty fast, knowing Mama. When she meant save, she really meant save, and she meant starting at the moment her decision was made. I bet she coasted down every hill between Liberty Creek Baptist Church and home just to save on gas. Mama had even been known to wash and reuse Dixie cups.

"Don't you go plotting and spending without talking it over with me first, Ezekiel Taylor. I know how you can be." So did Rita Jean and I, and we hoped just this once Daddy would do some tucking of his own, at least until after Christmas was over.

Mama went into the kitchen and began making cornbread to go along with the fried chicken, mashed potatoes, and blackeyed peas left over from Sunday dinner—dinner being what Ozzie and Harriet called lunch. Rita Jean, as always, began her thirty minutes of daily piano practicing, followed by a few minutes of trying to pick out the boogie she had heard that day.

"Where on earth did you hear that, Rita Jean?" Mama began putting supper on the table in the dining room where the piano was located.

"Daddy's old friend Mr. Silas Metcalf came by to visit this afternoon, and Daddy got him to play the piano for us." I was quick to interject the story before Rita Jean had a chance to answer.

"Boy, can he boogie!" This was Rita Jean's contribution.

Mama looked unimpressed with Rita Jean's remark, put her hands on her hips, and glared at Daddy. "And when did he get out of Parchman?"

My mouth flew open. Parchman was the state penitentiary about a two-hour drive away in the Delta, not nearly far enough in local people's minds. When convicts escaped from Parchman, something that happened way too often, it elicited fear and trembling in all of us and prompted Daddy to leave the keys in the car and truck, much to Mama's vexation, but Daddy stood firm on his reasoning and refused to give in to her arguments.

"I don't want no murderer breaking down my door and killing my family for a getaway vehicle. I can replace a car."

With this kind of fear of convicts, it was hard to believe that Daddy had welcomed one into our home. It was even harder to believe that he had lied about where his old boyhood friend had been.

"I thought you said he had been up north, Daddy?" questioned Rita Jean as she left the piano bench and sat down at the table.

"Well, he had for the last year or two, or so I thought. He was in Parchman before that. I never thought Silas would come back to Mississippi after he got in trouble."

"What'd he do, Daddy, to have to go to prison?" I sat down on the piano stool where the only convict, or ex-convict, I had ever met or hoped to meet had just a few hours before dazzled us with his talent. Scooting to the opposite end of the stool from where Silas sat, I acted as if his crime might be contagious.

"Silas Metcalf was nothing but a common thief. If he was in here today, we probably need to count the silver." Mama sounded angry, even though we didn't own any real silver.

"Silas may have done some things he shouldn't ought to, but deep down, he's a good man. We were best friends as boys. Ma can tell you about Silas."

Daddy looked up at Old Ma, who had just come in to eat supper. "Ma, tell the girls here about Silas. Irene seems to think he was bad through and through."

"Oh, Silas was all right. He had a hard life, was so poor he had to steal food to survive, at least until he and his grandpa moved to the Taylor place. Him and Zeke did everything together, and I was glad of it. Silas was big for his age, and watched after Zeke. He saved

Zeke's life when he was 'bout Rita Jean's age. Clay's big old bull caught your daddy between fences, trampled him right into the ground, and was about to gore him to death when Silas come running into that pasture and jumped on that old bull's neck, throwing him right to the ground. 'Run, Zeke!' he yelled, but your daddy couldn't do nothing but drag himself, moaning. Silas held onto that bull 'til your Uncle Bud come and drug your daddy out of the way. Silas had his faults, but I'll always be grateful to him for saving your daddy."

That was the last we talked about Silas that night, but the subject did surface again three days later when Mama was reading the *Bartonville Weekly*.

"Looks like there's been a lot of burglaries in Bartonville. Piggly Wiggly got broke into, and so did that service station on Highway 6. You don't think your old friend is up to his old tricks, do you, Zeke?"

"Don't even suggest such a thing, Irene. I swear. Just 'cause a man goes bad once in his life, folks think he's bad from then on. Let me see that paper." Daddy grabbed the paper from Mama's hands, took a few minutes to read the rest of the article, and then gave us a quick synopsis.

"Well, I guess they'll at least be knowing soon who robbed the service station, 'cause Joe Johnson that runs the place saw the burglar running out the back and shot at him with his .38. Says here the sheriff found a trail of blood left by the robber. Joe had locked up for the night and just happened to go back 'cause he left his lunchbox. Says here the robber didn't get but about fifty dollars that had been left in the drawer. Somebody paid a big price for just fifty bucks."

"Well, hero or not, I don't want Silas Metcalf hanging around here. Don't you girls let him in if he comes around. Hear me?"

Rita Jean and I nodded yes to Mama. I found it hard to believe that God could give so much talent to a person with such a sinful nature. I hoped Mama was wrong about Mr. Silas, since he saved Daddy from the bull.

The next day was Thanksgiving, and I headed to the fence post to put the red coffee can up. Since we wouldn't have our big meal until supper, I had the whole day to play with Liz Bess and Little Ben. I didn't like to share my time with Liz Bess with Ben tagging along, but we had no other choice. He adored Liz Bess, and she felt sorry for Little Ben because his mama had run off and left him. Since his daddy, Ben, Sr., worked away on the railroad, Little Ben had to live with Nagalee and Bay. Liz Bess could relate to Little Ben's dilemma and tried to take up the slack left by his sorry mother.

"I'm going to play in the gully, Mama. Can I take my lunch to eat there? I'll be back in time to take a bath before Thanksgiving supper." I made the promise as I rummaged through the pie safe for moon pies and crackers.

"I guess so, Sue Ann. At least you won't be in my way, or your sister's, while we're cooking. Watch the road, though. Mattie Lynn and Bob ought to be here by mid-afternoon. They're staying at Bob's parents' but will eat with us tonight. I can't wait to see my baby. It seems like she's been away forever."

Mama's baby was only sixteen years younger than Mama. Daddy and Mama had married at fifteen, with

Mattie Lynn born when Mama was just a kid herself.

When I got to the gully hideout, Little Ben was already there, standing beside the propped-open rusty tin doorway, staring in a silent, terrified stupor.

"What is it, Ben? Is it a snake? If it is, don't you move too sudden!" Approaching fast, thinking it must be a cottonmouth or a water moccasin, I jerked Ben away from the crude structure. We tumbled to the red clay dirt several feet from the hideout.

"Who dare?" A muffled deep voice came from inside the tin enclosure.

I stood not moving, not knowing what to do. This was no snake but could be just as deadly.

"Who dare?" The weak voice came again, this time a little louder. I had to look inside.

"Stay here, Ben, and wait for Liz Bess. If I yell, you run for help."

Gingerly, I creaked the tin door open wider and looked inside. Silas Metcalf lay in a bloody heap on the apple crates.

"Mr. Silas, what happened to you?" I stepped in and went to Mr. Silas's side.

"Get yo daddy! Get Zeke. Don't tell nobody else. Please, li'l miss."

"He ain't home right now, Mr. Silas. He went to town. You're hurt bad. I'll get Mama." As I turned to leave, Mr. Silas grabbed my leg.

"No! Just yo' daddy. Nobody else. I been here two days…another li'l bit won't kill me."

My mind raced to the article in the *Bartonville Weekly,* and I suspected there was a connection between the robbery at the service station and the dark red stain on the shirt that was dried and stuck to Mr.

Silas's side. My instincts told me to run fast and get Mama to call the sheriff, but in my mind I kept seeing Mr. Silas as a young teenager holding tight to a bull that was trying to kill my daddy.

"Here's some water, Mr. Silas." I pulled the fruit jar of ice water from the backpack Old Ma had sewed for me out of a flour sack, and helped Mr. Silas to hold his head up while he guzzled it. He poured some on his bloody handkerchief and laid it carefully over his wounded side.

I saw Liz Bess outside the door with Ben and motioned for her to come in.

"Mr. Silas, this is my friend Liz Bess. Liz Bess, this is my daddy's friend, Mr. Silas. He's hurt bad but won't let me get nobody to help him but Daddy. Liz Bess, we need to help Mr. Silas. Here, feed him some crackers and water. I'll go to the road and flag Daddy down before he gets to the house. Ben, you go stand watch on Red Mountain just like you do when we play Lone Ranger. If you see anybody coming other than Daddy or me, give the wolf call."

Liz Bess had no idea who this man was nor why I was helping him, but she trusted my instincts without question. I left Mr. Silas in her care and headed for the gravel road, knowing Daddy should be back from town any minute. Sure enough, ten minutes later, I saw his blue pickup stirring up dust as he came around the curve. He saw me waving furiously and came to an abrupt stop.

"What's wrong, Sudi Girl? You look like you seen Old Pa."

"Come quick, Daddy! Mr. Silas is hurt bad!"

Daddy pulled to the side of the road and followed

me to the gully hideout.

"Oh, lord, Silas. What have you gone and done?" Daddy bent over his friend and examined his wound. "I've got to get you to a doctor before you bleed to death."

"No doctor, Zeke. Make the children leave now. Don't tell nobody," mumbled Mr. Silas, pointing toward Liz Bess and me.

"You kids need to go on home now. I can't tell you not to tell your grandparents, Liz Bess. Wouldn't be Christian for me to tell you to keep secrets from your folks. I'll leave that decision up to you. I can tell you this. This man is my friend and he is a good man, regardless of what this looks like. Run on home now."

Liz Bess took Ben by the hand and hurried in the direction of her house. I refused to leave Daddy, offering to help.

"Sue Ann, I can't allow you to be involved in this. It wouldn't be right."

"Daddy, I'm already involved. Remember? Now what can I do?"

"Go to Nagalee's house and get a bucket of water and some clean rags. I'll patch him up best I can until I decide what to do."

As I neared Nagalee's house, I met her leaving her yard, heading in the direction of the gully. In her arms was a stack of clean cloths that looked like cut-up sheets, and two bottles: a bottle of ointment and a bottle of whiskey. Behind her, Bay carried a bucket of water. As I met them, Nagalee nodded but did not say a word.

Liz Bess and Ben met me at the door.

"Mama said she'd take care of everything, Sue Ann. Don't worry now."

The three of us sat in the swing on the porch of the board-and-batten house and did not talk. Less than an hour later, Daddy climbed out of the gully, got in the pickup, and headed for the house. I could stand the suspense no longer, so I headed home. No one was stirring outside the hideout as I passed on the rim of Red Mountain. The whole gully was deathly quiet.

Daddy and Mama were in the bedroom talking with the door closed when I got home, and in a few minutes, Daddy came out with the old worn-out suitcase in his hand. Stopping at the door, he gave me a quick pat before heading out in his pickup.

Mama came out of the bedroom, wiping her hands nervously on her apron, and reentered the kitchen.

"Sue Ann, I know you want to go play with Liz Bess, and after talking to your daddy, I've decided to allow you two to play together. But today I need you to help Rita Jean and me in the kitchen. Do you think you could follow a recipe and make those sweet potato croquettes you love so much?"

I smiled at Mama, grateful not only for her letting Liz Bess and me be friends but for acknowledging me as a real female member of the family. I turned to Rita Jean, who had her mouth open in disbelief, and stuck out my tongue as I began to read over the recipe.

Thanksgiving dinner was delicious that night, but Daddy was not there. Mama heaped a big plate full of chicken and dressing with all the trimmings and covered it with tinfoil for Daddy to eat at whatever hour or day he returned. She did not mention Silas Metcalf, and neither did I. Mama excused Daddy's absence by saying that he had a good job prospect he had to check out and had to go out of town.

After supper, we listened while Rita Jean played her recital pieces on the piano. I asked her to play the boogie she had taught herself, and she beat the piano in the familiar style of a bullfighter. For her last number, we sang with her as she played:

What a friend we have in Jesus,
All our sins and grief to bear.
What a privilege to carry
Everything to God in prayer.

.

Have we trials and temptations?
Is there trouble anywhere?
We should never be discouraged.
Take it to the Lord in prayer.

.

Are we weak and heavy laden?
Cumbered with a load of care?
Precious Savior, still our refuge
Take it to the Lord in prayer.

Chapter Six
The Rescue of Emmett Till

Mama turned her dream into reality with her entrance in Moler's Beauty College in Memphis the summer after I finished sixth grade, a new beginning not only for Mama but for our whole family. Since Daddy had gone to work on the pipeline, Mama decided it would be best if Old Ma, Rita Jean, and I all lived with her in the small apartment at Annie Belle's for the summer. I secretly wondered if she was just trying to keep me from spending the summer with Liz Bess, but it did seem to be a good idea, since Daddy wouldn't be there to help Old Ma with Rita Jean and me.

Tommy was tickled that I'd be living right next to him and didn't mind at all that I was a girl. In fact, his friend Glenn didn't seem to mind either, and we quickly became a threesome.

One day, Glenn came up with a really great idea, or so we thought. He wanted to ride the city buses and go to Beale Street, but added it would take a good bit of money because we would have to change buses three times to get there.

"What's so special about Beale Street?" I asked this knowing there had to be some really good reason for going to all that expense to get there.

"You don't know about Beale Street?" Glenn looked at Tommy and smiled his "shit-eatin'" grin, as

Daddy called it. "I thought everyone knew about Beale Street."

"She's a little country girl from Mississippi, remember? It's where the whores are, Sue Ann. Mostly at night, but you can see some of 'em during the daytime, too." Tommy shook his head and whistled. "Whoo…wee! Do they look tough."

"Oh," I said as if I knew what a whore was. I didn't want to give them the idea I was completely ignorant of city terminology. "How much money will I need for the bus rides?"

"Probably a couple of bucks. We get a discount 'cause we're kids. I bet Old Ma will give us the money."

Tommy asked Old Ma for bus fare and told her we wanted to go to the zoo. She thought it would be all right, since she had heard Annie Belle and Mama talking about wanting me to see the zoo while I was here.

"Are there many whores at the zoo?" I asked in my most knowledgeable, innocent voice as we left the house and headed to the bus stop. I thought it sounded like it might be a wild hoglike creature, maybe from an African jungle.

Tommy and Glenn laughed so hard that Glenn fell down and rolled around on the sidewalk, quite a sight on its own, since Glenn was short and pretty chubby.

"That's a good one, Sue Ann." Tommy hit me on the back to show he approved of my humor. I laughed, too, as if I knew how funny I was.

Being confused with all the bus changes and having no idea how Tommy and Glenn knew where we were going, I trusted them completely, a big mistake.

As we approached our last stop, I became aware of a section of the city that did not look at all like the zoo I remembered from the one time I went when I was four.

"Are you kids sure you know what you're doing, getting off here?" The bus driver looked questioningly at Tommy.

"It's okay. Our moms work here." Tommy and Glenn laughed and hit each other in their symbolic brotherhood fashion as they exited the bus. I was more confused than ever but decided not to say anything for fear of showing my "little country girl from Mississippi" ignorance again. It soon became obvious even to me that this was not the zoo, at least not the kind I thought it was.

Music blasted from the open doorways up and down the street and sounded like Leonia listening to WDIA—the colored station out of Memphis—on three different radios with three different tunes playing at the same time. I liked the beat of the music and tried to keep time to it as I walked down the sidewalk. There were many more Negroes on the street than there were whites, and everyone seemed to be having a good time.

"There's one!" Glenn was staring goo-goo-eyed at a beautiful but skinny young Negro girl leaning against a street sign. Glenn and Tommy headed in her direction, and I followed, not knowing what "one" was.

"One" had on the shortest skirt I'd ever seen, and it was so tight you could see every curve, or rather every bone, in her body. Her high-heeled red shoes looked more like stilts than shoes, and I wondered how in the world she walked on them, especially with her beanpole legs.

Just as we got within a few feet of the girl, a car

pulled up alongside her. Leaning into the car window, she began talking to the driver, who looked to be about the age of Daddy, and her short skirt hiked up to show flashy red panties beneath. I turned away in embarrassment for her. Tommy and Glenn did not. The girl opened the car door and got in, with the car speeding off almost before she closed the door.

"Told you we'd see some. Let's walk to the end of the street and see if we see any more."

Glenn gave his most mischievous grin and put his stubby little legs in high gear, making Tommy and me have to run to catch up. Passing several cafes with wonderful smells of barbecue and "chicken on a stick" made me wish we had asked Old Ma for more money.

The next part of Beale we came to was shabby, with stores that seemed to be held up only by the vibrations of the blues that emanated from every crack. Inside one place, exotic dancers' skimpily-clad bodies danced to the beat on the bars being used as makeshift stages. A man with a scruffy beard and the look of a gangster from New York stood guard at the door, and when he saw Glenn trying to sneak a peak inside, he looked down at him and warned, "Careful what you look at, son. You might go blind."

Just up from the open door was another young girl, but this one was white, dressed in the same fashion as the first. Once again, a car stopped, but before the girl could get in, a police car sped up, its siren screaming. Two policemen jumped out and grabbed the girl, handcuffing her hands behind her before shoving her into the police car.

Tommy looked scared.

"Quick! Get in this alley before that cop sees us."

This gave me my first indication that not only was this not the zoo, but it was a place we should not have been, at least not by ourselves. Running down the dirty alley, we saw a neon sign that blinked, "Madame Celia's Boarding House for Young Ladies," and we darted inside. A big-bosomed Negro lady in a fancy pink lace dress met us at the door. Her hair was glued to her head in a sea of blue-gray waves that hit the nape of her neck like a dark seashore.

"And who do we have here? You must be looking for the arcade, children." She threw back her head and laughed, and her heavy chest jumped up and down and jiggled like two giant cantaloupes trying to leap out of a pink grocery sack.

Glenn, as usual, was the one to take the lead in this awkward situation.

"I think my Aunt Virginia lives here."

"I don't think so, son. No Virginias here, but we do got some aunties." She laughed as she made this remark. "You children better be on your way before Madame Celia finds out you're here." Leaning down she whispered to Glenn, "This is not a place for children, you know."

"Oh, I'm sorry."

Glenn took on an apologetic expression as if it were an accident that we were there. He seemed proud the lady had picked him out to be the leader of the group and that she thought he understood whatever it was she was talking about.

As Glenn led us to the door, I looked around to discover a beautiful room very different from its shabby alley entrance. It was like we had stepped back in time to an earlier age, into a room filled with velvet chairs and sofas, marble-topped tables, and a huge chandelier with millions of tiny crystal teardrops cascading from it. It was just like one I'd seen in a western at the Palace Theatre in Bartonville, but that one was in an Old West saloon, not a boarding house. I really wanted to see what the rest of the place looked like, but we were being escorted out by the lady.

Just as we got to the front of the parlor, the door opened. A tall white man with dark glasses stepped inside, nodding to the lady.

"Madame Celia is waiting for you." Her eyes ushered him up the beautiful winding staircase.

He looked familiar to me, but I could not put a name to the face. Where had I seen this man before?

Glenn glanced to each side to make sure there were no policemen around before we stepped into the alley outside the boarding house.

"We better get back to the bus stop and get our tails home." Tommy had decided we had seen enough of Beale Street. I had no idea what I had seen, but I knew it was a world I was not accustomed to. I kept trying to figure out where I had seen that man before.

When we came out of the alley and back onto Beale, Tommy scanned each side of the street to make sure there were no police. Glenn, on the other hand, had his radar tuned to track down another "one."

"Wow! There's the best one yet!" Glenn was looking across the street at a young Negro woman with her red-dyed hair piled high on her head. She stood outside one of the open doors where music boomed, and was dressed in a purple sparkly blouse with a pair of pants that were surely tattooed on, black high heels, and a red leather jacket slung over her shoulder.

"Watch this."

Glenn, short on brains but long on guts, crossed the street before Tommy could stop him. I stood frozen, big-eyed, as my heart thumped much louder than the "thu…duh…dee…duh" of the bass guitar coming from behind the girl. Walking right up to her, Glenn stretched his short arm up and placed it around her shoulder. The girl stood motionless, void of expression, looking down into his chubby cheeks as if to say, "You best move if you know what's good for you." Tommy looked scared and motioned for Glenn to come away.

"How's about a date, baby?"

Glenn gave the girl a pretentious, adoring look but dropped his arm quickly, moving away, as a tough-looking tall black guy with dark glasses and greased, slicked-back hair came out of the open door. He slid over to Glenn, standing so close that his baggy striped suit jacket was rubbing against Glenn's T-shirt. Glenn was playing a game of freeze tag with the guy's belt that hit him at eye level, too frightened to move.

"You flirtin' wi' my girl, man?" Taking off his glasses, he breathed down into Glenn's face, which had transformed from flirt to fright and then to flight.

"Run, Glenn!" Tommy yelled, but did not wait to see if Glenn was heeding his warning.

The three of us took off at full speed toward the bus stop, with Glenn running down the opposite side of Beale, his chubby legs way ahead of his bulbous cheeks, which sloshed from side to side as his feet banged the pavement. I looked back over my shoulder to see if the man was running after Glenn. He was standing there with a small group of people who had obviously come out of the bar, since one of them was holding a guitar, and they were heehawing at the sight of the three of us running like the devil was chasing us. Tommy and Glenn didn't stop at the bus stop where we'd gotten off but kept running until we reached the street that runs beside the Mississippi River. Riverside Drive, the sign read. Panting and holding our sides, we finally reached a bus stop, where we bent over to catch our breaths as our lungs threatened to explode.

Tommy was furious with Glenn and pushed him to the ground.

"Are you crazy, Glenn? You could get yourself killed pulling stunts like that!"

Glenn did not fight back. He knew Tommy was right, and that what he had done was stupid.

We had to wait for about fifteen minutes for the bus to come, so we walked over to look at the historical river. Standing silent, not only still trying to catch our breaths but also in deep thought about what almost happened, we stood staring into the Mississippi River.

All I could see as I looked down into the muddy waters was the swollen, brutalized body of fourteen-year-old Emmett Till, a young boy a little older than Glenn who had flirted with a white lady, the same thing I had just witnessed but racially reversed. My heart raced and would not slow down as I kept watching toward Beale Street for the boyfriend. Would he drive up, snatch Glenn from us, and take him to the same fate as Emmett?

Where was that bus? Would the man follow the bus home and find out where Glenn lived? I decided I'd sit at the back of the bus and watch to make sure no cars followed us from Beale Street.

At long last, the brakes of the big city bus squealed

in front of us. Tommy and Glenn sat down near the front, but I made my way to the back. There was only one seat left at the back of the bus, and it was beside an elderly Negro lady with a pleasant smile that peeked from under a beautiful hat covered with red roses.

"May I sit with you?" The lady scooted over and patted the seat beside her.

As I sat down, I noticed that only Negroes were sitting at the back of the bus, except for one young man who sat toward the middle but more to the front. Tommy and Glenn kept motioning for me to come sit with them, but I just shook my head in refusal as I turned to watch out the back window for suspicious cars coming from Beale Street. No cars appeared, but I continued to look until we reached our next bus stop.

"Thank you." I smiled at the lady as I left the seat, and she nodded, returning my smile.

I could hear mumbling as I walked down the aisle to the front of the bus. There were only three people sitting in the front section, including Tommy and Glenn, which made no sense to me.

I decided that maybe Negroes liked to sit in the back. Maybe they were used to watching their backsides like I was doing.

"Sue Ann, are you nuts? White people don't sit at the back of the bus. That's for colored people." Tommy was furious with me for some reason, and I was beginning to wish I was back in Shadywood, in my gully where things weren't so complicated.

"Don't you listen to the news, Tommy? Colored people can sit anywhere they want now, thanks to that King man and Rosa Parks and the bus boycott in Montgomery. 'Course, it will probably take a few years for it to reach Memphis, except for that one guy on our bus. Probably a college student who thought he'd test the law." Glenn's daddy was a high school history teacher, so Glenn always knew what was happening news-wise.

On the way home on our last bus, we were all three quiet again, obviously thinking of the what-could-have-beens from Beale Street. I made myself think of something different and began thinking about Madame Celia's and how beautiful the inside of the boarding house was. Suddenly it came to me where I had seen that man.

"That man was J.T. Harvey!" I practically yelled my thought out.

"What man?"

"The man in Madame Celia's! He's the richest man in Bartonville. I wonder what business Mr. Harvey had with Madame Celia in a boarding house."

Tommy and Glenn looked at each other and began laughing again, making me believe I could be a comedian on television, they had laughed at me so much that day.

"You really don't know, do you, Sue Ann?"

"Know what, Tommy?" I copped an attitude and put my hands on my hips.

"That ain't no boarding house! That's a whorehouse, Sue Ann. Everybody knows that." Glenn could hardly speak for laughing.

"Oh, of course!" I spoke sharply, sick of the "everybody knows" remark.

Tommy and Glenn were getting too much enjoyment out of my lack of whore knowledge. I'd know soon, though, what was so funny. I'd ask Old Ma when I got back to the apartment. She'd know, but I couldn't tell Old Ma or anyone about Beale Street or about the crazy stunt Glenn had pulled. But I was still very uneasy about what might happen to Glenn, and I'd be listening for cars stopping on our street tonight.

"You know, Glenn, you better be careful, flirting with Negro ladies. Did you hear what happened to Emmett Till last year?" I was sure neither Tommy nor Glenn had ever heard of him and felt proud at the prospect of knowing something they didn't.

"Everybody knows who Emmett Till is, or I should say was. I remember seeing that redneck lawman on the news. When the reporter asked him if he knew what happened to the boy, he looked right at him and said, 'Well, I guess that nigga was trying to swim the Tallahatchie River with a gin fan tied round his neck.' My daddy didn't think it was one bit funny, and neither did I." Glenn crossed his arms and frowned to show his anger at the crude remark made by someone who was supposed to keep the law.

I should have known Glenn would know, but I felt bad that I had not known until Liz Bess told me, and I live in Mississippi just one county over from where Emmett was murdered. I vowed right then that I would start watching the news every day and would even read the *Bartonville Weekly* when it came in the mail.

"Aren't you afraid that girl's boyfriend might come drag you out of your home like those men did to Emmett?"

"It don't work that way in the South, Sue Ann. White folks can do or say anything they want to coloreds and they won't do nothing. The law would get them if they did, and they wouldn't get off like those two guys who murdered Emmett Till. My daddy calls it a 'double standard.' What's good for the Negroes is not the same for the whites. I'm not scared of her boyfriend, but don't you go telling your grandma or your mama, or my butt will be in big trouble if my daddy finds out. I *am* scared of him."

That afternoon I got a much bigger education from Old Ma than I ever got at Shadywood School. She was hesitant at first to explain to me what a whore was, but with my insistence, she gave in and gave me the dirty details in the best Baptist terminology she could. I also learned a lot more than I had known about how babies are born. My information was terribly limited, having come from little-girl talk and reading material on bathroom walls at school. This was the kind of information Mama should have shared with me but didn't.

"You know, Sudi, the only one I ever knowed about at home was Paragark Irma."

My mouth became a flytrap. Paragark Irma, as everyone called her, received her name because of drinking paregoric, a cheap substitute for whiskey that contained opium and could be bought over the counter at any little country store in the state. Irma, with her cheap, long, bleached white hair, walked the roads and highways and had always been a source of great fascination to me when I saw her, having no idea how she made her living until now. She was a non-person in our county. Nobody seemed to know anything about Paragark Irma, nor did they care. Mama used her name as a reference to really bad bleach jobs, swearing that when she was a beautician she would make sure no one left her beauty shop looking like Paragark Irma.

Sleep did not come easy that night, not just because I had to sleep with Old Ma, who was so heavy that I was constantly climbing back up on my side of the bed, but because of all the happenings of the day. Even though Glenn had tried to convince me not to worry, I still caught myself listening for cars on our street. When I heard one slow down, I would peep out the window beside the bed to make sure no one got out at Glenn's house. Images of Emmett Till surfaced in my mind, and when I did finally go to sleep, I dreamed of Liz Bess, Tommy, and me rescuing him from those awful men who kidnapped and murdered him.

We slipped Emmett from the barn where his kidnappers had taken him to be beaten and tortured, and then sneaked through the woods, leading Emmett to the shanty where Silas Metcalf lived. Mr. Silas hid Emmett in the floorboard of his car and drove him to Memphis, where he bought him a one-way ticket on the northbound City of New Orleans to Chicago. His mama met him at the train station, relieved to have her son back.

"You were right, Mama. Mississippi is no place for a black kid from Chicago. I'm real glad to be home safe with you." Emmett hugged his mama as they left the station.

If only dreams were true.

Chapter Seven
The Date

I started junior high without my cowboy boots. The image of Sue Ann the Cowboy seemed finally to be fading. It was hard for my family to believe, because I had worn boots ever since I was old enough to understand the western movies Daddy always took me to see at the Palace Theatre.

Rita Jean was thrilled but still could not believe I had actually requested a pair of black-and-white saddle oxfords for school. I was in a state of disbelief and shock myself and felt self-conscious the first day I wore them. All the girls my age were wearing saddle oxfords in Memphis, and I had noticed several wore them on American Bandstand, which I watched every day after school with Rita Jean.

My sister needed to learn the latest dances now that she was in high school, and needed me as a practice partner. Our dining room became Philadelphia at four o'clock each day as dance partners Bunny and Eddie, Arlene and Kenny, Carmen and Frank, and Rita Jean and Sue Ann bopped, hopped, cha-cha'd, and strolled to the Top 40.

The biggest surprise was that I could dance. Rita Jean told me I bopped just like Pat Moliterri. Not that I believed her, but I did like hearing it. I knew she was just trying to sway my interest from the gully and the barn hideout so she would have a dance partner. Rita Jean figured she was more the Bunny Gibson style of dancer and was just looking for her Eddie Kelly, Mr. Right.

My cowboy boots would have fit my feelings the first day of school extremely well, since I felt like I had a saddle between my legs. I had started my period, much to my chagrin. At least it didn't scare me when it happened, like it did some of my friends. This was one thing I knew all about from having two older sisters who always complained about "the curse" and "being on the rag."

I was so afraid someone would notice the big lump that I wore extra crinolines under the new skirts Mama had bought me for school. My favorite skirt had a poodle on it, another reason I was glad I had saddle oxfords. Boots and poodles just did not go together, and somehow, this year, it mattered.

Never in my wildest dreams did I think I, Sue Ann Taylor, would be a trendsetter, but a week after school started, all the girls in my class were wearing saddle oxfords.

Rita Jean, on the other hand, was always the one to start new fashions at school, and things were no different at Bartonville High.

On her first day, she sported a ducktail, a new short haircut Mama had learned how to cut at Moler's that was just like Elvis's. Rita Jean wore her collars turned up around her neck to really accentuate her ducktail, and it wasn't long until several girls had the same hairstyle, the same upturned collars, the first to follow suit being Lady Victoria Harvey. Rita Jean was furious when Lady V was pictured in an article in the school newspaper, of which she just happened to be editor, with the new "coiffure" for the year. This was to be the beginning of enmity and rivalry between the two girls that would last until Lady V graduated.

Even though I was changing, I had not outgrown Liz Bess. We still played in the gully and read Nancy Drew, although we were branching out a bit into other types of literature. We were both reading *Gone with the Wind* and frequently acted out scenes in the barn that had changed from the hideout to Taylor Little Theatre. It was evident from the start that Liz Bess was much better as Scarlet than I was, so I played sweet Melanie and sometimes Prissy. My favorite line was, "I don't know nothin' bout birthin' babies," and I used it along with, "I'll worry about it tomorrow" to excess, not only in the barn but at school and at home when a situation seemed to warrant it, at least in my way of thinking.

One Saturday, Rita Jean hit Mama and Daddy with a bombshell.

"Jerry Pearson asked me to go to the football game next Friday and to the dance afterward. Can I go, Mama?"

"I just don't think you're old enough to date yet, Rita Jean." It was Daddy who answered, even though the question was directed at Mama. Rita Jean thought Mama would be the difficult one to convince.

"I expected this to happen, but I don't know that I'm ready for it yet," replied Mama. "I still haven't gotten over the fact that Mattie Lynn married so young. I don't want that happening to you. You know I was married at your age, and I sure don't want you repeating my mistakes. The longer we can put off dating, the better, is my thinking."

"Mama, I'm not you, and I'm not Mattie Lynn. I've got better things to do with my life than get married and have babies. I plan to go to college and then become a famous actress."

This was the first I'd heard of college in Rita Jean's future plans, but in looking at the twinkle in Mama's eyes, it was obviously having the effect Rita Jean intended. Daddy's eyes were void of twinkle, however.

"I don't know this Pearson boy. Who's his folks?" Daddy started the third degree that was usually left to Mama.

"His daddy owns Pearson Dry Cleaners in Bartonville. He also owns two more over in the Delta. They are very well-to-do, and Jerry owns his own pickup." Rita Jean was now appealing to Mama's "betterin'" side.

"Owns his own pickup? How old is he, eighteen?" Daddy was about to lose one of his little girls, and I could tell he was going to fight it tooth and nail.

"He's just a year older than me, Daddy, and he's a member of First Baptist of Bartonville. He even goes to Training Union. I know 'cause I heard some girls talking about seeing him there. Oh, please, Daddy. I've never been to a football game."

Rita Jean was not missing a trick in arguing her case. She had hit Mama's logic on every front, even religion. Now she was appealing to Daddy's love of sports.

"What do you think, Daddy? It was bound to happen sooner or later. She's too pretty to sit home with her family forever."

I immediately took Mama's statement personally. I

bet she thought Sue Ann the Plain was going to be one of those old-maid daughters who lived with her parents until she was forty, never dating, just going to church outings with her decrepit old parents and taking canning classes from the county home demonstration agent when she really wanted some excitement. Well, she and Daddy would find out soon enough that I had a few plans of my own, with or without a man tagging along.

"I think Rita Jean should go. All the other girls her age are dating, and most of them are not as responsible as Rita Jean. I bet none of them help their mamas like she does. There's not another girl at Bartonville—probably not in the state—that can bake a red velvet cake that will melt in your mouth like Rita Jean's, and just look how she manages this house while you're at Moler's through the week, Mama. She's a teenager, Daddy, like it or not. She's even old enough to get her driver's license."

Was this me talking? That big blister I got from my saddle oxfords must have gotten infected and caused a red streak of blood poisoning to my brain. I don't ever remember taking up for Rita Jean before that moment. Rita Jean looked pretty surprised at my support and compliments and just sat there with her mouth open.

"I guess Sue Ann is right. We have unloaded a ton of responsibility on Rita Jean this year. What do you think, Mama? Are we ready to let our little girl go?"

My reasoning seemed to have had a positive effect on Daddy's decision-making. Mama looked at Daddy and then at Rita Jean.

"I guess it's okay. But we will have some strict rules you better follow if you want to continue dating, and you won't be out late, either. You'll have to be home by eleven o'clock, and not a minute later."

Rita Jean squealed and jumped out of her chair to run and hug Mama. Mama smiled with delight and looked as if she wanted to return the hug, but didn't. I was immediately reminded of the cold cream episode from my childhood and couldn't help but be both jealous and hurt by Mama's positive reaction to the first hug I'd ever seen Rita Jean give anyone.

That Friday, Rita Jean looked gorgeous as she nervously waited for her first date to pick her up. She had on a yellow wool skirt that was tight but fit her perfectly to show off her newly developing movie-star curves, all except her bosom, which she'd enhanced with a couple of my bobby socks.

With the skirt, she wore a white stiffly starched and ironed blouse with the collar standing firm under her swooped-back-to-perfection ducktail. Her matching yellow sweater hung loosely over her shoulders, and she wore her Sunday flats. They were just slippery enough that she knew she would be able to bop just like Bunny. Rita Jean hoped Jerry would arrive before Mama got home from Memphis, afraid she might give him the third degree, and was pleased when he knocked on the door ahead of Mama's arrival.

I was as nervous as Rita Jean and could not wait to be introduced to the new beau who my sister said was a "dreamboat" and looked just like Frankie Avalon. Rita Jean was terrified I would wear the boots and shorts I usually put on as soon as I got off the bus, but I surprised her by leaving my school clothes on until after they left.

Jerry Pearson was indeed handsome. I could see how Rita Jean could be the envy of all the ninth-grade girls at Bartonville High, as she claimed. I asked if I could take their picture with the new camera Daddy had bought me at a local pawn shop. Rita Jean and I had planned this before Jerry's arrival. Before I could take the picture, Jerry had to check himself in the big mirror hanging behind our couch, combing his hair back over his ears and further exposing his long, dark sideburns.

I felt a little tingle in the pit of my stomach as I gazed upon this likeness of Frankie Avalon, although I thought he looked more like Ricky Nelson, and was ashamed for being so normal. Rita Jean was beaming as the handsome couple posed for several shots.

I could not wait to hear how the date went, so stayed awake until Rita Jean got home promptly at eleven o'clock. Jerry honked the familiar "shave and a hair cut, six bits" honk as he rounded the curve by Old Ma's storehouse. Rita Jean giggled and then lit into the details of the night from the time they left to the quick goodnight kiss on the front porch.

My sister did not understand football one bit, since Shadywood only had basketball, and said she just cheered when everybody else did. The only time she ever knew the whereabouts of the football was when the pile formed. The cheerleaders were by far the best part of the game, along with "who was wearing what," or rather, "who was with whom wearing what."

My sister was actually talking to me like I was a fellow human being. We had both obviously grown since the days I was the Lone Ranger and the time Rita Jean chased me with a butcher knife because I made fun of Pinky Lee, her favorite TV star. It seemed I was no longer the obnoxious brat of our youth.

"Sue Ann, I was the best bopper at the dance.

Everybody said so. Jerry said he couldn't leave my side for a minute without some guy trying to take me away from him. Jerry's a good dancer, but the best dancer there was Caleb Perkins. He asked me to dance once, and everybody stopped dancing and just formed a circle around us and clapped. And guess who Caleb was with?"

I did not have a clue but didn't have time to guess anyway before Rita Jean blurted it out.

"Lady Victoria Harvey! You should have seen the look on her face when she came from the bathroom and saw Caleb and me dancing with everybody clapping. She had on a red outfit almost identical to mine, but everybody told me I had a lot better figure than she does. Every time she and Caleb got close to us on the dance floor, Caleb would look at me and wink when V wasn't looking. I had no idea high school would be this much fun."

Rita Jean was talking so fast that I had to blink constantly to stay with her.

I could tell it would be a long time before we went to sleep that night, until Mama yelled for us to be quiet. Even that did not stop my sister's exposé of the date of the century, with all the naughty details left intact.

"Okay, Mama," Rita Jean yelled as she left her bed and crawled in beside me so she could continue to whisper under the covers and tell me every bit of every minute of the night. This was a new act of sisterhood that I'd never anticipated but was enjoying immensely.

Rita Jean had refused to sleep in the bed with me when she turned thirteen. She always complained that I breathed too loud and kicked. There were two double beds in our room. One was supposed to be for guests that we never had, until Rita Jean demanded it become her bed. I was only eleven at the time and was heartbroken. This was like the death of childhood: no more tickling backs or telling ghost stories.

Besides, I was always afraid of the dark and felt secure with Rita Jean sleeping on the outside of the bed. I always imagined that if a murderer, probably an escapee from Parchman, stole into our bedroom, he would stab Rita Jean and would never suspect there was another potential victim hidden, completely submerged, under the chenille bedspread. After she moved to the other bed, I piled two teddy bears and a cheap doll on the outside and covered them, to fool any would-be murderers. I kept up this bedtime ritual until I outgrew it when I turned fourteen.

I was really surprised to hear of Rita Jean's infatuation with Caleb Perkins. He was sort of our neighbor. His daddy owned two hundred acres that adjoined our property. Caleb didn't actually live there. His parents divorced because of his daddy's drinking, and Caleb lived in Bartonville with his mother. Even with the drinking, the Perkinses had plenty of money. His daddy had inherited it, supposedly, but small-town folks liked to gossip and were always conjecturing that Mr. Perkins made it by selling whiskey illegally in dry counties all over the state.

One fact was sure—Caleb Perkins never lacked for money, and he drove a new red convertible around town, one that was outlined with shiny chrome and was further adorned with Lady Victoria Harvey melted and poured next to him like a statue of a Greek goddess.

"You will never guess what I saw Caleb do!" Once again, I did not have time to guess before Rita Jean blurted it out in an almost too-loud whisper.

"He had his hand inside her blouse, feeling of her breast! Can you imagine that, Sue Ann?"

Lady V obviously had no need for bobby socks, except maybe on her feet. This dispelled the "better figure than" notion, but I didn't say anything for fear of bursting Rita Jean's bubble, which seemed to be growing as the story continued.

"Of course, they had no idea that anyone was watching," Rita Jean continued without coming up for air. "They were over in a corner in the dark. I almost died when I saw it, and she looked like she was enjoying it, but that is not the worst part!"

There was more? I was shocked. How could any girl be so brazen? There was a part of me that did not want to hear more, but there was also the "normal" part that did. The normal won out.

"What could be worse than that?" My whisper got too loud with the shock, and Mama yelled at us again.

"Plenty! I kept watching them, and not only did she seem to be encouraging him, but she had her hand down the front of his jeans, trying to touch his thing!"

"No way, Rita Jean! I thought Lady Victoria was supposed to be nice, the envy of all of Bartonville. I bet her parents don't know she's like that."

"All I know is I didn't dance with Caleb Perkins anymore after that. He's really cute, but I wouldn't want to go out with a guy who might think every girl is like Lady V. Harvey even if he does look like Kookie. She should be ashamed of herself."

"So should he, Rita Jean. It was just as much his fault as it was hers. Maybe more." I began to think the term "double standard" fit where women were concerned, as well as Negroes.

"When Mama gave me 'the talk' after she decided I could go with Jerry, she told me things like that could happen, but if it did, it would be my fault. She said it's the girl's place to make sure she is respected and she should remember her Christian values."

"That's crap! Boys are supposed to be Christians, too. I can't believe God expects anything different from boys just 'cause he gave them a tallywhacker." I was adamant in this belief and could not believe anyone, especially Mama, could think any different.

"Anyway, Lady V and Caleb left right after that, to do heaven only knows what. I told Betty Jean and Dorothy what I saw, and they said they could believe it. They had already heard rumors about the two of them. Betty Jean's brother is a senior and is on the football team with Caleb. He said Caleb brags to the other boys about what he and V do."

"If everybody knows about it, how does Lady V stay so popular? I'd think nobody would want anything to do with her. Why, she's nothing more than Paragark Irma—worse, because she has money and doesn't have to do it to survive."

"I don't understand it at all, Sue Ann, but I know Lady V gave me some looks that could kill. I hope she won't use my dancing with Caleb to turn people against me at school."

The next week of school Rita Jean's worries were confirmed. Lady V was being especially snotty to Rita Jean and would point at her and laugh every time she saw her in the hall. What was worse, V's horde of friends laughed at her, too. The school newspaper came out that Wednesday, and Lady V's vengeance was evident in the gossip column that she wrote. Rita Jean came home in tears that day and showed me the column in the paper:

A certain sophomore boy must be hard up to have to rob the cradle for a little ninth grade country girl. Not only is she plain, but she dances like a yellow peacock. She didn't even have the sense to see that the crowds surrounding her when she danced were laughing, not cheering.

"How do you know this is you she's talking about?" I asked, feeling really sorry for my sister.

"I was the only one who wore yellow, Sue Ann, and the others only stopped to watch when Caleb and I danced. Besides, Jerry is on the school newspaper staff. He's the head photographer and told me she was teasing him about "robbing the cradle." It just isn't fair that someone like her can write something so hurtful and get away with it."

That wasn't the only thing in the paper that upset Rita Jean. There was a big article about a new club that was being formed called the Bartonville Debutantes Society. The new club was sponsored by the Harvey family and was selecting girls to become members who were from "notable southern heritage" and who possessed the qualities of "charm, proper etiquette, and strong character."

Invitations would be sent out during the next two weeks, with the deadline being Thanksgiving. The highlight of the new club would be the Christmas ball, where each girl would be presented to Bartonville society. This was to be a very formal occasion and the biggest event for Bartonville since the inaugural ball of Governor Winfred B. Harvey, J.T. Harvey's older brother, who was governor only briefly in the forties, having died a few months after taking office. Governor Harvey had chosen to have the ball in the family's antebellum home, Five Oaks, which was bigger and more beautiful than the governor's mansion in Jackson.

Five Oaks was also where J.T. Harvey had held his celebratory ball after he was elected to the Mississippi state legislature as a senator, a position he held for only two terms. He chose not to run after that because his "business endeavors were just too time- and energy-consuming," as the *Weekly* had reported his official statement, and he felt his constituents, the good people of Barton County, "deserved someone who could devote one hundred percent to the office." Five Oaks was now the home of former Senator J.T. and Annette Holden Harvey and their lovely daughter Lady Victoria, who by all accounts was no lady.

"This could be the most important event in my life, and I won't get an invitation because of that horrible Lady V." Rita Jean gushed tears again.

Sure enough, two weeks passed and there was no invitation in our mailbox. Rita Jean practically ran from the school bus to the mailbox each day to check, only to have her worst fears confirmed. Lady Vampire, as I renamed her, was getting her revenge on my sister. There were only two days left for Rita Jean to get an invitation, and she had given up hope.

Rita Jean moped around during the week we got out for Thanksgiving. It was evident by Wednesday, the last day before the two-day Thanksgiving holidays, that she would not be receiving an invitation. I could not understand why she would even want to be part of a club based on such fakery, but I was suffering with my sister. I did not like seeing her hurt. This newfound sisterly love was killing me. Being a boot-scootin', gully-climbing, muscadine-vine swinger had been so much easier, but there was no turning back now. The transformation was almost complete.

Chapter Eight
Revenge

Jerry brought Rita Jean home from school on the Wednesday before Thanksgiving. They were a real couple now. "Going steady" was what Rita Jean called it as she sported Jerry's initial ring held tightly on her finger by a half inch of sticky white adhesive tape wrapped around the band. Rita Jean did not rush to the mailbox because she did not want Jerry to see how heartbroken she was at not getting an invitation. I checked the mailbox but just laid the mail on the dining room table like always. Rita Jean could tell from my actions that there was no invitation in the stack of mail. Jerry sensed Rita Jean's disappointment.

"I think it's terrible how V is treating you, Rita Jean. She is such a spoiled brat. Some day she'll get what she deserves, and I hope I'm around to see it. I heard she was intentionally leaving you out of her club because of Caleb dancing with you that night. And what she wrote in that column was a big lie. I know she wrote it because I overheard her bragging about it in the school newspaper office the other day. You were the prettiest girl there, and the best dancer. V is just jealous because there's someone at Bartonville High now who's prettier than she is."

Rita Jean seemed to perk up with the compliments from this handsome young man. Maybe she would not be totally ostracized like she'd thought.

"There's a dance Saturday night. You want to go with me? Let's show her what a liar she is. How about it, Jeannie?"

No one had ever called my sister Jeannie before. She smiled her approval at this pet name.

"Okay, I'll go with you, but only if you promise to keep me dancing all night. I don't want to dance with anyone else this time."

Jerry was leaving just as Mama got home from Memphis.

"Hi, Miz Taylor. Hope it was okay if I brought Rita Jean home from school. Can I help you carry those in before I go?"

Mama was obviously impressed with Jerry's good manners and was glad to have extra help carrying in the carload of groceries she had bought for the preparation of our Thanksgiving feast. Mama said we had a load of blessings to be thankful for this year, and we were celebrating even though Mattie Lynn and Bob wouldn't be here. They were moving to Whitehaven, Tennessee, where Bob had finally gotten a good job as an engineer, his first job since graduating from college.

"Thank you, Jerry," Mama said as she handed him two sacks. "Rita Jean tells me you're a real good dancer."

"It's easy when you have a good dance partner. Is it okay if I take Rita Jean to another school dance this Saturday? I promise I'll have her home at eleven, just like always."

How could Mama refuse such a nice young man?

"I guess it's okay, but Rita Jean will miss a trip to Memphis to the hair styling convention that's going on at Ellis Auditorium on Saturday. Would you rather stay here with Old Ma and go to the dance, Rita Jean?"

There was no question as to which one she would rather do, and Jerry seemed pleased that Rita Jean had chosen him over Memphis. Rita Jean walked him to the car, but there was no goodbye kiss, just in case any twelve-year-old eyes were watching—which, of course, they were.

Mama was furious when she heard what all had transpired that week with "that wicked Harvey girl." She was also sad for Rita Jean and could not stand to see her daughter so hurt over not receiving an invitation to join the Debutantes Society.

"You may not get to be the belle of the Christmas ball, but you will be the belle of the dance Saturday night. Go look in those packages I brought from Goldsmith's."

Rita Jean tore into the boxes and found two of the most beautiful skirt-and-sweater sets I had ever seen. There was even an outfit for me, but with a full skirt rather than the tight ones for Rita Jean.

"Thank you, Mama. Now all I have to do is decide which one to wear Saturday night."

"Sue Ann, I just got you one outfit, since you're not dating yet. Hopefully, it will be a long time before I have to buy you clothes for that purpose."

With what I had witnessed with Rita Jean with just one date, I hoped it would be a long time, too.

On Thanksgiving morning, I went to get Liz Bess for a morning of picture taking in the woods. It was a late fall, and the colors were just now in their prime. Liz Bess and I had planned this ever since Daddy brought me the camera. We were going to take pictures of each other to give our parents for Christmas and had each brought a nice dress to change into before taking them.

"*Gone with the Wind* starts tomorrow at the Palace," I said to Liz Bess in disappointment. "I wish we could go see it together, but I guess we can't sit together unless we just do it like those demonstrators up north. But we might get our heads cracked. Maybe I could sneak up to the balcony and sit with you."

"It's okay, Sue Ann. Mother is coming to get me Saturday morning, and we're going to Memphis to shop. It's playing at the Malco, and Mama said she'd take me to see it before we come back home. I wish there was some way you could go with us. You know Negroes and whites go to some theatres in Memphis together now. Mama said they still don't sit together, exactly, but at least Negroes don't have to sit in a balcony like they do at the Palace."

"Adults must be smarter up north than they are in Mississippi."

Liz Bess and I made our way to the woods but passed the gully, our usual destination. We decided to go farther into the woods, to the Perkins place, where there were huge trees full of reds, yellows, and oranges, the perfect backdrop for pictures. We didn't know it, but the pictures we would end up with that morning would not need a backdrop of any kind to make a statement.

Just as we got to the top of the hill, we heard someone talking.

"Quick! Duck down, Liz Bess!" I whispered, not knowing if Mr. Perkins would get us for trespassing or not. He did have signs posted, but I had never seen anyone, the times Liz Bess and I had been in the woods.

We ducked behind some bushes that overlooked the hollow. Caleb Perkins and Lady V. Harvey were sitting on a stump.

They were laughing and talking for the first few minutes, but then their mood changed. They began kissing, and the next thing we knew they were undressing each other. Liz Bess's mouth flew open. I motioned for her to be quiet as I got out my camera and began clicking away. My plotting began. It was time for revenge!

Liz Bess covered her eyes for most of the escapades of the worldly young couple. I could not cover mine if I was to get perfect blackmailing pictures, but I wanted to. What I saw was too gross for words. Not that I would need words to describe the scene. The pictures would suffice. After what seemed like hours, the two once again sat on the stump, both as naked as birth.

"I bet your little Shadywood hick couldn't do that," said Lady V.

"Get over it, V. You know you're the only girl for me. I just danced with Rita Jean once, that's all. I don't know why you're still so worked up about it."

"Well, you won't be dancing with her at the Christmas ball. I took care of that."

"Don't you think that's mean, leaving her out like that? She didn't do anything to hurt you."

V stood up, nakedness and all, and slapped Caleb. She obviously did not like for her boyfriend to take Rita Jean's side in this matter. I clicked the camera again, getting a nice full-length shot of her in full swing, and there was more than her arm swinging. She definitely did not need bobby socks.

"What'd you go and do that for?" Caleb obviously had all the mandatory credentials, none of which I had ever seen before, nor did I want to see again, but he was certainly not acting very manly at this point.

Hurriedly, Lady V dressed and stormed out of the holler with Caleb still putting on his shirt as he tried to catch up.

"Oh, come on, V, don't be mad." He was following her like a puppy and begging for forgiveness, something she would be doing soon if my plotting worked.

Just as they got to the top of the hill, Caleb pulled Lady Vampire to him and kissed her.

"Still mad?"

The Vampire took his face in her hands and kissed him long and hard. Then they disappeared over the hill.

Liz Bess still had her eyes covered, and I had to pry her hands off.

"I'm sorry, Liz Bess, but we'll have to take pictures another time. I took up the rest of this roll of film."

"What do you want pictures of that for, Sue Ann? That was disgusting. They'll both go to hell for that, you know. That's what Mama tells Leonia."

"Blackmail, Liz Bess, blackmail! If I can figure out a way to get these developed, I'll just bet Rita Jean will have an invitation in the mail before you know it, even after the Thanksgiving deadline."

Liz Bess had no clue what I was talking about, so I had to explain all the details of Rita Jean's first date and Lady V's cruelty. Liz Bess could see how my idea just might work, but like me did not know how we would get the film developed. It would take weeks, sending it off, and besides, I would not want my name attached to these pictures. I thought it was probably against the law, but I knew it was against the Bible.

The answer to my dilemma was waiting at home for me. Jerry's car was in our driveway. He had brought Mama a bouquet of flowers for Thanksgiving like he did his mother.

Mama was genuinely touched, having never received flowers before in her life. This made me feel really bad. Maybe if she had a son, she would have gotten flowers. She did have a husband, but Zeke Taylor was not Jim Anderson from *Father Knows Best* and never thought about bringing his wife anything.

As Jerry was leaving, I had an idea. I rolled off the film in my camera and ran down the gravel road toward Liz Bess's house. As Jerry rounded the curve, I flagged him down.

"Jerry, did you mean it when you said you hoped Lady V. Harvey got what she deserved for hurting Rita Jean?"

"Of course, I meant it, Sue Ann. Why?"

"Do you know how to develop film?"

"I develop all the pictures for our school newspaper. I train other staff members to use the darkroom. What are you up to, girl, and why do you want to know?"

Quickly, I told Jerry about the pictures I had taken, but did not tell him all the sordid details. He would find out soon enough if he agreed to develop them for me.

"I guess I'll do it, but you have to promise not to tell anyone that I did this for you. I could get suspended from school for this. What are you going to do with the pictures?"

"You don't want to know, but I'll bet you one thing. I bet Rita Jean gets a personal invitation from Miss Lady Victoria Harvey to be a member of the Bartonville Debutantes Society."

"Then I guess it'll be worth taking the chance. I can't stand V or that Caleb Perkins."

"Here's the film. Now swear on spit that you won't breathe a word about this to anybody, especially not Rita Jean."

"I swear." Jerry spit in his hand and shook my already wet one.

"Don't go changing your mind about delivering those pictures back to me after you see them. They're really nasty. I know I'm not quite thirteen, but this is important to Rita Jean."

"I'll bring them to you first thing in the morning, and then you can do whatever dirty work you want with them."

The conspiracy was set.

Chapter Nine
"It just ain't fittin'!"

The next morning, Jerry came to the house. When Rita Jean went to ask Mama if she could go riding, Jerry pulled me aside and handed me an envelope.

"I can't believe I am handing so much filth into the hands of an almost-thirteen-year-old girl, but you have obviously already seen everything in here. I don't want to know anything more about this, Sue Ann. Remember, when you swear on spit, you take it to the grave with you. Right?"

"Right," I responded. "Thanks, Jerry."

"Good luck. I wish I could see their faces when they see these for the first time."

Rita Jean and Jerry left to go riding in Jerry's pickup. Now all I had to do was set up the rest of the conspiracy. I grabbed up scissors, paper, glue, and several copies of old *Progressive Farmers* and the *Bartonville Weekly* and headed for the barn hideout. I had told Liz Bess to meet me there at ten o'clock for the "biggest case of the Taylor & Donnelly Detective Agency yet." Trouble was, this time we were the criminals.

Liz Bess, though usually daring, had no desire to look at the pictures that Jerry had blown up much bigger than was necessary, so I picked out one that had both V and Caleb in it and put it inside a big envelope I had found in Mama's dresser drawer where she kept her bank statements and other business papers. I hid the rest of the pictures under the old hay in the loft. Then, the cut-and-paste part of the crime began.

Using the old *Progressive Farmers* and the newspapers, Liz Bess and I cut out words we could find for our message, glued them to paper, and then filled in the rest with what looked like first-grade printing. We couldn't risk writing the message in our own handwriting. That would be a clue to our identity. When we finished, we admired our handiwork and laughed. We had used expressions from *Gone with the Wind* to relay our message, some of Scarlet's, some of Rhett's, but mostly Mammy's. The demands read:

> Good gals don't show their bosom. It just ain't fittin'! It also ain't fittin' the way you been treating Rita Jean. You got one chance to make it right or you'll find pictures like this one nailed up all around Bartonville. I got some ready to mail to yo' mammy and pappy if you don't do what I say. Don't wait 'til tomorrow. It will be too late. By 6:30 this afternoon, an invitation to yo' high society club must be hand-delivered to Rita Jean Taylor. And in the next school newspaper, there better be a real genuine compliment for Rita Jean. Don't tell Rita Jean or anyone about this or the deal is off. When these conditions are met, the pictures will be destroyed. Don't fiddle-dee-dee this away or yo' "charm, proper etiquette, and strong character" just might be in question by the town of Bartonville. If you think this is unfair, you ain't seen nothin' yet!

We signed it: Friends of Rita Jean.

Now all I had to do was figure out how to get it to Lady Vampire. This could be the tricky part. Daddy provided the answer.

"Sue Ann, I'm going to Bartonville. Did you say you needed a ride to town?"

"Yep. I sure do. I'll be right there." I grabbed the envelope and headed for Daddy's truck. "Drop me off at the post office, Daddy."

"Okay. Meet me at the hardware store in about a half hour."

"What time does the mail run in town today?" I asked the postmaster.

"Ought to be going out any minute now," he replied. "You got something to mail?"

My envelope was addressed to Lady Victoria Harvey and was marked "Personal" and "Urgent" on the outside. I decided to chance giving it to the postmaster to get it to the vampire in time for the deadline to be met.

"I'll go on and put this in the Harvey's box. They don't get their mail on the route. They been in once for the mail today, so they probably won't pick it up again 'til tomorrow."

It was already one o'clock. This was not what I wanted to hear. V had to get the envelope today, and I did not want to risk the vampire's parents seeing it before she did. I decided I had to make a phone call.

I went to the phone booth outside, and in my gruffest, most disguised voice, I told V she had better check the mail before her parents did or she would be sorry. I hung up before V could ask any questions, then bought a vanilla Coke and sat in the drug store at a table where I could see the post office.

Sure enough, before I reached my last slurp, I saw Lady V heading into the post office in somewhat of a hurry. She left with the envelope in her hand.

"Success!" I thought as I headed to the hardware store, where I met Daddy on his way to the truck.

"Let me off at Liz Bess's house, Daddy. Mama said she could come up and play this afternoon, and I want to tell her." Life was much easier since Mama had given in to Liz Bess and me being friends, but she had made the stipulation that it was not for public knowledge. I guess she was afraid of the men in white sheets.

"Y'all not goin' to the gully on a beautiful afternoon like this?"

"Nope, we're just going to hang out at the house, maybe play in the Little Theatre."

Liz Bess and I hurried up the gully path and through the pecan grove to the house to await Rita Jean's invitation.

Two hours had passed since the vampire picked up the envelope, and I was beginning to get nervous that my plan was not going to work. Liz Bess and I went to the pecan grove to pick up pecans we'd missed earlier in the fall, and to watch the road. At five o'clock, we saw a familiar red convertible speeding up the road. We dropped our pecans and headed for the front porch.

Caleb Perkins got out of the car and sheepishly walked to the front porch.

"Can I help you?" I asked in my sweetest little girl voice.

"Is Rita Jean here?" he asked as he dug the toe of his shoe into the grass in the front yard.

"Rita Jean!" I yelled as loud as I could, to purposely startle the already nervous young man.

"What?" Rita Jean yelled back at me from inside the house.

"You got company!" I yelled back.

Rita Jean came out on the porch and did a double take as she saw Caleb Perkins standing there.

"Hi, Caleb. What brings you way out here to Hickville?" she asked, rudely making reference to the "country girl" quote from his girlfriend's column. I was very proud of my sister for not bowing down to "Kookie, Kookie, lend me your comb."

"Uh, my daddy got this letter in his mailbox by mistake. It's addressed to you."

Rita Jean took the letter and looked at the envelope. It was a very formal-looking letter with her name and address clearly written on the outside in calligraphy. Liz Bess and I hurried over to look over Rita Jean's shoulder at the envelope.

"Well, I wonder how that happened," Rita Jean pondered out loud.

"Well, his box is just two over from yours. It would be an easy mistake to make. Aren't you going to open it?" Caleb had obviously been given orders to wait and make sure Rita Jean opened the letter before he left. I guess he would be the witness, if needed.

Rita Jean carefully broke the seal on the envelope and opened the card inside. It read:

You are cordially invited to join the Bartonville Debutantes Society, a sisterhood honoring young ladies of "notable southern heritage, charm, proper etiquette, and strong character." We look forward to presenting you to Bartonville Society at the Christmas Debutantes Ball on December 22 at Five Oaks, the Harvey residence. Formal dress is required for you, your escort, and your parents.

> *RSVP*
> *Lady Victoria Harvey*
> *P.O. Box 32*
> *Bartonville, Mississippi*

"Thank you for delivering this, Caleb. Tell V I'll think about this and let her know if I want to join or not." Rita Jean was so cool, calm, and collected that I could not believe it was my sister.

"You mean you don't want to join, Rita Jean? V really wants you to be in the society."

"This has nothing to do with what your lady wants, Caleb. I don't know if I want to be part of a society that is headed by someone who low-rates people and lies about them in a school gossip column. Why did I get this, Caleb? I'm still just a plain little ninth grade country girl who dances like a yellow peacock. Was V trying to make me sweat thinking I wouldn't be invited?"

"No...I mean...V's real sorry she wrote that, Rita Jean. She didn't mean it. She was just jealous 'cause I danced with you. Come on, Rita Jean, say you'll be in her debutante thing." Caleb was grasping for words, afraid that if Rita Jean didn't accept the invitation, her friends might think he and V didn't go through with their end of the bargain. My sister had him squirming.

"I tell you what. You deliver this message to Madame Victoria Harvey." Rita Jean facetiously distorted V's name to show she was not bowing to her—or "kissing butt," as Daddy would put it—debutante or not.

"You tell her to come out here and apologize to me in person, and I'll accept this invitation. Otherwise, the answer is no."

Caleb got in his convertible and left. Liz Bess and I clapped and cheered.

"You told him, girl! That was great, Rita Jean. I didn't know you had it in you. But are you really not going to accept the invitation?" I hoped this whole escapade was not for naught.

"Nope, not unless she apologizes. My mind is made up." Rita Jean turned and walked into the house like she could care less about the Bartonville Debutantes Society.

My sister had some realistic values after all. I'm sure the fact that the best-looking boy in the school was still her boyfriend helped her self-image immensely.

Liz Bess did not want to leave, but it was getting late.

"Don't worry, Liz Bess. If the vampire shows, I'll memorize every word of the apology and tell you tomorrow."

Jerry came over to watch television that night. Rita Jean told Jerry about the visit from Caleb and about the invitation, and Jerry glanced over at me and winked. He told Rita Jean he was really glad she had stood up to Lady V and hoped he would be around for the apology if it should come.

Jerry was in luck. It wasn't more than an hour later that the red convertible drove up, this time with both the vampire and her favorite victim.

"Hello, V, Caleb. Would you like to come in?"

94

Rita Jean stood back to let the couple enter.

"We can only stay a minute, Rita Jean. Got a family dinner to go to. I just came by to say I'm sorry for acting like such a butt. I promise I'll never write anything ugly about you in the school newspaper again. I really do want you to accept the invitation to the Debutantes Society."

Rita Jean was enjoying this immensely, and so was Jerry, who had come and put his arm around Rita Jean so he could get the full effect of Lady V's groveling. I could hardly wait to tell Liz Bess tomorrow and was replaying the vampire's words over again and again in my head so I could remember them.

"Okay, V, I accept your apology, and I accept the invitation to join the Debutantes Society. I look forward to the Christmas ball. Thank you for coming by."

Rita Jean left Jerry to escort the two relieved-looking teenagers out. As she turned toward Jerry and me, she jerked her fist downward and screamed a whispered, "Yes!" Jerry grabbed Rita Jean, and they began bopping without music.

"Come on, little sister!" Pulling me onto the living room dance floor, the three of us danced, with Jerry giving me another big wink as if to say, "Well done," when Rita Jean wasn't looking.

Mama and Daddy came in shortly after, and Rita Jean told them all about the apology and how the invitation had been delivered to Mr. Perkins by mistake. She showed Mama the elegant invitation.

"I'm glad you got invited, Rita Jean. I guess we'll be shopping for formals soon. This says formal attire for your parents, too. Does that mean I get to wear a formal and your daddy has to wear a tuxedo? Now, won't that be something?"

Daddy just let out a big moan as he settled into his easy chair to watch the football game. There would be many moans ahead for Daddy, with three girls. He said he didn't miss having a son but would certainly have felt more comfortable watching a child on the football field than in a fancy ballroom.

Mama was visibly pleased. You could see her mind just dancing with visions of the better life. The Taylor family was definitely on its way up.

Chapter Ten
Graceland

Christmas vacation began with only one thought for the Taylor family, buying a formal for Rita Jean's social debut. Mama had opted to borrow a formal, once again sacrificing her pleasure so that her daughter could afford a formal that would "knock the stinkin' spoiled socks off that rotten little Lady Victoria Harvey," as Mama put it. Even Mattie Lynn got hung up in the excitement of the "Better Life" and insisted that she take Rita Jean shopping for a formal, something that had been left out of Mattie Lynn's life in high school when the school would not allow her to take her college boyfriend/fiancé/husband to either her junior or senior prom. Mama was happy for Mattie Lynn to take on this job and agreed Rita Jean and I could come as soon as Christmas break began.

Rita Jean had her driver's license now, and Daddy actually let us take the car by ourselves to Whitehaven, with the promise that we would not drive it once we got there, especially not in Memphis city limits, where the traffic was way too busy for little country girls. Mattie Lynn agreed to drive us downtown to shop for Rita Jean's formal, and, call me crazy, but I was actually excited about the shopping adventure.

Mattie Lynn and Bob had bought a house in Whitehaven, a brick house, a "real" brick house, with two bathrooms. When my sister reached the middle, she reached it in style. When we got to Mattie and Bob's house, I noticed my oldest sister's face was riddled with smiles, the kind of smiles that say, "I've got a secret." She helped us get our bags into the guest bedroom and then told us we had to sit down because she had an unbelievable surprise for us. I looked at Rita Jean, and we both jumped on the bed while our sister sat in the chair beside us. Mattie gave a little thrill shake, clapped her hands in rapid succession and dove right in.

"My neighbor, Rose, is the niece of Mr. Byrd, who just happens to be the gatekeeper at Graceland. Rose has two teenage daughters who go to Graceland a couple of times a week to private parties that Elvis throws for the teenagers of the Memphis area after midnight. She told me if you two came up during Christmas, she'd get you in to at least one of his parties." Mattie watched to see our reaction and was not disappointed when we shrieked, covered our mouths, and jumped from the bed and continued jumping up and down and holding our hands over our mouths to hold back the screams.

"You're going to Graceland tonight!" Mattie Lynn jumped up ready to collect us if we fainted or went any more insane. She would not be disappointed.

Rita Jean screamed so loud I was sure the cops would arrive any minute with sirens blazing. Then she jumped in the middle of the bed and began running in place…with her shoes on! I fell down in the chair my sister had exited, in a pretend faint like the one Rita Jean would probably do for real when she saw Elvis that night.

Good things were certainly happening to the Taylor

family, and I had no idea what we had done to deserve it. Rita Jean immediately started planning what she would wear. I did not have to think about it since I had only brought two outfits that would be suitable for such an occasion. The trunk of the Mercury would hold quite a bit, but Rita Jean had brought three big suitcases, one filled with nothing but shoes, makeup, hair rollers, and her hair dryer. My one suitcase had to go on the back seat.

"Well, you have until ten o'clock tonight to figure out what you're wearing, because that's when Rose and I will be taking you to Graceland. I have to admit, I'm pretty excited about it myself. Rose has been a lot, and she said she'll show me around inside the mansion before we leave you." Mattie was so excited she had to stop and catch her breath. "Bob and I will be back there to pick you up around three in the morning. Daddy would probably kill me if he knew I was doing this, but it's a risk worth taking."

We followed Mattie to the living room with her yakking the whole time and giving several more body tremors.

"I mean, how many girls from Shadywood get to party with Elvis?" Mattie's voice was shaking with excitement. At this, Rita Jean started screaming again, and I grabbed her and started bopping while singing, appropriately, "A Whole Lot of Shaking Going On." I ended it with the famous stiff right leg Elvis jerk and twitched my upper lip to excess.

It took Rita Jean two solid hours to get dressed that night, and this was after doing her hair. She changed clothes several times and even had to change her nail polish when she changed from a red skirt and sweater to a pink one at the last minute. Mattie Lynn kept rushing her, sure she wouldn't be ready by ten o'clock. Rita Jean was glad she had gone back to the ducktail Mama had given her at the beginning of the year. She had used half a can of hair spray making sure it was slicked back to Elvis perfection.

Both of my sisters decided I needed help with my hair, lots of help, so I would not look "so Shadywood," and before I could protest, my curls were stretched over gigantic brush rollers and I was sitting under Rita Jean's hair dryer that looked like a plastic shower cap with a long vacuum cleaner hose attached. It was torture sitting still for that long, but I had to admit I liked the results. My curls were straightened out into smooth long strands that flipped up on the end. Even my bangs were fluffy rather than in the tight "doo-doo rolls" that usually formed naturally whether I wanted them to or not. Mattie Lynn was so proud of the new me that she insisted I wear a little lipstick, light pink, which she applied for me, knowing I had no experience in such things. She was right. There were no mirrors in the gully, or the barn hideout. Of course, I had to pinky-swear not to tell Mama that Mattie had put lipstick on me.

I could not believe the fuss Rita Jean went to with her hair and makeup, but the end results made her look like she was from Hollywood, not Shadywood. Just before she put on her tight pink sweater, she took out an extra pair of nylon stockings from her suitcase.

"Oh, no, you don't!" I began backing up holding my hands up for protection. "I'm not wearing those. My bobby socks are just fine!"

"They're not for you, silly." Rita Jean wadded

them up and stuck one in each cup of her already padded bra.

It was then that I noticed Rita Jean had really filled out since her first date just a few months ago. She had gone from bobby socks to stockings. Later that year Frankie Avalon came out with a song that I was sure had been inspired by Rita Jean's blossoming bosom.

Rose and her daughters picked us up at ten o'clock sharp. Rita Jean had warned me not to embarrass her by appearing too excited in front of Rose's daughters. She didn't want them to know we were not accustomed to such activities. As it turned out, the city girls barely spoke to us. As soon as we entered the front door of Graceland, the girls joined their boyfriends, and we never saw them again. Rose and Mattie Lynn went to the kitchen, where they sat at the table and drank coffee. Mattie Lynn could not get over the fact that they used Pet Milk straight out of the can in Elvis's kitchen. I guess she thought Elvis would have a solid gold cream pitcher...perhaps one that played "Hound Dog" when you tipped it over. Mattie and Rose didn't stay long before leaving Rita Jean and me to wander the bottom floor of Graceland, anxiously awaiting the appearance of the King.

Rita Jean tried to act nonchalant, like we had been there many times before. We wandered around secretly absorbing every detail of the downstairs so we could share the information with our friends when we got back home. No one was allowed upstairs where Elvis lived. One of his bodyguards stood at the bottom of the stairs to prevent anyone from trying to invade his boss's privacy. Elvis slept most of the day, according to what we heard later, and came down right before midnight to lead a caravan of teenage fans to whatever destination he had rented for his private entertainment.

We followed a couple down a flight of stairs to the basement recreation room, where the walls were covered in gold records and albums. I was hoping there would be a time when I could touch one of the records, but I never got a chance with so many teeny boppers around. Rita Jean went over to a soda bar in one corner of the room and fixed herself a strawberry soda. I followed suit and prepared an orange one like I knew what I was doing. In my mind, this was my house and these were all my guests, entertaining themselves while waiting for the big party to start. Since I couldn't sing very well, I was imagining myself as a great novelist who had made millions off a series of Susan Taylor mysteries that had been turned into a weekly television show. Hobnobbing with the rich and famous had never been something I dreamed of, but Graceland triggered unusual thoughts in my thirteen-year-old imagination.

At eleven thirty, the King descended the stairs. He spoke pertly to his guests who had gathered in the front parlor and made his way to the white baby grand piano that was just off the main room. Teddy bears were everywhere in both rooms, lined up on the sofa and down on the white fluffy carpet that was like stepping on a thick layer of marshmallows.

Elvis sat down at the piano and cracked his knuckles, pretending to be a concert pianist. We all laughed as if Elvis was comedian of the year.

"This is for my cousin Bobby. It's his day." Elvis then sang "Happy Birthday" but in a fashion I'd never heard before, a combination of gospel and rock and roll.

I looked around, trying to locate this cousin Bobby,

but the room seemed to be full of cousin Bobbies, all with greased-back black hair and sideburns, obviously Elvis wannabes, but all looking more like rednecks from Tupelo than rich relatives from Memphis. None of them came close to being as handsome as the young singer/musician who sat at the beautiful baby grand piano.

Elvis disappeared shortly after his dedication, and Rita Jean and I decided to walk outside to see the famous kidney-shaped pool. As we rounded the corner, we stopped when we saw Elvis, famous-gorgeous Elvis, standing all alone beside the pool, looking up at the zillions of stars overhead. Rita Jean was quietly swooning as we watched from behind the shrubs, but as I stared at the beautiful young man, I felt his sadness. I thought of the loss of his mother whom he adored and wondered how one so famous ever finds solace, or thinking time, or time for "self" when surrounded by so many noisy fans and cousins, all vying for suffocation privileges. In a few minutes, one of the bodyguards who had been lurking in the shadows told his boss it was time. With one more look at the stars, perhaps searching for his mama, he gave a big sigh and returned to his mansion prison. I wiped a tear from my eye and followed on my sister's heels, not to be left behind.

At exactly twelve o'clock, the caravan left Graceland, with Elvis and his bodyguards in the leading limousine. Rita Jean and I had begged a ride with a couple in a plain old Chevy, third in line in the convoy. When we drove through the gate leaving Graceland, I rolled down my window and waved at the crowd. The driver turned and blessed me out, telling me to roll the window up and stop making a fool of myself. Rita Jean looked very embarrassed and punched me in the ribs with her elbow.

The convoy stopped at Rainbow Skating Rink, which Elvis had rented for the rest of the night, and Rita Jean looked worried. Neither of us could roller skate. As it turned out, not many of the group got to skate anyway. Elvis and his cousins and bodyguards used the entire rink as a battlefield to play a form of very violent football on wheels. They ran together, tearing at each other, tackling and slinging, with Elvis right in the middle of it. I kept my eyes shut most of the time, while the crowd cheered Elvis on and booed those who knocked the King down. The game was so rough Elvis split the whole seat out of his tight black pants and had to leave the floor. One of his bodyguards returned to Graceland and got another pair for him.

The best part of the night was when Elvis came up into the bleachers and demonstrated karate moves for his drooling audience. Rita Jean and I were sitting close, mesmerized by the beauty of this man. His eyes were hazel and seemed to sparkle as rink lights reflected in them. When he performed a karate chop or a kick, the jet-black kiss curl danced on his forehead, and I could see why all the girls swooned over him. Had I not been such a strong, in-control kind of girl, I might have fainted, too, just watching him.

As we filed out the door of the skating rink to load into the caravan on our return to Graceland, we each passed single file by Elvis. He stopped Rita Jean with his hand on her arm, stared into her face and said, "I like your hair." Rita Jean was so surprised with his touch she could only choke out a soft, half-swallowed "Thank you." Rita Jean, speechless! This was one for the records.

I remembered my manners as I passed Elvis and said, "I had a nice time."

"Glad you did, baby." He puckered his full, perfect lips in a kissing gesture that made my stomach churn as I hurried out the door. If I hadn't known better, I would have thought I was in love.

Bob and Mattie Lynn were waiting on us when we got back to Graceland. Rita Jean and I fought for airtime as we replayed every second of the night. Mattie Lynn promised we could go again the next night.

I took more pains, without prompting from Rita Jean, on getting ready for the second night at Graceland. Once again I was shackled to the hair dryer and even let Mattie Lynn apply some clear polish to my stubby fingernails, which were bitten into the quick the night before.

The second night was not as exciting as the first but was still unforgettable. What else could a night with Elvis Presley be? We caught a ride in a car that was already pretty full and was close to the end of the caravan. One of Elvis's greasy cousins with bad teeth and even worse breath rode in the backseat and put his arm around Rita Jean, who moved in closer—not because the guy was handsome but because he was the cousin of Elvis Presley. Go figure!

This time Elvis had rented the Memphian, a movie theatre downtown, where we saw two race car movies, one of which was called "That Dangerous Hairpin Curve." Elvis sat in front of us, surrounded by bodyguards and slick cousins. Neither Rita Jean nor I watched the movies; we just watched Elvis watch the movies. He was totally engrossed in the action and made loud comments all through both shows. If we had not been sitting behind Elvis Presley, it would have been considered an uneventful night watching two boring guy flicks. As we passed by our host on our way out the door of the theatre, I handed Elvis a pen, which I had sneaked into my pocket before leaving Mattie Lynn's, and asked if he would sign my white blouse. He smiled and said, "Sure," and signed "TCB. Love ya, Elvis Presley" right across my left shoulder on the back. I swore I'd never wash it and would keep it forever.

Later that week, after we got home, Mama washed my blouse even though she knew how excited I was about the autograph. Even in our present comfortable financial condition, Mama just could not bear the thought of wasting a perfectly good blouse. I was devastated and never forgave her for giving in to what I called her Depression mentality.

I had never been a big Elvis fan up until that time, but he had stirred emotions in me that I had not thought possible. The King pushed me from adolescence to my teenage years, hastening my maturity with a teasing kiss, a karate move, and the warmth of his hand on my shoulder as he signed his famous autograph. Later, I would think this was God's way of helping prepare me for changes that could be better dealt with as a young adult than as a child. Who but Sue Ann Taylor would think of my adventure with Elvis and Graceland as more of God's stepping stones into maturity?

Chapter Eleven
Victorian Lady

I missed her at first glance,
A derelict with shoulders stooped,
Eyes lowered in shame.
She hid, obscured by awry oaks
And honeysuckle falsely sweet, poison oak
*   entangled.*
Her eyes found refuge in the ground
And seldom, near never, looked eye to eye at
*   passersby.*
Her shawl, once white, now mildewed, rotted,
Kissed the earth for want
Of prideful looking up long since passed.
Shoes overrun,
Dress faded, much worn,
Lace dirty, ragged,
Torn away in dispassionate greed.
Heart and body defiled by drunken youths.
.
I paused.
Why did I stop?
She lifted her veil, salt-stained, tattered.
Eyes, sad but gentle, beckoned, "Save me!"
I saw deep,
Deep beyond present agony.
I saw the Victorian lady as she had been, could be.

PROUD, ROMANTIC, RESPLENDENT!
I held out my hand.
The lady was reborn.

(March 8, 1958)

.

Mama did it! She finished Moler's at the end of January, bypassing the high school diploma she'd missed out on, to become an educated, professional woman and a business owner.

She opened Irene's House of Style on Valentine's Day. The old building, which had been a bank at one time, was restored by Daddy to far past its original glory, with Chinese wallpaper reminiscent of the paper in the asbestos house, set off by mahogany facings and moldings that had been refinished to show their natural patina and then covered with clear, shiny varnish to protect it "for all time and eternity," as Daddy described it.

Mama furnished it all in antiques, with a Queen Anne sofa and three wing-backed chairs forming the waiting area for the many customers she envisioned arriving for their appointments. She had bought the pieces cheap because they were in such terrible condition, but she restored and then upholstered them in velvet or tapestry to match the elegance of the walls.

The sitting area was complemented with mahogany tables she had refinished, and there was one exquisite oak teardrop table rescued from the dump. The table was covered in magazines, arranged meticulously, with many showing the latest hairstyles, all of which Mama was proficient in reproducing for the ladies of Bartonville, none of whom would look like the models in the pictures regardless of the attention Mama paid to detail.

The shop looked like something that should have been in Memphis, and I couldn't help but be reminded of a certain boarding house just off Beale Street. I could see why Mama began referring to it as a salon rather than a shop. As she explained it, "A beauty shop is a box built out of plywood, sheetrock, or cheap paneling, and linoleum, the bare necessities needed in a place designed just to help a woman's outward appearance."

Mama had a way of associating building materials with stature and divine purpose. Irene's was a salon and reeked of elegance and pampering. It began the miracle makeover of each woman from the inside out as she entered its doorway, even before the final dramatic outward transformation.

Mama used the old bank's mahogany counter, which matched the trim perfectly after she refinished it, to separate the waiting area from the work area. The utilitarian portion of the salon had three stations, each outfitted with a hair-washing sink, a hair-dressing table with an ornate beveled mirror hanging over it, and a big metal hair dryer that looked like a barrel from Mars turned upside down, under which each customer sat for up to an hour.

Always determined on "bettering" herself, even in the wake of existing success, Mama fully intended for this business to make it big. She was set up to hire two more hairstylists even though, to start off, she would run it by herself and build up business.

Rita Jean was more excited about the new business than Mama was, or at least she showed it more. Every day after school, she worked as the manicurist, soaking, filing to perfect shape, and polishing the fingernails of the clients, many of whom had nails so long they looked like the bonepickers of the Choctaws that I read about in my Mississippi history class, who used their long nails to pick the flesh from the bones of the dead.

Daddy, too, added to the Taylor socioeconomic pinnacle and purchased the bulldozer he had talked about for months, starting his own dirt-moving business. Already he couldn't keep up with the jobs he had scheduled and, like Mama, was thinking of hiring an assistant, one for the other dozer he was going to buy.

One Saturday afternoon in early March, Daddy told me to get in the truck. He had something he wanted to show me. We headed for Bartonville but drove straight through town, past Irene's House of Style, where Mama had been steadily "twisting hair," as she called it, since 7:30 that morning, and down Harvey Road, an unlined paved county road on the outskirts of town.

The old Ford headed onto a rough dirt pig trail that seemed to go straight through what had once been a cotton patch, with hills of cotton rows still discernible as judged by the bump, bump, thud of Daddy's truck. The dried, prickly cotton stalks and hulls, long since stripped of their precious commodity, stood with their heads held high over choking sage grass and thick weeds, as if trying desperately to survive this attack by their formidable enemies.

The road turned abruptly uphill and ended in front of a massive tangle of vines, honeysuckle, overgrown hedges, and bushes that had once been a yard. Peeking out of the vines was a large, rundown house, ancient and forgotten.

"This is the old Parrish Place. My daddy used to

talk about going to parties here when he was a young man, before he and Ma got married. It was a real beauty in its day." Daddy grabbed my arm when he saw I was about to step up onto what was left of the porch. "Be real careful, Sudi. Step in my footsteps. The porches have all rotted away, so you have to walk across on the floor joists."

Looking like tightrope walkers from the circus that came to Bartonville every fall, Daddy and I walked precariously across the narrow joists of the side porch. An old concrete-and-brick cistern protruded through the rotting floorboards. Lifting the wood covering to the cistern, I stared squeamishly down into black water that must have stood stagnant for decades.

Daddy creaked open the old wooden side door, making an arched scrape on the floor as it opened just enough for us to squeeze inside.

"Isn't this a beauty?"

Daddy stepped aside to allow me to enter the room whose ceiling reached into forever. The ancient flowered wallpaper hung from the walls like torn skin, displaying cheesecloth flesh beneath, held to the walls by millions of tiny, rusty tacks. The fireplace, devoid of its mantel obviously stolen by other seeming lovers of antiquities long ago, was piled high with beer and whiskey bottles and mounds of cigarette butts. A de-clawed clawfoot tub was all that remained in the old bathroom, and it looked as if someone had tried unsuccessfully to steal it, having been dragged to the doorway of the bathroom before being abandoned and relieved of its decorative feet.

"I wonder why they didn't take the rest of the tub," I mused. I had seen old tubs like this pictured in some of the magazines Mama had in the beauty shop. It was popular to restore them and use them in modern homes.

"Why don't you go and lift one end, and I think you'll see why the thieves gave up."

I took Daddy up on the suggestion, but when I tried to lift it I found it would not budge even a fraction of an inch. The dead daddy-long-legs lying in its permanently stained, rust-colored bottom must have been an elephant in disguise. The tub weighed a ton.

"Look at these wide plank floors, Sue Ann. That's heart pine, and they are as sound as the day they were put down in 1880."

All I could see was layer upon layer of dirt, with more bottles, cans, and cigarette butts strewn from corner to corner, leftovers of the youths who had ravaged the old lady.

It even looked as if someone had tried to start a fire in the middle of the room, where the floor was black. None of this seemed to matter to Daddy, who was totally enamored with the old house and able to see through the grime to the majesty of what had been, what could be again.

We looked room by room through the rest of the house and discovered there was a fireplace in every room except the kitchen. Only one mantel remained, a relatively plain one, obviously its saving grace. The ornate tiles had been pulled away or had fallen from around the outside of the fireplace, but I could still imagine how regal this house must have been with all its fine details.

"How long since anybody lived here, Daddy?"

"Oh, it's been about twenty years, I reckon. Ain't it a shame to let something this beautiful go down like this?" Daddy shook his head in disbelief at such a sinful act of neglect. The old house had become personified in his mind.

Daddy's enthusiasm was contagious, and I began to revel in the beauty of what was once a Victorian mansion—a mansion from a Taylor's perspective, that is. I was even becoming attached to the ragged walls that looked like neglected flower gardens just begging to be pruned or replanted. The house lacked in comparison to Five Oaks, a real mansion, but then, the home of the Harveys was Antebellum, not Victorian, and remained part of a huge plantation.

The Parrish family were cousins of the Harveys but had not inherited as much of the wealth of the family as did the father of J.T. and Winfred. Five Oaks stood in its magnificence across the road from the Parrish Place, in the middle of hundreds of acres of land, not visible from the road except for its long, winding driveway overlapped with magnolias on each side, like giants holding hands, allowing visitors to pass through the rich, green tunnel beneath.

"Where do these stairs go, Daddy? This is not a two-story house, is it?"

I had become brave enough to explore without Daddy right beside me. Old houses had always fascinated me, but this was my first one to explore, and I wanted to absorb every inch of it.

"What a great ghost story this would make, or better still, the setting for a Susan Taylor thriller." Thinking aloud, I looked up the long staircase.

"Must be an attic room. Go on up and have a look, if you want, but be careful. I think it's pretty sound once you get away from the porches, but you might test the floor before you put your whole weight on it." Daddy continued to devour the downstairs portion of the house.

In eager anticipation, I creaked up the stairs with just a little fright of what lay at the top. Very little light came into the attic room, which gave the stairs a creepy aura, but I continued on in the brave tradition of the "Susan Taylor" façade I took on in moments like this.

As I stepped into the attic room, I heard a rustling noise behind me, and I jumped and gave a muted shriek. A huge gray rat scurried out from under a pile of rags and papers heaped up in the corner.

"Give me a few minutes, and I'll give you back your home." I laughed when I realized I was carrying on a conversation with a rat.

As I turned around, I received a much bigger fright. A shadow of another presence appeared on the wall that slanted steeply from its high-pitched, pointed ceiling to the floor. This time I screamed loud enough that Daddy ascended the stairs two at a time to come to my rescue.

"What is it, Sue Ann?" Daddy was puffing hard from climbing the stairs so fast.

As I pointed to the figure that had made the shadow, we both laughed. An old dress form stood guard over the attic room. Though small in stature, with a tiny waist typical of the Victorian era, she cast a big shadow. Daylight filtered in only slightly from the attic's one window shaded by several tall oaks.

"I wonder what's in this old trunk." Careful of what might be inside, I lifted the lid as Daddy continued looking around, kicking through treasured trash on the floor.

"Oh, my gosh! Look at this dress! It looks like

something from the Roaring Twenties!"

Holding up a hot pink satin dress with a scooped neck and a dropped waistline accentuated by moth holes, I danced the Charleston just like Mama had taught me, as Daddy slapped his thighs laughing.

"Do you think it's okay if I take this with me, Daddy? Obviously no one cares about it, or they wouldn't have left it here to rot. I bet it would bring back some memories for Mama."

Daddy hesitated before answering.

"Actually, Sue Ann, I guess it's yours now anyway."

"What do you mean, Daddy?" With a questioning stare, I waited for Daddy's explanation.

"This place is ours now. Your mama and I signed the papers on it yesterday. We're gonna restore it. We'll be living in it by late this summer. I've already hired a contractor."

Holding the dress, I stared at Daddy as if waiting for him to say he was joking. My speakeasy crumbled to the ground and my emotions were as tangled as the vines and honeysuckle that were sucking the life out of the old lady. Knowing Daddy never did anything like this without an ulterior motive, I should have sensed this was more than an adventure. Though the house was awesome, or could be, I couldn't imagine living in it, at least not now.

"What about school? Does this mean no more Shadywood for me?"

"That's right, but don't worry. You'll make friends fast, just like Rita Jean has at high school. Besides, you don't have but one more year at Shadywood. Your old friends will be following you in a year."

"What about Liz Bess, Daddy? How is she going to follow me? What will you do with our old house? And what about Old Ma?"

I needed questions answered before I could feel comfortable about the Victorian lady, and from the look on Daddy's face, he couldn't or wouldn't answer them all right now.

"It will all work out, Sue Ann. You'll see. We better head back now. Your mama ought to be home soon."

Just as we turned to go back down the stairs, I caught a movement by the window and screamed, grabbing Daddy's arm and holding on for dear life. A long, thick black snake with a distinct pattern on its back stretched full-length on the back wall and took his time before slithering out through the slightly raised window, as if letting us know this was his domain and he would come and go as he pleased.

"It's just a rat snake, Sue Ann. He's protecting the place for us, getting rid of the rats. I heard that Old Man Parrish used to keep a rat snake just for that purpose. Maybe that guy's a descendant."

I hated snakes, and so did Daddy usually, but he loved the old house so much he could even overlook the snakes. I just hoped it wasn't an omen.

As we walked through the massive living room of the derelict house on our way out, I stopped and took one more long contemplative look around. The conflicting thoughts from my head ricocheted off the twelve-foot ceiling and bounced back to land directly in my heart, which was turning emotional somersaults of its own.

"Welcome home, Sue Ann!" My whisper echoed,

heard only by the ghost of the Victorian lady who would become known as Parrish Oaks.

Chapter Twelve
Tomorrow

The Coasters "yakety-yakked" from our new twenty-inch television with Liz Bess and me bopping and twirling as *Bandstand* worked its Saturday afternoon magic. Leonia rocked to the beat of the "honky" music, as she called it, from the back of the ironing board where she spent most of her Saturdays, working for Rita Jean's hand-me-downs plus an additional eight dollars that Mama now paid with the success of her business. Nagalee was ailing, too, "stowed up," as she described the arthritis that was fast making her a cripple, and, like it or not, Leonia had taken over her mother's old job.

"That ain't how you do that, girl. Here, let me show you."

Leonia left the ironing board, took my dance partner away from me, and showed me how to pull Liz Bess under her arm and back again and then twirl her continuously as she moved her partner around the living room dance floor like a wind-up ballerina on a music box I had seen once in Sterling's Five and Dime.

"Oh, I see. Thanks, Leonia."

Why I practiced the maneuver was uncertain, as if there would ever be an occasion for Liz Bess and me to show off our dancing in front of our peers.

Mama and Rita Jean came through the back door,

making their way to the living room, where Mama dropped to the couch. Rita Jean followed suit as if she had worked as hard as Mama in the salon. Liz Bess and I stopped dancing, uncomfortable with how Mama might react to such close contact between races.

"Turn that thing off, Sue Ann," Mama yelled. "I've had enough noise out of those two old biddies I had to give permanent waves to this afternoon. I swear. I've got to hire another beauty operator so I can have Saturdays off. I'm worn to a frazzle." Mama kicked her shoes off and laid her head back.

Mama had already hired Carolyn, a young hairdresser right out of beauty school, but the two of them still could not keep up with the demands of Bartonville society. In fact, Mama was taking business away, "right and left" as she put it, from all the ordinary beauty shops in town. Mama had been right. Women preferred mahogany to plywood, velvet to vinyl.

"I like your hair. How'd you get it to do that?" Rita Jean stared at Leonia and surprised us all by giving her a compliment. "It looks almost like a ducktail."

Leonia smoothed one side of her short hair over her ear with her non-ironing hand and looked pleased not only that Rita Jean had complimented her but that she had talked to her at all. Usually, Rita Jean just came in and went about her business without even acknowledging Leonia's presence.

"Thank ya. Did it myself. Copied it from a picture of Carlotta Walls." Leonia seemed proud, though shocked, to be carrying on a conversation with this white princess.

"Who in the world is Carlotta Walls?" Rita Jean took on more of her usual demeaning teenage role, used

119

with anyone she felt was beneath her, black or white.

"She one of the Little Rock Nine." Leonia responded with pride, knowing Rita Jean probably didn't have a clue who the Little Rock Nine were.

"They were the nine Negro students who desegregated Little Rock Central High School last fall." I jumped in and explained this to Rita Jean before changing the subject even faster to deter any hostilities sure to develop between the two opinionated teens. "I love that fingernail polish, Rita Jean. What color is it?"

My question redirected Rita Jean into a long discourse about new colors for the fall, how many manicures she had done today, and how much she got in tips. She then hurried off to take a bath and get ready for her date with her new boyfriend, William David Hamilton, the Third—Will D., as his friends called him. It seemed everyone in Bartonville went by an initial rather than the double names typical of the South. I wondered when my sister would become Rita J.

Mama didn't look to be in a very good mood, so Liz Bess and I went to the front porch to swing until Leonia finished ironing. We could hear Mama talking to Leonia.

"What would a 'do' like that cost you in a colored beauty shop, Leonia?"

"Probably fifty bucks, with the perm, the cut, and the curl." Leonia never looked up from her ironing. "A lot more than I could ever save. Some day I'll have my own shop like you, Miz Tayla, and I be in style all the time, like Lena Horne."

"I've heard colored shops make a lot more money than white ones. I guess it cost a lot with all that processing you have to do to make your hair look like

120

white folks' hair." Though back to her old tactless self, Mama seemed genuinely interested in what Leonia had to say.

"We ain't got no choice. Can't get nowhere with corn rows and nappy heads in today's world." Leonia played to Mama's curiosity and possible sympathy for her plight as a "colored" girl with bad hair who just wanted to get ahead.

Liz Bess told me that Leonia had ruined her hair one time trying to straighten it with a mixture she concocted out of Red Devil Lye and potatoes. In fact, she burned her scalp with the mixture so bad they were afraid she would lose her hair. Ever since that incident, Miss Lucille made sure her little sister had plenty of real hair care products, and she took Leonia for a complete makeover and new hairdo in a Memphis beauty salon when she turned sixteen.

"My sister Lucille say she gonna send me to beauty school when I finish high school. She say I got natural talent when it come to hair fixin'. Iff'n I could find a way, I wouldn't wait 'til then."

"It must be a good business to get into. There's a colored shop over on Plessy Lane, and I swear she stays open 'til midnight or later every night. She must be raking in the money being the only colored shop around."

"There ain't many places we can go to get our hair fixed. A lot of women do it in their homes round here, but they ain't got no license. Lucille told me never to go to none of them." Leonia folded the piece she had finished ironing and grabbed another. "There's a barber at Terza that does women's hair if ya don't mind gettin' scalped. That shop in Memphis my sista took me to sho

121

wuz somethin'! My sista spent almos' a hundred bucks on me 'fore we left there. I don't know where dat beauty operator come up with so many Negro women with dat kind of money, but she do. That woman driving a pink Cadillac like that Elvis man."

The wheels in Mama's head seemed to be turning as she listened attentively to what Leonia had to say.

"You go after that dream of yours, Leonia, just like I did. Some day you might just work for me."

Liz Bess and I looked at each other, shocked, when we heard Mama's conversation. She wasn't implying that Leonia clean up or iron. She was suggesting Leonia might be a beautician in a shop owned by her. What in the world was my mama plotting now? One thing for sure—it would make money, if Mama had anything to do with it.

Parrish Oaks would become my new home in two weeks, and Liz Bess and I had spent the entire summer latched on to each other like there was no tomorrow, which was very likely under the circumstances. Old Ma had opted not to move with us but was going to live with her daughter in the Delta. The thought of losing both Liz Bess and Old Ma was almost too much for me to bear.

At least Daddy was not going to sell our old house for a while, having decided to rent it out instead. Selling it would be too much of a break with his family heritage, and he was going to keep the board-and-batten house so Liz Bess and her family would be able to stay. Daddy promised he would find a way for Liz Bess and me to see each other.

The days passed, and I tried not to think of the move to Parrish Oaks, but leaving Liz Bess was always in the back of my mind. Early one Saturday morning in mid August, as I was hanging out wash in order to free up the day for play-acting, I noticed a car from the sheriff's office pull up at Liz Bess's house. Nervous, I slowed down so I could watch, hidden behind my clothesline that looked like a Fab advertisement from *Post*. The sheriff's deputy did not stand on the porch as was customary, but took his hat off and went inside.

Screams burst from the house, sending spasms of terror up my spine. I recognized one of the screams as belonging to Liz Bess, and I dropped the laundry and ran to the gully path. I took the front steps two at a time and made my way through the open wood door that exposed pandemonium inside.

Nagalee and Bay sat on the side of the bed hugging and rocking Liz Bess, who sobbed uncontrollably. Leonia was on her knees crying, "Lord, no, it can't be!" This seemed to be an exclamation of disbelief more than a prayer. Little Ben sat on the floor crying, more out of not understanding what was transpiring than from real fear.

"What's wrong? Oh, God, Liz Bess, what is it?"

The deputy took me by the arm and led me back out onto the porch.

"Lucille Donnelly is dead. Murdered last night in Memphis. Don't know no details. Just had to deliver the message to her parents."

The deputy, ill at ease, didn't seem to know how to help. The old color line once again acted as a barrier to any display of empathy that this young deputy obviously felt for the family. Calling Bay out to the porch, he told him someone would be coming from Memphis later that day to give them more details.

"I'm sorry for your loss." The deputy headed to his car.

"Thank you for comin' to tell us, sir."

The tearful father's worst fears had come true. I remembered his words to Miss Lucille on that first day I met her, "Take care of yo'self. You know you mighty precious to Mama and me."

Reentering the house, I took my place within the family embrace to share the grief of my friend.

Daddy went with me to Miss Lucille's funeral a week later. We sat on the back row in the church even though Bay had invited us to the front to sit behind the grieving family. Daddy did not want to intrude or take up space designated for family. He warned me that this funeral would be very different from Old Pa's, which I could barely remember since I was only six at the time he died. It didn't take long to see what he meant.

The open display of emotion appeared exaggerated by white standards, but it seemed genuine. The church was filled mostly with people from the Delta, all displaying grief and personal hurt by this tragedy. Most were given to loud moaning and praying followed in many instances by fainting. Women dressed in white and wearing white gloves hurried to the sides of mourners overcome with grief and on the verge of fainting, trying to help them to their seats before they collapsed.

One very large lady, enwrapped from head to toe in black satin embellished with black lace, wept loud, mournful sobs and was lowered to her seat by three of the women in white just before she would have fallen to the floor. After the funeral, she got into a long black car with a Tennessee tag.

Limousines lined the road in front of the small church, obviously Miss Lucille's friends and business acquaintances from Memphis, all bearing sprays and huge bouquets of flowers. Flowers covered the front of the church, not plastic ones like so many that were at Old Pa's funeral, but fresh-cut flowers that Daddy said cost a fortune.

A big controversy had stirred over where Miss Lucille's body would be interred. Her request was to be buried in the all-white Liberty Creek Baptist cemetery, the largest in the county and one where many rural dignitaries were buried, but the pastor and deacons had refused. After much haggling by Negro lawyers from Memphis with the church leaders, a deal was made. The church received a large but undisclosed amount of money paid by an anonymous donor, and in return, Miss Lucille was buried on church property just outside the old part of the cemetery, with a fence separating her from her deceased white neighbors, her grave to be maintained by the church's cemetery committee.

Liz Bess told me later that during the graveside service several cars and pickups loaded with angry-looking white men constantly rode past, staring, causing many mourners to leave early. One truck parked just up the road from the cemetery, and three men sat on the tailgate drinking beer and watching as if they were specially chosen as guardians of the elite dead. With their country music blasting, they laughed and hooted, showing disrespect and contempt for the scene that was transpiring in the old, historical, previously all-white cemetery.

We did not follow the procession to the cemetery. Daddy had heard there might be trouble and did not want me to witness it or be seen by the hostile element, but he took Liz Bess and me to Miss Lucille's grave a few days later. Daddy went to the newer part of the cemetery across the road to visit the graves of Old Pa and Uncle T.D., who was killed in the war, in order to give my friend and me time to grieve together.

Miss Lucille's tombstone, one of the largest in the cemetery, was already in place, much to the surprise of everyone, since it usually takes months for this to happen. It had a pink cast to it—Miss Lucille's favorite color—with an angel on top. In the middle was an oval picture of Miss Lucille dressed in a long, formal, green velvet gown reminding me of Scarlet O'Hara from the scene where Mammy made her a dress from the living room draperies so she could dazzle and manipulate Rhett Butler. Liz Bess seemed pleased with the likeness of her mother and expressed how beautiful she was in the picture.

"She looks just like a queen, Elizabeth." I used the name Miss Lucille preferred for her daughter. "The tombstone is beautiful."

"Mother would be pleased. I just wish we knew who to thank for it. Mama and Daddy Bay were worried she would never have one. They couldn't afford it, but when we came out here the other day, there it was." Liz Bess caressed her mother's picture, wiped her tears one more time, and turned to leave.

As we walked through the old part of the cemetery on our way to Daddy's truck, we read some of the inscriptions on tombstones. Many were killed during the Civil War, fighting for the Confederacy, including one Taylor and two Harveys. The Taylor man was one of my great-great-grandfather's brothers, Benjamin

Taylor. Daddy had told me about him. He said his great-grandmother loved history and used to spend every dime she had buying history books from traveling salesmen. She gave all her sons historical names. There was Thomas Jefferson Taylor, Benjamin Franklin Taylor, Henry Clay Taylor, who my grandfather was named after, and George Washington Taylor. She lost two of her sons in the Civil War. The other son was buried in a trench grave at Shiloh. His body was never recovered for burial here.

What a strange twist of fate! A Negro lady who seemed to feel most of her own people were inferior, buried in the same cemetery with white men who fought a war based on the belief that all Negroes were inferior and thus should be subject to white men. Ironically, Miss Lucille had more in common with these Civil War veterans than she did with her own people.

"What will happen to you, Liz Bess, now that your mother is gone?"

"I don't know. I keep asking Mama and Daddy Bay, but they don't answer me. I'm afraid, Sue Ann."

The answer came within a week when Miss Lucille's lawyer from Memphis brought her will and read it to Nagalee and Bay on their front porch. Miss Lucille had left an inheritance for Liz Bess that would pay for her to be educated in a girls' boarding school up north, and she would be leaving the first of September, accompanied by a female lawyer from the firm. He insisted to her grandparents that it would be the best thing for Liz Bess and she would be well provided for financially.

"Money don't comfort and money don't love, Mr.

Smith. Der's a reason it be called cold cash."

Nagalee slowly rose to leave the porch, helped out of her chair by her husband. The disheartened, stooped grandmother held to the walls and door as she took refuge from the lawyer's words in her house. Her daughter's death, coupled with her debilitating disease, was taking a terrible toll on the proud woman, and her daughter's last wishes aggravated the mother's frailty even more. She would lose Liz Bess—not just her grandchild, as these impersonal papers identified her, but her real-life child, a precious piece of her heart.

****

Liz Bess and I shared our last gully climb together at the end of August. Big changes were coming to both our lives, Liz Bess in the North and me in Bartonville. We took an oath in spit that day, promising never to forget each other and to always be best friends regardless of the miles separating us. I gave Liz Bess a silver locket—half a locket, actually—a heart that had been cut in half, with "Friends" on one side and "Forever" on the other, each half on its own chain. Behind my half was engraved "Honta," behind my friend's, "Saca."

We tore down the gully hideout that day, scattered the tin, and broke apart the apple crates, slinging each board as far as we could in a vain attempt to relieve some of our frustration. No one else would be allowed to use it, not our sanctuary, not our solace from a southern reality that wouldn't allow us to share the same row in school, eat ice cream at Nelly's together, or watch a movie in adjoining seats at the Palace Theatre.

As we climbed to the rim of the gully for the last

time, Liz Bess on her side and me on mine, I raised my forward fist and gestured a final, heart-wrenching farewell with eyes and heart overflowing. My friend Honta responded likewise and lowered her small fist to her heart. We turned down our gully path, one to a board-and-batten house, the other through a cherished pecan grove, both moving away from childhood.

There were no escapes left now, and no time for putting off.

Tomorrow had arrived.

Chapter Thirteen
The Feeling

My voice singing "Pink Shoe Laces" sounded nothing like Dodie Stevens as it echoed off the tall ceiling of my new, much-oversized bedroom at Parrish Oaks. Even though I missed my old house and the pecan grove, the Lady had become a cherished friend as soon as I allowed her into my soul.

Mama had decorated my room with antique oak furniture, complete with a tall bed that required a big leap just to get into it at night, made even taller by the flock of geese who provided the down for the featherbed. Each morning, I forced myself to fold it over in four directions and pound until the feathers fought back, each one waving its little fingers in protest, resulting in a battlefield of fluff. It was also worth it, considering the warmth it provided in what would otherwise be a very cold, drafty old house.

The best part of the Lady was the way she stirred my imagination. My creative juices flowed like the Yocona River during the rainy season and, though sometimes muddy, were ever present. My room large enough for a desk, but Mama could not find just the right one in the price range she wanted, so I used an old wooden table we had salvaged from a one-room log cabin in the woods at the back of our thirty-five acres. The table, like the cabin, was probably left over from the days of slavery and barely stood without leaning considerably.

Made out of poplar, the table was held together with wooden pegs that had receded so much, from age and from being left out in the elements for decades, that Daddy had to reinforce the legs with nails just to get it to stand without swaying. I loved that wooden table, primitive by antique standards, and told Mama I did not want a regular desk. An old straight chair with a sunken cane bottom that I had also found in the log cabin provided the chair for my desk after I filled in the seat with a thick cushion retrieved from Old Ma's storehouse.

As I sat at the table, I tried to imagine what life was like for the family that had used it over a hundred years earlier—what their pain must have been like for want of freedom, and what their joys might have been inside the log walls when their family was away from the eyes of master or overseer. The table, like Parrish Oaks, added extra flavor to my inventiveness, stirring emotions not previously perceived by this teenaged white mentality.

Another of my favorite pieces of decor was the Roaring Twenties dress now displayed on the old dress form I had found in the attic the first day I was in Parrish Oaks. I squeezed in the waist and bust of the dress form to accommodate the small size of the dress, and Sally, as I called her, now stood guard in one corner of my bedroom. Sally became my constant companion, the easiest member of my family to talk to—something I did far too often, in retrospect—but then, she was there more than the others.

The Taylors had come a long way from their unpainted board-and-batten beginning. The new lifestyle suited all of us. We still came together at mealtime every once in a while, but each had our own space for exercising our uniqueness the rest of the time. Mama and Daddy, consumed by their businesses, had little spare time to enjoy our new surroundings, and Rita Jean was busy driving and dating, with a little manicuring added in to give her extra money for gas and clothes. I found myself alone most of the time with the Lady and Sally.

During this new and very different stage of my life, I finally got "the feeling" and joined the church right after my fifteenth birthday. I had this revelation not as a Baptist but as a Methodist. We left Liberty Creek Baptist and joined Parrish Methodist Church, named for Reverend Joseph Parrish, its founder and also the original owner and builder of our house. Parrish Methodist was a short distance from our house, and at one time had been on the large acreage owned by Brother Parrish.

Our new church was much larger than Liberty Creek Baptist and had been established about the same time, just prior to the Civil War. Brother Parrish used slaves, some owned by him but most loaned to him by his cousins on the Harvey plantation, to build the church, but he showed unusual brotherly love for the slaves and concern for their souls by fixing it so they could worship at church along with their white owners.

The church had a balcony, like the one at the Palace Theatre, where the slaves sat, but they had no access from the inside. The Negro worshipers climbed a tall ladder on the outside of the church and entered the balcony by way of a small door. After Reconstruction, no Negroes were allowed to attend the church, not that they would have wanted to anyway; they had their own churches by that time.

The balcony was preserved, as was the small door, although that had since been nailed shut. A steep, narrow staircase had been built just inside the foyer and led to the upper area, added after World War II at a time when the membership of the church had grown so large that the balcony was needed for extra seating.

The boxed-in pews designated each member family's seating, and we Taylors, being latecomers to the church, were assigned a short pew toward the back of the sanctuary. At one time, the Harveys had been members and, of course, had the pew of honor at the front, but they had long since moved their membership to the much bigger First Baptist of Bartonville, more suitable to the high-society taste of Annette Holden Harvey's Delta upbringing. Thank goodness! I just didn't think I could concentrate on a sermon if I had to look at Lady Victoria Harvey.

Mama, pleased with my "public profession of faith," was not satisfied with my baptism, the mere sprinkling of water customary for the Methodists. Accustomed to the full dunking of the Baptists, and perhaps sensing that my sins were many, she felt it would take a full immersion to wash away their severity. The following summer, at Mama's insistence, I was re-baptized at the point where the Yocona River flowed into Enid Lake. As things tended to happen where I was concerned, it was a traumatic experience.

"I baptize you, Sue Ann Taylor, in the name of the Father, the Son, and the Holy Ghost." Brother Alvin leaned me back into the holy Yocona waters. At that very moment, a huge catfish sideswiped his leg, obviously scared out of its hole in the bank nearby and thinking it was about to be grabbled into submission, a feeling similar to my own, I must confess. Brother Alvin went down with me, and we both had to be rescued by Daddy, who could not contain his laughter at the sight of us coming up spitting water and gasping for breath. Mama did not think it was the least bit funny, and felt it was sacrilege rather than a true religious experience.

But regardless of the reverent atmosphere of Parrish Methodist, "the feeling" did not come about as a result of the church. It also did not happen as a result of Mama's constant chiding for my not making that "public profession of faith," it being three years overdue, according to her belief. It was the simple faith of an old Negro lady who made me "see the light."

I had purposely kept my distance from our old place, had not even gone out to pick pecans from the orchard that fall, not wanting to be reminded of the painful memories left behind, especially memories of the friend I missed greatly. For reasons unknown but later believed to be fate, I decided to go, one cool, clear fall afternoon shortly after I turned fifteen, for a reunion with my old feelings. Even though I did not have a driver's license, I was allowed to drive an old red-and-black '46 Dodge pickup with an oak cattle frame on the back that Daddy had purchased for a farm runabout. The only rule Daddy made was that I had to stick to the gravel roads.

Walking around in the pecan grove, I paused for a long time at the old barn. It was now stooping, its mossy green and gray weathered boards leaning so far it looked like the barn was doing a side bend in an attempt to touch the ground. I really wanted to be able to sit up there in the opening and gaze at the precious panorama of my garden, grove, and gully, but it was too near gone to risk climbing into the loft where I had once hid from my chores and Mama's wrath.

I walked instead to the edge of the grove, to the post still standing, though rotted, where I had once hung a red coffee can to signal a secret meeting. Gazing nostalgically into our gully, Liz Bess's and mine, I imagined I could hear the sounds of apple crates pinging against rusty tin as they were stacked and restacked and moved about as redecorating ensued. The tracks of mountain climbers had been washed away so that only trenches of hardened red clay were left to mark the trails of old.

Looking down, I saw the edge of a rusty, faded red can hidden beneath the honeysuckle vines. "Folgers," though parts of the letters were worn off, could be deciphered through the tangle, and I dug it out to be taken to my new home, cleaned up, and placed in the old trunk Daddy and I had found in the attic and claimed by me as my "hopeless chest."

As I turned to leave, I saw Bay waving from the porch of the board-and-batten house. I waved back and then headed for the path leading to his house. Bay reached for my hand, smiling as I neared the steps, probably afraid I would hug him if he didn't put this distance between us with his outstretched hand, something he would not have been comfortable with from a young white girl.

"Lord musta heered Nagalee's thoughts. She been talkin' 'bout you and Liz Bess all afta'noon."

Bay held the wooden door open, and I walked

inside to the familiar woody smoke smell of the fireplace and a faint but lingering smell of Leonia's hair ointment. Nagalee, now bedridden, looked feeble as she reached out her bony, deformed hand to me.

"Miss Sue Ann, I been thinkin' on you an' missin' you like I misses ma baby Liz Bess. How ya'll been? Set here on da bed and tell me 'bout yo new house."

I sat on the featherbed beside Nagalee and told her all about Parrish Oaks, Mama's business, and about high school. My thoughts were of Liz Bess, but I asked first about Little Ben and Leonia, although I had already heard they had both left Shadywood.

"Lil Ben be wit' his daddy whar he oughta ben from da start. Leonia be in beauty school down in Jackson. She livin' wit' a cousin down there. Lucille left her some money so's she can larn to fix hair and make a good livin'. She didn't wait ta finish high school 'fore decidin' ta go. Tain't nobody lef' here but us two old souls, an' one of us ain't long fo' dis worl'."

"Don't you be talkin' like dat, Nagalee. You ain't goin' no place." Bay was quick to correct his wife, but the sad look in his eyes told what she was saying just might be true.

"How's Liz Bess? Does she like high school?" I wanted to know but was afraid she had completely forgotten about me.

"We got a letta from her. She don't say much, but she knows me and Daddy can't read much no way. She say it okay and she gots plenty. Some fam'ly take a likin' to her and she go der on weekends." Nagalee's voice was getting weaker the more she talked. "It be for da bes' dat she went away. Lord knows what's bes' iff'n we jes' listen and let Him 'lone."

"I miss her, Nagalee. I don't think it's best for me that Liz Bess had to go. I guess, truth be, I'm mad at God for taking her away."

"Sho it bes'. Ya'll see iff'n ya jes' try. Ya jes' needed Liz Bess a li'l while to make ya see how thangs oughta be. Liz Bess taught ya der ain't no color in God's kingdom. Love ain't black and love ain't white, it jes' is. Lord sent you to Liz Bess when she so lonesome her wanna die. I pray for Him to send her a friend 'cause de colored chillun at school don't 'cept her and be mean to her. I neva thought 'bout Him sendin' no white chile, but you da answer to dat prayer. I knowed it da fus day I seen you playing queen wi' my Liz Bess. Movin' to dis ole house was God's doin'. I be mos' thankful you done come in our life. I neva thought could be sech a blessin' at th'utha end uh dat gully path."

I looked away to keep Nagalee from seeing the moisture in my eyes. I had always known Liz Bess was a blessing to me, but I never thought about myself as being a blessing to her. I underestimated God, not thinking He took notice of little things like childhood friendships.

As I left Nagalee, I promised I'd come again soon, but I had come just in time. Later, I knew it was no coincidence I had come that day.

It was dusk, and the sky was the most magnificent orange I had ever seen. It cast a brilliant glow on the already crimson gully and, for a moment, I expected a pathway to open up leading straight to heaven. As my tears flowed, I looked into the blaze and prayed:

"God, I know you're there now, and I know Liz Bess was a gift to me, although I didn't deserve her.

Watch over her, Lord, and please bring us together again some day. Help me to understand where I fit in Your great plan, and forgive me for not listening for You before. I'm here now. And thank You, God, for letting me be somebody's blessing."

Nagalee died that night, with her beloved Bay by her side reading from the Bible as best he could. There were no crowds of mourners or church full of flowers at her funeral, and no line of limousines in front of the church. But there was a chorus of angels singing above her, welcoming her home into God's fold, and there was a strong man who loved her, weeping beside her grave, bidding her a mournful goodbye. She was buried the way she lived, quietly, beside her precious daughter, but with no controversy and no demonstrations of disrespect.

Chapter Fourteen
Fast Track

My fifth week of high school as a freshman, I suddenly became a sophomore. Because of my excellent grades, I was placed in the experimental Fast Track program and would complete high school in three years rather than four. Rita Jean was not keen on the idea of her little sister catching up with her. She was quick to figure out that I would be taking some of the same classes she did her senior year if I was able to stay in the program.

"If you want to be a pen head, go ahead. You're already a bookworm. It won't add to your popularity, for sure."

My sister made the remark to get me to change my mind even though she knew that popularity was not one of my priorities. I had already told her I did not want to join the Debutante Club, but she assured me I'd get an invitation anyway, thinking I'd surely change my mind. Mama hoped I would change my mind, too.

It was nice having people I knew from my old school in Shadywood in school with me, but now that I was in Fast Track, I hardly ever saw them. All of my classes had been changed, and I was with new people I didn't know very well at all.

One girl I seemed to have a lot in common with was Jules Steiner, who everyone called "Baby." Her uncle owned the ritzy clothing store in town, and her daddy managed it for his brother, but Baby didn't act ritzy at all.

What I liked about her was she was not obsessed with clothes or boys. Like me, she was a voracious reader and dabbled at writing, too, though not to the extent I did. Art was her passion.

If she had a shortfall, it was her sarcasm. I almost didn't let myself get to know her because of her nasty attitude, which surfaced every once in a while.

One day when I walked into advanced literature class, she was trying to be cute in front of a group of kids and yelled out, "Sue-ee, Sue-ee, Pig, Pig!" She then proceeded to snort as she and the others hit each other, laughing.

I walked straight over to her and said, "Are you calling me...Jew Baby?" I hesitated. Immediately, I became furious at myself for stooping to her level and for making fun of her race—or was it her religion? Baby and her family tried to cover up the fact they were Jewish, since Jews were often condemned in the South. Her family attended the Presbyterian Church.

"I'm sorry, Baby. That was mean of me."

Baby laughed. "Actually, I deserved it. It was a good comeback. For some strange reason, I like it. Who'd a thunk it?"

And that was that. Baby, who hated the fact that her family was Jewish, became "Jew Baby" to me, and every once in a while, just to show she hadn't really changed, I was "Suey" to my new best friend in high school.

Just before Christmas break, I headed Daddy's old Dodge truck to Terza to watch the Christmas parade.

Baby was supposed to meet me there but seemed to be making another of the non-appearances she was famous for, so I stood alone.

The streets were lined with children—white children—wild with the anticipation of seeing Santa Claus. Over behind one group of whites, Snuffy Kuykendall had his family of five small children, the only Negroes at the parade, at least in the downtown area. When Santa did arrive in the town's fire truck, Snuffy's children's faces lit up like the Christmas lights on the town square. I watched as Santa threw candy and a "ho, ho, ho" in the direction of every child—every white child—along his route. He looked toward Snuffy but never threw candy to his children. Their little faces fell as Santa passed in total disregard, and so did my seasonal spirits, as well as my faith in the jolly one.

Furious with Santa's actions, I moved up the street, following him as he continued throwing out candy, and gathered up handfuls of candy canes, bubble gum, and jawbreakers until my pockets wouldn't hold anymore. When I got back to my original location, I walked straight over to Snuffy's family and began passing out candy to the children, while many white spectators looked on disapprovingly, muttering to each other as if I couldn't hear with my back turned, or maybe hoping I'd hear their mean remarks.

"Santa asked me to bring you this candy. He thought you might not reach any from back here. He asked if you had been good girls and boys, and I told him you looked like you were really good children. Was I right?"

"Yes, ma'am! We been real good," the oldest little girl told me as she unwrapped a candy cane and popped it into her mouth.

"Tell the lady thank you, kids. We bes' be goin'." Snuffy headed his family away from the square.

As the children crawled into the back of their daddy's dilapidated pulpwood truck, he looked at me and said, "Thank you."

"My pleasure."

I got into my truck to leave, having had enough Christmas cheer, and didn't wait for Jew Baby. Before I had a chance to close my truck door, Booger Melton came up and slammed it. I had to jerk my leg in fast to keep the door from hitting me.

"Still nigga lovin', Sue Ann?" Booger stuck his ugly head in the window, breathing his nasty tobacco breath in my face. "Didn't I teach you nothin' that day when we wuz kids? Better watch it, or I'll tell my uncle, and he'll have the Klan after you."

"Ooh…I'm so scared, Booger!" I droned sarcastically, not flinching or even moving away from the stench of his breath hot on my cheek, refusing to give him the satisfaction of knowing he scared me. No way would I submit to his harassment. I put the truck in reverse and stomped the accelerator. Booger hit his head on the truck's window frame as he jerked back.

The bogus redneck cursed me, using all of his four-letter words, pretty much his entire vocabulary, and shot me the finger as I pulled away. As he stiffened his middle finger, he tightened his jaw over clenched teeth to add impetus to the rage I elicited in him just by my presence.

I was furious with Booger, and remembered Daddy trying to excuse his actions so long ago when I tried to protect Liz Bess and Ben from the bully. Daddy had talked about families who had to pick cotton for a living, like Booger Melton's family, and made me feel very fortunate that my parents were "betterin's," and Rita Jean and I had never had to know such deprivation or desperate means of survival.

Booger had quit high school at the beginning of the school year and claimed he was joining the Army. I couldn't imagine how he would fare in the military, since it was integrated, and imagined him returning with many battles scars not received in battle. I couldn't help but hope he would get a really good butt-kickin' or two.

Every time I'd gotten close to him in high school, which was not very often since he was in remedial classes and I was in Fast Track (not to mention the fact that I steered clear of him as much as possible), he would taunt me with "nigger lover." I just ignored him. After all, it was true, since I prided myself in choosing whom I loved based on character, not skin color.

Just as I was about to leave town, I saw Jew Baby running toward me. After picking her up, I told her about my encounter with Booger.

"You better keep out of his way, Sue Ann. I know for a fact he and his family are big-time Klan. My uncle keeps up with all that, him being Jewish and all."

I laughed at her reference to "him being Jewish" as if there were no blood relation between them.

****

Much to the disappointment of my mother and sister, I chose not to be presented to Bartonville Society. The Bartonville Debutante Christmas ball was held without me. At least I had scruples where the Harveys were concerned. I chose to stay at home that night with Sally and prepare two plays I had written to send to the *Progressive Farmer* to see if they might be interested in publishing them to sell in their catalog order department: "An Angel for Every Occasion" and "Peggy Plans Her Future."

"Peggy Plans Her Future" had taken second place at the state Future Business Leaders of America competition. That was not enough for scholarship money but did give me billing in the *Bartonville Weekly*.

Two months later, Mr. Davidson, our principal, called my name before an assembly program in the auditorium and asked me to stand. I had no idea why he was calling on me.

"I am proud to announce that Sue Ann has sold two plays to the *Progressive Farmer* magazine, which is going to publish them. The editor called me just before I came into the auditorium to make sure Sue Ann was indeed a student here. Let's show Sue Ann how proud we are of her."

I was overwhelmed as everyone clapped and cheered. I felt rich later when I got the two checks for my plays, one for thirty dollars and the other for twenty-five, but it was not the money that made me proud. It was seeing my name in print on the copies of the plays I had created, a feeling of great accomplishment for a small-town girl.

Rita Jean had her own accomplishments the following spring. She and Lady Victoria, even though debutante sisters, were once again in competition, this time for Sweetheart of the Future Farmers of America at Bartonville High. According to Jerry, who was president of FFA, Rita Jean was a shoo-in, but when the final vote was tabulated, the Vampire had beaten her by three votes. Rita Jean was devastated but too proud to demand a recount. There was certainly reason to be bothered, since Caleb Perkins was one of the committee of two counting the votes.

Taking it all in stride, she chose to save her energy for the most important honor in Bartonville, the role of Miss Hospitality, which was chosen by the mayor and the Board of Aldermen each May. Miss Hospitality would represent the best of Bartonville's young ladies with qualifications that sounded like they were copied right out of the Bartonville Debutante's Creed. As usual, Lady V also had her name in the pot, even though I knew her character was questionable. As it turned out, the two girls were finalists for the honor.

That May, Mama and Daddy tried to prepare Rita Jean for the inevitable. They couldn't compete with the money and prestige of the Harvey family and felt Rita Jean was setting herself up for another disappointment. Each girl had to prepare a speech to give to the mayor and the aldermen, and had to expound on the reasons they should be chosen to represent Bartonville for the next year. I helped Rita Jean to write her speech, and it was a masterpiece. No way could a Harvey or anyone in Bartonville top it.

But Mama came home from the salon early the next day and pretty much busted our bubble. She had heard from a reliable source, as if there is such a thing in a beauty shop, that Annette Holden was buying votes for her daughter among some of the aldermen. She also said Lady V had her friends spreading vicious rumors about Rita Jean which might cause the aldermen and anyone who believed the rumors to question her character. Mama begged Rita Jean to withdraw from the competition, but she refused.

"Dadgum it all!" I thought. "If I hadn't joined the church, I could probably do something really shady and get the Vampire to lay off Rita Jean and run an honest competition."

The two competitors gave their speeches to an open assembly on Friday night, the day before Miss Hospitality would be selected. Lady Victoria gave her speech first and sounded more like Scarlet than Victoria as she dropped her r's like she was from the Delta, not the hills, and drawled on and on about her family's heritage and position of leadership in Bartonville society. She practically had mint julep running out the corners of her mouth, and the aldermen, who sat smiling and nodding their heads in agreement, were obviously taken with her "southe'n cha'm."

Annette Harvey sat like a dignitary, head held high, smiling royally. J.T. Harvey looked like he would as soon be sitting in a bed of red ants as here and never looked up through his sunglasses as his daughter dripped syrup to her adoring audience of aldermen, who lapped up each attribute expounded upon as if it were actually true. When she finished, she sat down with the confidence of a winner. My nerves were on edge for Rita Jean.

Rita Jean did not put on airs. She was Rita Jean Taylor, the daughter of Zeke and Irene Taylor, hard-working, God-fearing parents who held high standards for themselves and their children. Rita Jean talked of her ethics, her religious beliefs, and the high moral values she lived by. She was brilliant! It was the perfect speech, and the aldermen listened attentively but without the slightest hint of emotion or nodding of approval or belief. They had been taken in by the "notable southe'n heritage" and "strong characta'" of Lady Victoria The Slut.

I watched the audience during both speeches and felt Rita Jean had the support of the majority of the audience, but they were not the ones making the final choice. My sister was swamped with well wishers and people congratulating her on an excellent speech as we made our way out of the auditorium. Mama and Daddy were especially proud of her and the way she had expressed pride in her family, especially her parents.

We left with high hopes for Rita Jean becoming the next Miss Hospitality, but deep down we all knew it was hopeless. It would take a miracle for a Taylor to defeat a Harvey, and Sue Ann the Fast-Tracker was not devilish enough to help…this time.

Chapter Fifteen
The Tornado

I could not sleep that night worrying about my sister being hurt again. It just was not fair that one girl could be allowed to cause so much heartache. Lady V had enough honors, with everything she had stolen from Rita Jean since we moved to Bartonville.

The only time my sister had actually beaten her in anything was when the two of them ran for president of Future Homemakers of America, the most popular club at school, due to the trip its members got to take during school each fall to the Midsouth Fair in Memphis. Rita Jean beat V Harvey by a landslide, thanks to the efforts of the home economics teacher, Miss Nell, who we heard had said she was tired of Lady V winning everything and had solicited votes for Rita Jean. It was fitting that Rita Jean be president. Her red velvet cake had taken a blue ribbon at the fair her first year in FHA, and she was by far the champion future homemaker in the school.

When I finally did drop off to sleep, I woke up, startled, to Daddy shaking me hard.

"Get up, Sue Ann! There's a storm!"

Daddy was terrified of storms. When I was little, he would get us up, herd us into the car, and drive us to a spot under a bridge overpass. His thinking was that getting under the bridge would somehow prevent a tornado, if the storm developed into one, from blowing us away. We'd sit there scared to death as the car shook, waiting for the storm to subside.

One time, the storm hit before Daddy could get us into the car. He nearly killed me trying to shove me under the lowest bed in the house, putting a big knot on my head. We got so tickled during this ordeal that it finally broke the spell of the storm, and we rode it out like normal people, huddled in the dark comfort of our beds.

One of the things Daddy had liked about Parrish Oaks was that it had a storm shelter built under the house. This is where we headed now when storms threatened. I was more afraid of snakes in the shelter than I was of the storm, and begged to be left in my bed every time he got me up.

All I could think about as I followed Mama and Rita Jean down into the storm shelter was that big black snake Daddy and I had seen in the attic that day. While Parrish Oaks was being restored, the carpenters had killed twenty-nine snakes in and around the old house. Daddy finally had every bush in the massive yard surrounding the house, regardless of how old and rare, bulldozed away to get rid of "snake habitat," much to Mama's disappointment. She loved the old plants and bushes and had planned to salvage all she could.

As we sat in the shelter, shivering even though it was May and already very warm, we heard what sounded like a giant locomotive roaring overhead, followed by surreal silence. Daddy wouldn't let us leave until he was sure the storm was over. When we threw open the double doors leading up into the yard, we saw debris everywhere. The electricity was off, but the moon and stars were already shining brightly, as if nothing had happened. Several shingles from the roof were lying on the ground beside the house, as well as numerous limbs from the massive oaks that gave our house its name. We sat in candlelight for a long time that night, too nervous to go to bed. Daddy said he was sure it was a tornado we heard and we should thank God in our prayers tonight for keeping our house and family safe.

The next day, we rode through the county to see the aftermath of the storm. A tornado had cut a path from just south of Shadywood through Terza and Bartonville, with the worst of it hitting Shadywood. Mama, Rita Jean, and I rode with Daddy, anxious to see how our old house had fared.

"Thank goodness!" Daddy exclaimed. "The house is still standing."

Several of the pecan trees had been uprooted, but both our old house and the board-and-batten house seemed untouched except for a few shingles blown off.

"Oh, no!" I yelled. "The barn is gone!"

The spot where the old barn had stood was as clean as if there had never been a barn there. Not a weathered board nor a sprig of hay remained, and the two pecan trees closest to the barn lay on their sides with their massive roots reaching for the sun.

It was so strange how the tornado had jumped from spot to spot, taking the barn but leaving the house just a few yards away. Some of our neighbors were not as lucky. The Williford house had been damaged, but no one was hurt. They had left and gone to their neighbors', the Browns', storm shelter when the storm first started. In Terza, several people were hurt and three homes were flattened. Luckily, no one was killed.

On the Channel 5 news, it was reported that debris was strewn for twenty miles. A Bible from one home that was destroyed was found ten miles away and was returned to its owner with not a page torn from it. There were many stories like this, some funny.

One family's outhouse from Terza showed up sitting in the front yard of a well-to-do doctor in Bartonville. The doctor, who was known for his good humor, hung a "For Rent" sign on the outhouse and left it there for a few days. A picture of it made the front page of the *Weekly*.

The strangest thing to come out of the storm, though, was a collection of several pictures that were found in Terza and Bartonville, awful pictures of a teenaged girl and boy, naked as jaybirds, doing things only whispered about in the Bible Belt. Some pictures were torn, giving a partial story of what was happening, a leg here, a boob there.

One redneck fisherman reported that he lost a cooler of beer when he nearly overturned his boat trying to rescue a picture he saw in a limb hanging over his favorite fishing hole on the Yocona River. He laughed and said it was wet and a little faded but worth the effort, even with losing his beer.

News traveled fast in Barton County, where the faces of the teens were all too identifiable. By Saturday afternoon, it seemed that already everyone had either seen one of the pictures or knew someone who had, and the whispers and chuckles continued for months. A couple of the pictures were turned in to the sheriff, who delivered them to the home of J.T. and Annette Harvey and their lovely daughter Lady Victoria, probably for their family scrapbook.

The Harveys—both mother and daughter—were noticeably absent during the ceremony that evening, when Rita Jean was crowned Miss Hospitality. It was said that Annette and Lady Victoria were on a cruise to Panama, one of V's graduation presents from her parents. Lady V also missed her high school graduation ceremony, foregoing an opportunity to give her speech as salutatorian, second in her class in academic achievement behind Valedictorian Sophia Langston. Sophia graduated a year early and had been the inspiration for the Fast Track Program. However, being an illegitimate country girl from Shadywood, she had never received an invitation to join the Bartonville Debutante Society.

The Lord works in mysterious ways.

"Oh, surely not." I giggled as I placed the worn-out second-hand camera in the hopeless chest.

Chapter Sixteen
The Fire Talker

"Sue Ann, I need you to go up to Mr. Charlie Smith's and pick up some mustard greens for me. I swear he has the best green patch in the county. You know it's your daddy's birthday this weekend, and all he wants is some of my good home cooking. It's been so long since I cooked a big meal, I don't know if I can remember how. He ordered mustard greens, white navy beans, creamed potatoes, fried chicken, cornbread, and muscadine pudding with white sauce."

"Sounds yummy. I bet you haven't forgotten. Make a big muscadine pudding, Mama. You know it's my favorite, too."

I could already taste the tart/sweet combination of Mama's muscadine pudding. That, along with fried peach pies and sweet potato pie, were Mama's trademark sweets. As I headed for the old truck that Daddy allowed me to drive, Baby drove up and got out of her dad's big Buick.

"Where you off to, Suey?"

"Come on, Jew Baby, and ride with me. I'm going over to Mr. Charlie's."

We jumped into Daddy's old Dodge truck and headed up the gravel road, the long way to Mr. Charlie's that went by our old house. The leaves were beginning to turn, and I loved driving the curvy country roads with their shoulders covered with yellow and orange leaves mixed with cotton that had loosed itself from the cotton wagons heading for the gin. The gin stood silent now, finished for the year. All that was left was for the factories to complete the metamorphosis of cotton boll to bolt of cloth.

As Jew Baby and I pulled in to Mr. Charlie's driveway, we were alarmed to see flames shooting up out of the raised hood of Mr. Charlie's truck. The elderly man was frantically beating the blaze with his hands. I jumped from my truck and grabbed a 'toe sack from the back, ran over, and started beating down the flames. The fire subsided.

"Mr. Charlie, your hands are burned!" I yelled as I helped him into a chair in his yard. I picked up a towel lying on the porch and wet it at his hydrant. Carefully, I wrapped his burned hands in it, feeling great empathy for him as he groaned in pain.

"Come get in my truck, and I'll take you to the hospital."

"No! No doctor. Take me to Ruth."

"Miss Ruth?" I repeated, questioning. "This is pretty serious. You think she can help you?"

"Yes, she can talk the fire out of it quicker than any doctor could do anything."

I knew what Mr. Charlie was talking about. Once when Mattie Lynn was in high school, she and a group of her friends had gone to the dam to sunbathe. Mattie Lynn burned so badly that her back burst into huge water blisters, and she couldn't wear clothes for two days. When she began to run a fever, Mama took her to Miss Ruth, who talked the fire out of her body to the point that she was able to go home, put her clothes on, and go back to school the next day.

"Scoot over, Jew Baby, and let Mr. Charlie in. You are about to witness something very different from your ordinary little life."

"A fire talker? You've got to be kidding," she whispered as she scooted to the middle of the truck seat.

Jew Baby and I sat in the swing on Miss Ruth's porch and watched in hypnotic silence as Miss Ruth worked her miracle. She never said anything out loud but was obviously chanting or reciting something to herself as she held each of Mr. Charlie's hands, passing her hand over each one and keeping a distance of about two inches above his burn. She would make a slow, methodical pass with her cupped hand and then blow gently on the wound. She repeated this process for several minutes on each hand.

When she'd finished, Mr. Charlie swore his hands were no longer in pain. He still did not want to go to the doctor, so I took him back to his house. Just as I was leaving, he ran out of the house holding a sack filled with Mama's mess of greens. In the excitement, I'd completely forgotten why I had come in the first place.

"How did she do that?" asked Baby, who was awestruck by the actions of the miracle worker.

"Mama told me Miss Ruth learned to fire talk from her mother and it is always passed from mother to child. The gift comes from the Bible, but only Miss Ruth knows what it is. Mama really admires Miss Ruth, as does the whole community. Can you imagine the faith it must take for her to put into practice this God-given gift? It is so fascinating."

"Fascinating and strange," Baby replied, but

admitted she was glad she had been with me to experience this firsthand.

We rode quietly down Harvey Road on our way to town as we tried to comprehend what we had witnessed. Just after we passed the Harvey plantation and the Taylor thirty-five acres, we both screamed, nearly jumping out of our skin as an ambulance pulled right up on our tail with its siren blasting, warning us to move to the side, before passing us and speeding toward town.

"I wonder where that came from?" I asked as I took a deep breath, trying to rid my body of the goose bumps and slow my fast heartbeat caused by the siren. I pulled back out onto the road but knew it would do me no good to try to chase it; the old Dodge would not go faster than forty miles per hour. An instant later, Jew Baby and I screamed again as a car horn sounded right behind us just before flying by, obviously following the ambulance.

"That was Mr. Harvey's Cadillac!" I yelled in disbelief. "I've never seen him drive like that. What in the world is going on?"

When I dropped Baby off at her uncle's store, we found out what all the commotion was about. Annette Harvey had been rushed to the hospital. An hour later we heard that she had died.

I felt both sympathy and remorse as I thought of Lady Victoria being without her mother. Even someone as selfish and hateful as V must surely have feelings. I couldn't imagine what it would be like to lose your mother and hoped I didn't have to find out for a long, long time. Probably I wouldn't, since all of the women in Mama's family lived to be centurions, or at least into their nineties.

When Mama got home from the beauty salon, we got all the details. Whether they were one hundred percent gospel truth or not, I could not swear. Annette Harvey was an alcoholic, had been all of her adult life, from all accounts, although few people in Bartonville knew about it. It was rumored that she died from liver failure, but in the *Bartonville Weekly*, it stated she died of heart problems.

Years later, it would be disclosed that it was indeed her heart, not from any physical malfunction of the organ itself, but from living a life exhausted by overwhelming loneliness and despondency. She was buried in her family cemetery at her Delta plantation at Beeville with its antebellum, columned mansion, her final request.

****

Times were changing. As hard as the citizens of Bartonville tried to keep things the same, the more it became apparent that change was inevitable.

Within the Taylor family, change was also happening. Rita Jean graduated from high school and was in college…preparing for a career she would probably never use. School, high school or college, had never been as important to her as it was to me. Her main focus was finding a husband, a task that took up most of the time she should have used in studying.

Only a year after watching my sister graduate from high school, I found myself walking down that same aisle but with very different results. I was Valedictorian of my class and had my pick of state colleges as a scholarship recipient. Even though I was a very young high school graduate, my focus was career, career,

career...secretly! I had a side attachment, my high school boyfriend, a state college man, who thought he was my main focus and should be the deciding factor in where I went to college. The compromise, or so he thought, was Mississippi State College for Women, "the W." I had always dreamed of going to the W and, as luck would have it, it just happened to be twenty miles from Starkville, where Mississippi State, the predominantly male college, was located.

My college years would finalize my "morphing" into an outspoken rebellious activist...an unstoppable free spirit. No regrets.

Book II

Where the Gully Path Ends

Chapter Seventeen
Crisis in Black and White

My parents shed no tears as I pulled out of the driveway with Dailey, my only boyfriend from my high school years, heading for my college debut. But even though my parents did not cry, they still stood, looking forlorn, on the porch of Parrish Oaks, their now-empty nest. They continued waving as we left the driveway and turned onto the highway. I was on my way to Columbus, to Mississippi State College for Women. I was not sad and could hardly contain my excitement at being a college girl.

College proved to be extremely different from high school, a good difference. The W was wonderful with its melting pot of girls from many different backgrounds and with many seditious ideas and philosophies like my own, at least where Mississippi law and practices were concerned. One girl I particularly liked, though we never became close friends, was named Jon, a name that reeked of noncompliance and uniqueness.

Jon wore antique wire-rimmed glasses that had belonged to her grandfather but were adapted to fit her prescription. Her hair was butt-length, and she wore it in braids most of the time, with her outfits consisting of long skirts imported from India and loose flannel shirts secured around the waist with whatever she desired to set off the decadence of the outfit: sometimes rope, sometimes real belts made from silver conches. Being from Memphis, she was considered a total dissident as she condemned southern laws that prevented Negro students from enrolling in state universities. She openly canvassed for a new Republican Party in the state but was a staunch supporter of Democratic President Kennedy in his support for the Civil Rights Movement.

During free afternoons when we were not in classes, students spent time huddled in groups in "The Goose," the recreational room and snack bar, a place where boys from Mississippi State were allowed during designated times. I loved going to the Goose on the afternoons when Dailey did not come over from State College, so I could join with the discussion group that Jon always had going. It usually included some of the young professors from the political science department, making it not only interesting but a good way to get brownie points if you were in one of their classes. In these discussions in the Goose, I first heard the name James Meredith.

James Meredith, a Negro, tried for a year to be admitted to all-white Ole Miss. Finally, backed by a Supreme Court decision, he was to be admitted on Monday, October 1. Jon was elated and planned to be at Ole Miss to witness the historic event. I was envious but knew better than to ask Dailey to take me there, he being my only means of transportation. Besides, Daddy would have a hissy fit if he thought I was anywhere near a potential scene of violence, and violence was assured with Governor Barnett adding fuel to the fire with his promise to "bar the door." As it turned out, it would have been good training ground for my future life.

Though Dailey was not a racist in the extreme definition of the term, he was opposed to desegregation of schools and colleges and was prejudiced. We talked little of such matters because of the arguments these discussions generated, but he knew how I felt.

As we drove through Oxford late that Sunday afternoon on our way back to Columbus and Starkville, the mob was already forming. I convinced Dailey to drive through the Ole Miss campus, where we saw federal marshals surrounding the Lyceum Building in preparation for Meredith's admission the next morning.

Not only were groups of students forming, but many pickup trucks and cars plastered in rebel flags were parked all around the campus. Leaning against them were hordes of mostly young men who did not have the demeanor or dress typical of Ole Miss students, often referred to by State Bulldog fans as "the social club." These rednecks were the outside agitators that would be blamed for the ensuing riot by the locals in the days following the perilous night. Dailey could not leave the campus fast enough, since it was obvious that the fuse was lit and trouble was brewing. He had no intention of being anywhere near when the dynamite exploded.

No one went to class the next morning. Huddled in front of the television in the dorm lobby, we watched the reports of the Ole Miss riot that left two people dead and hundreds hurt.

Regardless of the casualties and the severity of the violence that was finally quelled by the deployment of National Guard troops to Oxford, James Meredith was admitted to Ole Miss that morning, and history was made. Many students, obvious sympathizers for the "southern way," wore black armbands in mourning for the death of an era that had lasted since before Mississippi became a state in 1817.

Jon entered the lobby later that afternoon, face flushed and looking tired, but bubbling over with the details of the riot and the historic moment she had witnessed. Many of the Ole Miss sympathizers got up and left the room when she began her review of the night.

Booger Melton and the KKK could not have dragged me away as I sat mesmerized by her expressive discourse. She had stood near a construction site on campus, watching rioters load up with bricks to be thrown at the marshals when the sound of gunfire opened up. Feeling like she was in a battle scene from World War II, Jon hit the ground in an attempt to dodge bullets. When a break in the deadly noise occurred, she noticed a young man lying on the pile of construction materials. As she ran to him, he was quickly surrounded by others, some his friends, who pushed her aside and began screaming for help. Later, we heard the spectator, a young man from Oxford, had died.

Jon, though terrified, refused to leave as she watched the rest of the night from her car. When daylight finally came, the riot was over, but the debris strewn everywhere made the Grove look like a tornado had been through. The National Guard surrounded the Lyceum as James Meredith climbed the steps to be formally admitted at eight o'clock that morning.

Poetic and passionate, the young dissident took a deep breath and exclaimed, "He passed through the huge Lyceum doors riddled with bullet holes, leaving the old state of Mississippi behind; when he reappeared, he stepped out into a new state."

It was a new era, but Mississippi still had a long way to go before it would really be a "new" state, and many more lives were yet to be sacrificed, both black and white.

At home in Bartonville, Mama had black-and-white crises of her own transpiring. One afternoon, she left the salon early, just generally worn out and "needing an afternoon to rest." As she entered the side door of Parrish Oaks, she heard a terrible commotion, like someone running through the house, overturning furniture as he or she ran. Mama, never afraid of much in her life, forgot how tired she was and tore out in the direction of the sound, passing dresser drawers pulled out and dumped on the floor, chairs overturned, and closets ransacked. As she rounded the corner of the kitchen, she saw long legs leaping through the back door.

Mama pursued the would-be thief, a young Negro teenager, a big strapping boy, as she described him, running as fast as his big frame would carry him across the yard. Stopping at the edge of the yard knowing she would be unable to catch him, she screamed at him in her most demanding, angry voice, "You get yourself back here this instant!"

For reasons nobody could figure out, the boy stopped, turned to face Mama, and slowly recounted his steps, his arms laden and his head held down in shame. Mama then made him reenter the house and cower at the kitchen table while she called the sheriff. After finding out who he was, she called his mother, who lived a couple of miles down Harvey Road. The mother was horrified with her son's shenanigans and assured

Mama he had never done anything like this before.

"Luke's always been a good boy," she swore to Mama, but she was unable to sway Mama from her decision to report him to the sheriff.

The sheriff searched the teenager and found he had taken several pieces of Mama's and Rita Jean's jewelry, as well as a six-pack of Cokes and a carton of Daddy's Camels that Mama had taken back when he entered the kitchen. Mama's anger peaked when she recognized her Moler's pin as part of the loot the sheriff took from Luke's pockets.

Mama refused to let the sheriff keep the little silver razor pin as evidence, but she did let him take the rest of the jewelry. Sheriff Bowman knew better than to argue with her. He could not get over the fact that Luke had come back at Mama's command even though he was twice her size. Laughingly, the lawman offered Mama a job as a deputy, should she ever decide to leave the hair business. The next year he would remember that offer and make it once again, this time for a different one of the many Irene exploits, a more serious one.

Mama had other problems during this first week in October. Her Negro beauty salon, named Ebony Styling Salon, was very successful. In fact, it was making more money than Irene's House of Style and had three full-time stylists working.

One day, Miss Minnie, who was a stylist as well as manager at the Ebony, came to Mama and announced she would be leaving at the end of the month, moving to Jackson, where she planned to open a salon of her own. Mama offered her more money, but she declined. Mama didn't know what she would do without Minnie, but two days later the answer to her prayer walked through the door of the House of Style. Mama laughed as she recounted the story to us at dinner that night.

"The young Negro woman looked familiar to me, but I could not place where I'd seen her. She was obviously a city woman, dressed in a royal blue wool suit with matching shoes and hat. Her hair had been permed and styled in soft curls, probably one of the new products on the market, maybe Ultra Sheen."

" 'You don't 'memba me, do you, Miz Taylor?' she said, with a charming smile. I had to admit, I really had no idea. Then she said, 'I'm Leonia Donnelly, Nagalee's daughter.'

" 'Leonia, my goodness, what a pretty woman you made! Look at you!' I looked her up and down, shaking my head with approval. 'I heard you were living in Jackson. What brings you back to Barton County?'

" 'I'm looking for work, Miz Taylor,' she explained. 'I a hair stylist now. Been managing a shop in Clinton for the last year and heard you owned a shop over in Plessy Lane and needed a manager.' " Mama used her best Leonia dialect in telling the story.

" 'How old are you, Leonia? Seems you weren't much older than my Rita Jean. You're awful young to be managing a shop, especially one with three operators.'

" 'My last shop had four operators. Here, I brung a letter of reference from my former employer. I jes' turned twenty-three, but I been working ever since I left here and finish beauty school almos' five years ago.'

"I read the letter and was impressed with the recommendation. Neither of the other two operators at Ebony have any desire to manage the shop, even with the extra salary. They don't want the responsibility of the bookkeeping and handling of the money that's collected each night at closing time, so after a quick deliberation, I decided to give Leonia a try. She starts tomorrow. I know it's quick, but I don't have any one else beating down my door for the job."

It would be a decision Mama would never regret. Not only would Leonia prove to be her most valued hair stylist and a good manager, but she remained loyal to Mama until they both retired from the business many decades later.

Leonia helped Mama make decisions that would add to the success of her Negro salon. For instance, there was the time she convinced Mama to stop using Revlon products, a white company, and change completely to Johnson and Walker products, black-owned hair care products companies. She argued that colored clients knew the difference and this would increase business. Leonia was right, and Ebony had to stay open later just to accommodate the many new customers.

Later, Mama had to admit Leonia's tenure was not without its problems, but that is another chapter in the family history.

Chapter Eighteen
COFO? No, No!

He walked in a bounce, stretching each step full-length from heel to toe, pausing to balance on his toes like my nephew had done when first learning to walk, probably an attempt to make himself appear taller than his short stature. Even though the young man wasn't Tarzan or Superman, he had a countenance about him that mesmerized me as I watched him walking toward me and past, on the sidewalk of downtown Bartonville.

Our eyes met briefly, and we returned smiles as if we were casual schoolmates in an everyday chance meeting. After he passed, I turned to get one more look and met his eyes again as he, too, turned to get one more look at me. Embarrassed, I turned around quickly and hurried to get off the sidewalk.

I almost missed the seat of Daddy's old Jeep as I got in, still staring at the stranger's back as he continued down the sidewalk. Obviously, he was not from the South with his faded, worn jeans and his brogan-looking work boots. His blond, curly hair hung long over his ears, more Beatles than Elvis, and was definitely a contradiction to the flat tops still prevalent in Mississippi. His hair rubbed against the collar of the bold plaid flannel shirt he wore with the sleeves rolled up.

"A flannel shirt in June. Definitely not from

Mississippi," I said to myself as I attempted to pry my stare loose.

But my gaze was petrified, and I didn't even realize that Jew Baby had already gotten in on the other side of the Jeep and was waiting for me to crank up.

"I would be careful at who I was goo-goo-eyeing, Sue-ee. He's probably one of those COFO workers. The county's full of 'em, down here tryin' to save Mississippi."

"Reckon?" I asked as if any of the acronyms suffocating Mississippi would stop what I was thinking. "I don't care if he's COFO, SNCC, NAACP, or YMCA, he's gorgeous!"

"You know, Sue Ann, you could wait until the print of Dailey's ring on your left hand has tanned equal to the rest of your hand before you go drooling after some Yankee do-gooder. I guess there's a period of mourning that is appropriate after going with someone for four years, isn't there? I have no experience in such matters myself."

Jew Baby smiled her usual mischievous grin. She had never liked Dailey and was certainly not trying to protect his interest. This was just her way to play the rascal and try to confuse my thoughts.

But it was true. After four years of "going steady" with Dailey Bailey, I should have some sense of remorse, but I didn't. It had taken the last year of dating him to realize that, nice guy that he was, he was still just a possession, or an old habit, and not someone I wanted to spend the rest of my life with. Why it took two years of high school and two years of college for me to figure this out was beyond me. We had gone together for so long, people thought we looked alike.

I figured I had one year of college left before I had to become a responsible, boring adult, and no way would I limit myself to one person, not even if it was the ever-doting Dailey and not even if my mother was devastated by the breakup. It had taken a week of calls and rejections for Dailey to finally realize we were truly an item of the past, but it would take longer for my mother. Dailey moved to south Mississippi to work in his uncle's furniture business and to "try to move on" as he said when he called to bid me that last goodbye.

"Let's follow him and see where he's going," I whispered, as if afraid the outdoorsy stud, one of my cowboy terms not to be confused with a more worldly definition, might hear me from a block away.

Driving a beat-up Army Jeep from World War II that had no top made it a little difficult to be discreet. I drove slowly, never having to shift gears, in an attempt to stay far enough back that he would not sense he was being pursued.

Looking in the mirror, my reflection screamed at me—no makeup, and my hair hanging in crinkly braids, long extensions of the foot or so of washboard waves that did not, could not lie flat on my scalp but were a reprieve from the thick mass of long, tangled curls that I usually wore in my attempt to look like Cher. I had picked Jew Baby up at her uncle's store, and we were on our way to ride Queen, the horse Daddy had bought me in high school.

"I think you should pull right up beside him and offer him a ride." Baby made the suggestion, sarcastic as usual, with that devilish twinkle in her eyes she was famous for.

"Is that horse manure I smell on those cowboy

167

boots of yours?" Baby continued. "Surely you care about your looks when on a mission of such magnitude."

"Oh, darn it! You're right!"

I hit my brake in a pretense of actually caring about what I looked like before gunning the motor and pulling right up beside him. After all, I had to do the unexpected that was expected of me by my friend who knew me too well.

"Hi, there. Need a ride?"

Nervously, Jew Baby glanced around to see if any locals were watching us as I yelled.

"Sure." Just like the athlete I knew he'd be, the handsome young man leaped into the back of the Jeep without opening the door.

"Where you headed?" I asked before remembering that introductions were in order. "Oh, I'm sorry. I'm Sue Ann Taylor, and this is Jew Baby, uh, rather, Baby Steiner."

"Nice to meet you. Thanks for the ride. Didn't expect one, especially not from two good-looking southern girls. I'm Tate Douglas. I'm heading out River Road, if it's not too much out of the way for you."

Jew Baby and I were not surprised to hear a northern accent. I wanted to know more, a lot more, about this handsome young man, but was almost afraid to ask. But then, I didn't have to with Baby along.

"What organization brings you to our humble town?" asked Baby, still in sarcastic mode. As always, she succeeded in embarrassing me with her brazenness.

"Very perceptive, Baby. Is that your real name?" he asked, but I suspected it was either an attempt to change the subject or was retaliation for Baby's sarcasm.

"Don't ask. She'll get all riled up. If it makes you more comfortable, you can call her Jules, but she doesn't like that either. If you really want to be her friend, just call her Jew Baby like I do."

"Are you Jewish?" We both expected this question next, and I could never wait to hear how Baby would answer.

"Only at family funerals, and even that depends on which half." Baby answered matter-of-factly. "The rest of the time I'm Presbyterian. Now, back to you. Which part of the alphabet do you belong to?"

"C-O-F-O." Tate spelled it out without a hint of hesitation as he pulled a stack of leaflets from his pocket and handed one to each of us.

"You're going to drop me off at River Road Missionary Baptist, if you're brave enough. I'm running a Freedom School there."

"Aren't you terrified of the Klan?" I asked into the mirror, totally fascinated and impressed with the handsome though idealistic young crusader. "Especially after those three COFO workers disappeared down in Philadelphia. Any word on them?"

"Yes and no. Yes, I'm terrified of the Klan, and no, we have no word on the fate of Schwerner, Goodman, and Chaney. You can let me out here. The school is usually being watched. It's really not a good idea for you two to be seen letting me out there." Tate indicated that we should stop a good quarter mile from the church.

"Are you insinuating that girls can't be brave too?" Baby came alive and was ready to tangle with the Yankee boy.

169

"Not at all. It's just that the white girls I know who work for COFO are all from the North. One of them is even Jewish, and not just at family funerals." Tate winked at me as I looked back at him in the mirror. I blushed, an obvious chemical reaction to the tingling that had developed in my stomach.

"We've come this far. We'll take ya'll all the way." I drawled my answer, accentuating the "ya'll" for Tate's sake, wanting him to know I was no coward even though I was southern. After all, I already had a reputation for being a rebel. One more little episode would only add to my status.

I pulled right up in front of River Road Missionary Baptist to let Tate out. A handmade sign that read "Freedom School" hung across the front of the church. Jew Baby looked frightened as she glanced around for pickups with shotguns mounted in back windows. Seeing none, she sat taller in her seat.

"It was a pleasure, Mr. Douglas. I hope you enjoy your stay in our fair state and are overwhelmed with our southe'n hospitality." Baby continued being sarcastic, but with what I sensed had a sincere warning and wish behind it.

"Thanks for the ride. Hope to see you around." Tate exited on my side of the Jeep and gave me another wink before turning to go up the steps to the church.

I made a donut turn in front of the church and waved to Tate as I headed back toward town. I noticed Roweena Pugh standing in the doorway and waved a second time to her. She waved back, giving a pleasant, toothy smile.

As we rode Queen over the acreage at Parrish Oaks, Baby and I talked about Tate and about the possibility of violence in Barton County.

"True, most of the county wants whites and blacks to stay segregated, but I don't think the Klan is big here. I've never heard of any violence in Barton County, have you, Baby? No lynchings, anyway."

"Do you think they print that kind of news in the *Bartonville Weekly*, Sue Ann? Of course there has been violence, just not as much as there is in other parts of the state. We just don't know about it. I can tell you for sure that my parents have gotten hate calls. The KKK is not just against Negroes, you know. They hate Jews—even Presbyterian half-Jews who don't practice Judaism—Catholics, foreigners of any kind, and they especially hate white people like you who defend Negroes. It's just a matter of time before you start getting threatening phone calls. If you're determined to pursue this Tate thing, you better either be prepared for the worst or keep it very quiet."

"What do you mean, 'this Tate thing?' I probably won't ever run into him again."

"Sue Ann, this is Jew Baby, your friend. I know you well enough to know this is not the end of it. You just better be careful. If my family thought you were even thinking about seeing a COFO, they'd put a stop to our friendship even though they're both crazy about you. They try to be so southern. My daddy's terrified of being thought of as a Jew rather than a 'good ole boy' and not being accepted around here."

We rode for a few minutes in silence, just enjoying being out in the woods. I wanted to see if Daddy had finished the roof on the old cabin. He had promised the cabin could be mine when I graduated from high school, but he never got around to renovating it.

"Oh, look! It's finished."

The one-room cabin looked like it belonged in Alaska except for the huge magnolia tree whose branches overlapped the tin roof like a protective mother smothering her infant in her tight embrace.

We dismounted and I tied Queen to the hitching post Daddy had made in front of the cabin. I felt just like a kid in the gully again, when Liz Bess and I had first built the hideout out of apple crates and old tin. Daddy had hired a local handyman to re-chink the logs and put a new tin roof on the cabin, but the rest would be left up to me.

I knew what I would do next. The primitive table in my bedroom would be returned to its rightful home, and I'd furnish the rest of the cabin with primitive pieces I'd been collecting for the last two years: a rope bed, a meal bin, a walnut jelly cupboard complete with rusty, tin-covered rat hole, and a couple more straight chairs. All I had to do was load up Daddy's old Dodge truck and move in.

There was no electricity in the cabin, being too far from the service, but that didn't bother me. I'd use kerosene lanterns and candles if I ever wanted to be there at night, but it would be mostly used as my writing studio during the day. The return to a primitive era was completed with an outhouse out back that had also been renovated, complete with its original two-hole seat.

"Thank goodness I still have my old manual typewriter. I'd be up a creek if all I had was an electric one. You gonna help me set up my studio, Jew Baby?"

I knew the answer before asking. Baby loved decorating, although using primitive antiques was a new type of decorating for her. When she was little, she liked building playhouses; not playing in them, just building them, and once finished with each one, she'd tear it down and build another one. Baby combined her talent in art with architecture and interior decorating, a double major at Mississippi Southern. We decided we would start the "redecorating" the next weekend, since she had to work the rest of the week in her uncle's store.

The next day, Jew Baby proved to be right again. I just happened to be riding past River Road Missionary Baptist Church, alias Freedom School, when I saw Tate outside playing ball with a group of black children. As I hoped would happen, he flagged me down.

"Want to play a little softball, Sue Ann? We're short one player."

"Why not?"

I got out of the Jeep and took third base. We had been playing for about twenty minutes when I noticed an old, battered, brown Buick creeping by. A man wearing a floppy hat and sunglasses was slumped down in the car, obviously trying to conceal his identity. It was unnerving, but I pretended not to pay any attention.

What's the big deal? I thought. Daddy and Old Ma had talked about the games that used to go on in the pasture between Daddy and Uncle Bud and the children of the tenants. In fact, it was a favorite Sunday afternoon activity. Many times, all the children in the neighborhood would take part, with parents, black and white, cheering their teams on. Still, somehow I knew this was not being construed as an innocent pasture game.

"I've had enough, kids. Let's call it a day."

Tate took up the bats and balls and ushered me to the Jeep amidst the moans and groans of the kids who did not want their fun to end.

"Sue Ann, I think you better leave. We've seen that car pass here often lately. I don't think he's up to any good. He followed me for a long way yesterday when I was in the car loaned to us by the church. I know he was trying to see where I was staying, but I finally lost him by going pretty fast, kind of dangerous on these curvy gravel roads. I appreciate you stopping, and the kids need to see this kind of interaction, but I don't want to jeopardize your safety."

"That's my decision, Tate. I'm not afraid. You don't know me, but I'm considered a bit of a rebel myself."

"I know. Roweena told me about you. She saw you fight a bully one time when you were little, trying to protect some black children."

"Really? I didn't know she was there. That was a long time ago."

"She also told me that when you were in high school at a Christmas parade you picked up candy thrown by Santa to the white children and took it over to give the Negro children in the back who were being ignored."

"How did she know that? Only Snuffy and his bunch of kids were standing in the back. They were the only black family there."

"Snuffy told everybody. You have a reputation in the Negro community that you don't even know about. You should be proud for taking up for black children like that."

"Someone else told me that the day I attacked

Booger Melton...the bully you were talking about. Has nothing to do with pride...just being human, is all."

Tate continued edging me toward the Jeep in an attempt to make me leave.

"What if I don't want to leave, Tate?"

"Sue Ann, I'd like nothing better than to be with you, but I am afraid for you. I have no right to put you in harm's way."

"Let me be the judge of that. It's my skin. Do you like to ride horses?"

"Don't know. I've never ridden one."

"I'll pick you up tomorrow. What time's good for you?"

When Jew Baby was right, she was right. The "Tate thing" was definitely being pursued, but I would not discuss this with my family. Rita Jean was at summer school at Ole Miss, so I couldn't talk to her—not that she would understand anyway—and my parents would not receive such information pleasantly.

Even though they had both come a long way in their thinking, they still basically believed there was a white world and there was a black world and the two did not mix socially. Liz Bess and I had been an exception. I heard both of my parents express distaste for the college students invading our county from northern universities, "stirring up unnecessary trouble for blacks and whites."

Call it fate, but if I'd had any thought of telling them about Tate, I would have changed my mind after the discussion we had at the supper table that night.

"Zeke, I've heard that Sadie and her family are mixed up with that COFO Freedom School. If that's the case, I'm not offering my housecleaning job to her. I'll have to find someone else. I don't want anybody causing those KKK crazies to come snooping around my house."

"I don't know nobody else that's not already working. Are you sure it's Sadie? I heard her daughter Roweena has been seen hanging around the church where they meet on River Road, but I hadn't heard nothin' about Sadie. Offer it to her, but let her know if she's part of that COFO operation, she can't have the job. That's simple enough."

"Well, I guess Sadie can't be responsible for what her daughter is doing. I heard from Leonia that Roweena's pregnant. I guess that'll be another grandchild she'll have to raise. She probably needs to work. I'll talk to her tomorrow."

"Sue Ann, you're mighty quiet tonight. Wrote any good books lately?"

This was Daddy's favorite line to use with me and usually got a reaction, but tonight I was not in a prideful mood, torn between a new interest in my life and my desire to keep the pride of my parents that I had fought so hard to earn. I changed the subject to one I could be honest and enthusiastic about—the cabin.

"Jew Baby and I rode Queen over and looked at the cabin today. It looks great, Daddy. We plan to move my primitive pieces in this weekend. Thanks for fixing it for me."

"Sue Ann, I wish you wouldn't call her Jew Baby. It sounds so…so…"

"What, Mama? Jewish?" Daddy and I looked at each other and laughed. Mama did not.

"Billy has a little bit to finish on the back wall, but he'll get it tomorrow. Then, it's all yours." Daddy changed the subject in a hurry because Mama always got mad when we laughed at her.

"Just promise me that when you write that novel of yours, you'll make me appear even smarter and more handsome than I am in real life."

"Make him wealthy, too, Sue Ann, so I don't have to work so hard." Mama laughed when she made this remark. I knew it was a joke because Mama enjoyed her work, especially now that she owned three beauty salons and had plans to open one farther north, closer to Memphis. We were all proud of her success, but most important, Mama felt good about herself.

After supper, I picked up the *Bartonville Weekly* to scan for anything newsworthy. Mostly filled with community news like who's visiting who and what revivals or all-day-singings and dinners-on-the-ground are being held at what churches, it didn't take me long to scan. Toward the back of the paper, there was a half-page ad that did catch my interest. In big, bold letters across the top was written the caption:

COFO! NO! NO!

Underneath it was a long treatise written by someone "who knows the truth" behind the organization. The author claimed the Communists were financially backing these students from liberal northern universities to come to Mississippi, with the sole purpose of causing an insurrection on our "southern way of life" in order to "bankrupt our economy and make us easy prey for foreigners and northern carpetbaggers."

It went on to warn our "young gentle southern women" to "beware these smooth-talking Yankee males" who will attempt to sway them from their

Christian ideals. The ad also condemned northern white females, who were being paid big money to join with these Communists in "destroying all that is right and good about the South. They are nothing but prostitutes who would do anything for money."

It ended with a Bible verse:

For the love of money is a root of all kinds of evil, for which some have strayed from the faith in their greediness, and pierced themselves through with many sorrows. 1 Timothy 6:10.

Chapter Nineteen
Departure and Reunion

I parked the Jeep out of sight on a rough dirt road that was actually on Harvey land but led to the back of our property. Queen was tied to a tree at the end of the road, and I mounted first.

"You'll have to ride behind me since you don't know how to ride. Put your foot in the stirrup, hold onto the saddle horn, and swing up. I wanna show you something pretty special to me. It's not far."

Tate took my instructions like a man, like I knew he would. This reminded me of when I was little, telling Daddy that my husband would have to let me drive the motorcycle and ride behind me. But I didn't want to get ahead of myself. I barely knew this "Yankee do-gooder," as Baby called him, but I planned to.

As we approached the back side of our acreage, I turned Queen down into the woods.

"Watch your head. We're going under some limbs." I leaned to the left so Tate could see the approaching limbs. He was only a few inches taller than I was.

"Here it is! My little cabin in the woods, just not in Alaska."

"You want to go to Alaska, too? It's been one of my dreams since I read *White Fang* as a boy. I'm going someday, maybe after I get my law degree."

Law made sense with someone so active in constitutional rights. I could imagine Tate taking many pro bono cases for the underprivileged and mistreated, a real champion of the underdog.

Tate was in awe of the little cabin and, just as I always did, let his imagination run wild with historical scenarios that could possibly have taken place over a hundred years ago.

"Look at this, Tate." I got on my knees to show him initials and a date carved on one of the bottom logs near the floor.

"T.P. Decimbur 1862," read Tate, spelling out December as the carver had. "Far out! I bet some slave child did this from his pallet where he slept at night."

"I have this theory that it was a slave boy whose family took the last name Parrish, same as their owner, like many slaves did in those days, and that he got that pocketknife for Christmas, probably belonged to his daddy. He could obviously read and write, which was not uncommon on the Parrish and Harvey plantations, though it was the exception in the South. Both were kind slave-owners, an oxymoron, as if it's possible to be such a thing, but the Parrish wives taught the slave children to read and write. I pretend his name was Toby Parrish and plan to write a book about him some day."

"You write, too?" Tate sat with his back to the wall and looked at me, smiling. "You're a woman of many talents, Sue Ann Taylor." Before I knew what was happening, Tate pulled me into a sitting position facing him and kissed me.

More stunned than embarrassed, I pulled away, giving Tate the false impression that I didn't enjoy his impulsive action.

"I'm sorry, Sue Ann. That was presumptuous of me. I guess I'm moving this relationship too fast, but I'm really attracted to you and thought you were to me."

Looking into his eyes, I smiled my most mischievous grin before putting my arms around his neck. He gave me a confused look until I spoke.

"Relationship? Guess kissing is in order, then."

I kissed him even more passionately than he had kissed me. As I withdrew, he held me at arm's length, looking at me as if trying to figure out where this was headed. Threading his fingers through my loose curls, he pulled my face to his.

What came next took my breath away—the deepest most passionate kiss I had ever experienced in my short romantic life. It far surpassed the teenage kisses I'd shared with Dailey, and I sensed Tate Douglas would be the ultimate test to my strict Christian upbringing.

My body attempted to remain rigid, but with one out-of-control shiver, I melted into his arms, lifeless as he laid me back on the floor. With his body tight against mine, he continued kissing me as his left hand moved under my shirt. Regaining my will, I pulled away from him.

"No, Tate! This is not right. I can't do this." As I jumped to my feet, he followed me, moving between me and the door.

"Please! Don't leave, Sue Ann. I'm sorry! It won't happen again, not unless you want it to. I promise." Tate had one hand on my arm, and with his free hand he made a cross over his heart.

I looked down, embarrassed and uncertain as to what I should do.

"It's my fault. I know you thought you had the go-ahead when I kissed you. It's just…I'm still…a…a…"

"A virgin? Far out!"

Tate ran his fingers through his curly hair and stared at me with wonder as if he had come in contact with a rare endangered species. "Okay. I can deal with that." He backed up, holding me at arm's length, and gave me a serious look followed by a smile that melted away all doubts. "I want to know you, Sue Ann, as much as you'll let me, but I promise it won't be more than you're willing. Right now, I just want to kiss you again. Is that all right?"

And kiss we did. True to his word, he did not make sexual advances, but his kiss said plenty, making full use of his tongue to let me know how he felt. I knew it was just a matter of time before this would not be enough, but for the moment, it gave me tingles and sensations I had never experienced.

"As much as I hate to end this, I've got to get back to the school. When can I see you again, Sue Ann?"

"When do you want? I'm free until late August, when I have to go back to the W, but I hope you won't wait that long."

"The W?"

"Mississippi State College for Women. In Columbus—the oldest state-supported college for women, actually, if you want the full description."

"Oh!" He put his hand on my cheek and gave it an affectionate rub, using the back of his fingers. "How about tomorrow?" He paused. "Are you afraid to be with me at the cabin again? I feel like we're safe here. We can't meet in public, Sue Ann. It's too risky. In fact, while we're talking about it…kissing in private, yes, but in public, I don't want you to even acknowledge that you know me."

I started to protest, but Tate moved his finger over my lips.

"We received some pretty serious warnings today from Bob Moses, our leader at main headquarters. Klan activity is high all over the state. Many of our coworkers have been beaten, and so have the people who have helped us. We still don't know what happened to Schwerner, Chaney, and Goodman, but we were told to be on guard at all times. In fact, I shouldn't even be with you right now without one of my coworkers with me. For your own safety, you have to promise me you'll keep our meetings secret. Deal?" Tate took both my hands in his and locked his eyes on mine, waiting for my reply.

I shook my head in agreement and was relieved that I didn't have to explain to him why I took back roads and did not ask him to come to my house. This arrangement would work well as far as my parents were concerned, too. I would have to make Baby swear an oath of secrecy, though. We were past the spit-in-the-hand stage that had been so important to Liz Bess and me, but Jew Baby's word was just as good as spit. Besides, she would not want her parents to find out about Tate and me anyway.

I offered to take Tate home, but he wouldn't allow it. He said he was protecting me as well as the black family sacrificing their safety by letting him stay with them. I was disappointed that he did not trust me enough to tell me where he was staying, but I let him out down River Road, not far from the church.

Tate and I met almost every day at the cabin, but I

was not allowed to pick him up anymore. In fact, he made me stop coming to the Freedom School at all after the church was vandalized one night by the Klan, who left their calling card, a burning cross. Windows were broken, chairs and pews were axed to pieces, and "Go home Nigger lovers" was smeared over the walls and ceiling in red paint.

The church members were pleased it had not been burned to the ground like many other churches in Mississippi where the schools were being held.

The COFO workers and Negroes were not the Klan's only prey. Late one night shortly after the church was vandalized, I had a terrifying telephone call from Baby.

"Sue Ann, can you come and get me?" Baby whispered into the phone like she thought someone was listening in on her conversation. "I'm here by myself, and I'm scared. I just had a telephone call that said to get out of the house if I didn't want to burn. Why do they do this to us? We're Presbyterians, for God's sake!"

"I'll be right there, Jew Baby. Lock yourself in and don't open the door to anybody but me."

I jumped into the Jeep and drove as fast as I could to the road on the other side of Bartonville where the Steiner house was located. It was dark at the house except for one small light that I knew was coming from Baby's bedroom upstairs. Racing to the side door nearest to the bedroom, I pounded on it, yelling for Baby.

"Open up, Baby, it's me, Sue Ann!"

There was no sound from inside the house. Frantically, I began banging again, so hard I knew my fists would be black and blue, until I heard faint footsteps inside the house. At the same time, I heard a scurrying sound in the bushes behind me. Grabbing a leaf rake that stood beside the door, I forced myself to turn and face the bushes, lashing out at the would-be criminals.

"I'm not afraid, you redneck devils! Come on out and show me how manly you are to hide behind your wife's sheets and scare young girls!"

My adrenaline was overflowing, and at that instant I felt I could charge into the bushes in a demonic rage, screaming and thrashing, pulling white hoods off overgrown redneck heads. Just as the door opened behind me, the culprit lunged at me from the bushes, knocking me off my feet as we both tumbled into the Steiner home.

"Get off me, Muffin, you big goon! You scared me to death."

Jew Baby, though still shaken from the telephone call, held her sides laughing at the sight of me trying to get the huge dog off as we lay on the entry floor. When I finally got my balance, I, too began laughing at the cussin' I had given the poor hound, who now sat at my feet with his paw up as if to say, "Let's shake and make up."

"Let's go, Jew Baby, before something real happens. I think I used up all my adrenaline on Muffin."

The next morning, the sheriff came to our house and asked Daddy if he knew where Jules Steiner was. There had been a cross-burning in the Steiner yard the night before. Mr. and Mrs. Steiner were out of town and had told the sheriff to check on the house because Jules would be there alone. The sheriff was really worried when he couldn't get anyone to the door and had broken in only to find the house empty.

"Let me ask Sue Ann if she knows where Baby is."

Daddy walked down the hall to my bedroom and was relieved to find Baby and me sound asleep, buried in my featherbed with the air conditioner going full bore in order to make it cold enough in the room not to suffocate in the mountain of fluff that was more like a volcano than a mountain in the hot Mississippi summer.

The sheriff was grateful to hear Jules was safe, and it wasn't long before Baby's parents called my house. This time Daddy had to wake Baby up so she could talk to her parents. She told them about my daring rescue and my encounter with Muffin, the newest KKK member, but stopped laughing when she heard that the Klan had in fact visited their home in the night as forewarned.

Jew Baby left Bartonville two days later, headed for her grandmother's house in New Jersey to spend the rest of the summer. Her parents were afraid for their daughter and were even contemplating moving out of the state. The only reason they decided to stay was Baby wanted to finish her degree at Mississippi Southern the next year.

Every morning during the rest of the summer, I waited by the telephone at 10:00 for Tate to call me. It was our usual time to talk, when my parents weren't home, and the time when we could plan our meetings at the cabin. One day in late summer, Tate did not call, and I became frantic. After waiting an extra hour, I could stand it no longer and headed the Jeep toward the Freedom School. Roweena stood out front with two other people I did not know.

"Where's Tate, Roweena?"

"I don't know. He and some of the others went to town to recruit, but they're not back yet."

I could tell by her expression that she thought something was wrong.

"Damn this old Jeep!" I cursed aloud as I floorboarded the Jeep to Bartonville.

A crowd had formed around the square, and I sensed trouble as I parked and practically ran to see what was causing the commotion. It took several minutes to push through the crowd of onlookers before I could see the source of their curiosity. What I saw terrified me.

Tate and two young black high school students were seated on the sidewalk with their hands handcuffed behind them. A deputy stood between them and the crowd, several of whom shouted "nigga lover" and "Go home, damn Yankee" as well as other obscenities.

One heckler pushed past the deputy and jumped on Tate, knocking him onto his back and punching him hard in the face several times. Quickly, the deputy grabbed the man and pushed him hard back into the crowd.

"Go on home, Booger, 'fore I have to haul you into jail. We'll handle this."

"Yeah! Put me in the cell with that curly-headed son-of-a-bitch and let me finish him off! I'll show him what we think uh nigga lovin' Yankees in Mississippi!"

I pushed harder, getting within six feet of Tate, and almost screamed when I saw the blood running from his mouth and nose. His eyes met mine and he frowned, shaking his head vehemently, silently demanding that I not get involved as he coughed and spat blood. Ignoring Tate's warning, I stepped toward the deputy, but was stopped as someone grabbed my arm.

Turning, I looked up to see Daddy glaring at me.

"Let's go home, Sue Ann. You got no business here." Daddy didn't give me a chance to respond as he ushered me through the crowd.

I glanced back over my shoulder at Tate, and he smiled to reassure me that everything would be okay.

"Who is he, Sue Ann? What's your interest in him? And don't go making up a pack of lies, 'cause I'm your daddy and you know I'll know just by looking at your face."

"He's a friend, Daddy. His name is Tate Douglas. Baby and I met him this summer. He's a good guy, Daddy. I know you don't agree with what he's doing, but he thinks it's the right thing to do. When I was little you told me to follow my heart. Well, that's what Tate is doing here. His heart is just in a different place from yours and just about everyone else from Mississippi, it seems."

"I don't want you anywhere near him or any COFO, Sue Ann. You see how crazy that crowd is? Friend or no friend, you stay away from him."

"Then you've got to help him—he's hurt! Please, Daddy!"

"If I go back and talk to the sheriff, will you go home and stay there?"

"Yes, Daddy. I promise."

"Well, that'll have to do for now. We'll talk about this later when your mama's not around. I don't want her worrying."

Going home that afternoon was a hard thing for me to do, but I knew Daddy would help Tate if he could. All afternoon, I imagined Tate in a jail cell or worse, even his death at the hands of Booger Melton and the Klan. I could see myself crying with his parents like I had seen happen on the news way too many times in the last few weeks. Two hours later the phone rang.

"Tate? Are you all right? They didn't hurt you anymore, did they?"

"I'm okay. The sheriff released us after your dad talked to him. Some of us were giving out leaflets on the square, trying to get more Negroes to register to vote or to at least come to our training sessions, and the sheriff arrested us. He held us until he had a chance to see if we were breaking any laws by giving out leaflets for the Freedom School. I just got released a few minutes ago. I know it doesn't make sense, but what does, this summer?"

"I was so worried when you didn't call. Seeing you in handcuffs terrified me, Tate, and I thought Booger Melton was going to kill you."

"I know. It showed in your eyes. I need to see you, Sue Ann. Can you meet me at the cabin in a few minutes?"

When I walked through the door, Tate was already there. He sat straddling a straight chair and looking as if nothing had happened even though his lip was bruised and swollen.

"How can you sit there like it's just a normal day?" I paced while admonishing Tate. "You were arrested and beaten, almost shared a cell with Booger Melton, who makes two of you, not to mention he's mean as a yard dog, as if you don't already know. You scared me to death, Tate!" I stopped and folded my arms, never taking my eyes off him.

"I'm sorry, Sue Ann, but it's part of the risks we take. I don't want to end up like my three coworkers at Philadelphia, but I believe in what I'm doing or I wouldn't stay in Mississippi."

Crossing to me, he took me in his arms and hugged me, caressing my hair.

"That's not altogether true. Truth is, I don't ever want to leave Mississippi because of you. I love you, Sue Ann. I've known it from that first day here at the cabin, but today cinched it when I saw you ready to take on that deputy for me. Thank goodness your daddy showed up. And that's what we need to talk about."

"What do you mean, Tate?"

"Your daddy gave me a ride back to the school. He knows about us. I'm sure about it even though he never said so exactly. But he made me think about the dangerous position I'm putting you in."

"I told him you were a friend and asked him to help you. He's known the sheriff all his life. They were friends as children."

"He told me, and he asked me not to see you anymore, in a roundabout way. His exact words were, 'If you care enough about someone, you'd do anything to protect them, even if it meant never seeing them again.' "

"Don't even think about it. I have to see you. I'm in love with you, too." I searched his eyes as my tears fell, trying to understand what he was telling me, trying to console myself.

"They've asked me to transfer to another county. I didn't want to because of you, but now I feel I have to take the transfer because of you."

"No, Tate!" I turned away, wiping my eyes with my hand.

"Listen to me, Sue Ann. I can't stay here and not see you, but if I see you, I'm putting you at risk, and I won't do that. If I'm in another county, I can see you when you're at the W and nobody will know I'm COFO." Tate put his arms around me and held me tight. "I won't give you up, Sue Ann, but I will protect you, even if it means not seeing you. Can you understand what I'm saying?"

"No, I don't. I don't want you to leave. I'm not afraid." I shook my head and pushed away from Tate to sit on the edge of the rope bed.

"I know you're not, but I'm afraid for you. I've already called and told them I'll transfer."

"When do you have to leave?"

"Some time this month. I'll know for sure in a couple of days. Please, Sue Ann, try to understand. I love you." Tate sat beside me and put his arm around me, pulling my head to his chest. His heartbeat was like a slow-paced metronome…calming, soothing away all pain for the moment, making me forget everything except Tate and me and the moment.

As we kissed with the passion I'd felt only with him, I knew I was losing the battle I fought with myself. I wanted him, and I planned then to give myself to him totally before he left Barton County.

Two days later, Tate called.

"Can you meet me at the cabin late this afternoon? I need to talk to you. I've got a favor to ask."

My nerves were on edge for some reason that day, and I didn't know why. I saddled up Queen and took her for a long ride on the Harveys' property that adjoined ours and planned to get to the cabin earlier than scheduled just to have time to think and maybe do a little writing, although I knew I couldn't concentrate enough to write. I wondered what the favor was that Tate was going to ask.

As I led Queen through a thick grove of woods, I heard voices up ahead. After tying her to a tree, I sneaked closer to the sounds to try and make out whose voices it was.

"I don't care how dangerous it is, I want you there in the middle of it. I want to know every move they're thinking about making. No mistakes. Those damned COFOs! You report back to me the minute you know something."

"I will, Mr. Harvey. You can count on it. I haven't failed you so far, have I?"

I hid as the two men walked down the dirt road that Tate and I took to meet at the cabin. We would have to be more careful using this road in the future, now that I knew someone else used it, especially someone who hated COFOs.

I wondered what reason Mr. Harvey had for hating them. He didn't strike me as the "nigger-hatin'" type usually associated with the Klan, but Tate had told me I would be surprised at the number of "fine, upstanding citizens" in the state who were active in the KKK.

I assumed most upper-class racists belonged to the White Citizens' Council, nicknamed the "Country Club Klan" by the press. This council was formed in the '50s after the Supreme Court handed down the Brown Decision that demanded desegregation of white schools. The Citizens' Council had as its motto, "States

Rights and Separation of the Races" and vowed to use political power to prevent Brown from ever being enacted in Mississippi. They had been successful so far.

I caught a glimpse of the two men as they passed by where I was hiding. The younger man stopped to get a rock out of his boot, a fancy black-and-white snake boot, python, like the snake I had seen on *Nyoka the Jungle Girl* as a child. Where had I seen those boots before?

It was dark by the time Tate made it to the cabin. I was becoming more alarmed as time passed, afraid he had had another run-in with Booger or some other Klansman. Anxiously, I sat on the porch watching for him and was relieved when I saw him approach. Running to him, I threw my arms around him.

"You're late! Stop scaring me like this!"

"I'm sorry, Sue Ann. I had to wait until dark. There's been a lot of suspicious traffic by the school this afternoon, and I couldn't risk anyone seeing me coming here." Tate took my hand as we walked to the cabin.

"I know. We'll have to be careful meeting here. Mr. Harvey and another man were on the road, the one we usually take to get here. First time I've seen anybody on that road."

As we stepped inside the cabin, Tate turned to me with a look of dread on his face.

"We probably won't be meeting here anymore, Sue Ann. That's what I needed to talk to you about." Tate took my hand and led me to the rope bed, our spot for talking and making out, coming shy of lovemaking.

"COFO is transferring me to Paxton to run a new Freedom School that's opening there."

"I guess we're over, huh? It's just as well. I have to go back to the W at the end of this month anyway. I'll do my student teaching spring semester."

Trying to be nonchalant about the whole conversation didn't work. My heart was breaking. Tate was my first real love, a forbidden love, at that. But then, maybe that was what was so mesmeric about the whole thing, with its secret meeting place, stolen kisses, and provocative, though casual to onlookers, glances when accidentally meeting in Bartonville.

"Over? No way. I love you, Sue Ann." Tate held me tight in his arms, rubbing his chin against my head. "I can't think about us being over. We'll find a way to see each other. Besides, Paxton is closer to Columbus than Bartonville is."

"Don't make promises you might not be able to keep. Your parents want you to go back to college this fall, and I can't blame them. They must be terrified with you in the middle of this. Eventually, they will convince you."

"I'll finish what I've started here. I think the cause is worth it. Besides, I can see you if I stay."

"What's the favor?" I asked the question, not wanting to prolong the conversation of Tate's leaving. Tate moved from the bed to the chair and pulled it over in front of me. He took my hands and enclosed them in his, rubbing the backs of mine with his fingertips. When he looked up into my eyes, I sensed an urgency.

"I didn't want to tell you this, but I was chased by someone, possibly several someones, last night when I left the church; that same old brown Buick that kept passing the school. I drove thirty miles before I lost them. Drove all the way into Quitman County. When I got back to the house where I was staying, there was a cross burning in the yard. They had thrown bricks through the windows with hate messages attached and shot a flare through the back window, almost catching the house on fire. The people I was staying with managed to put it out before any serious damage was done. That's another reason I have to leave Barton County. I can't ask this family to jeopardize their safety any longer."

"So you're leaving?" I looked deep into Tate's eyes. Tate became silent for a few seconds and looked away.

"Yes. I don't have a choice." Tate redirected his eyes to mine. "The church leaders don't want COFO using their car anymore, so I was wondering if there was any way you could take me to Paxton. I'll pay for the gas and everything. We can stay at a safe house, a new one no one knows about but COFO. I hate to ask you to do this, but I thought maybe we could spend some time together, too, somewhere that nobody knows us and we don't have to hide. What the hell, we might even go out to eat and to a movie like normal couples do." Tate smiled, the first real smile I had seen on this afternoon of bad surprises.

"I'll have to come up with something to tell Mama and Daddy. Actually, you might be in luck. Daddy just bought me a '57 Chevy for my senior year. He said I'd need a car for my student teaching. We could really be incognito." I moved my hand to Tate's hair, combing my fingers through his curls.

"Good! Then it's a date. I can't wait to spend a whole weekend with you, sweetheart."

It was the first time Tate had called me a pet name,

and it sent cold chills over me. I knew then I'd go ahead with what I had been plotting for some time. As the darkness enveloped the cabin, Tate lit the kerosene lamp on the primitive table.

The next few seconds found us wrapped in each other's arms on the rope bed. Tate kissed me, dancing his tongue against mine more erotically than ever. As he eased his hand under my shirt, what had become his way of asking permission without words, I lay back without protesting. Pulling away, he looked down at me wondering why I didn't stop him as I always had before.

"Make love to me, Tate." I smiled at the shocked expression on Tate's face.

"Are you sure, baby?" Confusion and disbelief outlined the scowl on Tate's forehead.

"I've never been more sure of anything in my life."

"It's awfully hot in here." Tate's scowl changed to a broad grin.

"It'll get hotter." I smiled to reassure him.

Tate left the bed and opened the door wide to allow the little bit of breeze that was blowing to enter the cabin. Sensing my modesty, he turned down the lamp before undressing. I had been quick in removing my own clothing and had stopped to rub my hand over the wedding ring pattern of the quilt in a "make-a-wish" gesture. I waited, anxious to feel Tate's body next to mine.

"You know your first time can be painful, sweetheart?" Tate slid under the covers and cuddled me in his arms as he warned me, but I could tell he would be hesitant not to continue, at this point.

"So I've heard. So hurt me, my love. I'm ready." I

locked my fingers in his blond curls and pulled his lips to mine.

"I love you, Sue Ann. I'll never forget this night."

The magnolia leaves rustled over us, providing background music for the long-dreamed-of love scene. Moonlight filtered through the shaking leaves and played across our enraptured bodies, casting elfish shadows on the log wall beside our bed like a warning, a foreboding, but it went unheeded.

It was my choice to spend Tate's last night in the county in our secret place, the old log cabin at the back of Parrish Oaks. There, on the cotton-filled mattress of the primitive, antique rope bed, above the carved initials of a slave child, I witnessed the passing of my youth, my purity. No regrets.

****

Early on the morning of August 10th, I picked Tate up at the house where he had been staying since first coming to Bartonville, a house with a back room partially charred by grown men hiding their identities in silly white sheets, men full of hatred and contempt. Removed to one side of the front yard were the remains of a burnt cross. The home belonged to Sadie and Roweena Pugh and Roweena's new baby boy.

I held the baby and gushed over him for Roweena's sake even though he was not a pretty baby. I also asked both Sadie and Roweena not to mention to my parents that I even knew Tate or where I was going. Sadie had just started working for Mama a few weeks before and did not want to jeopardize her new job by letting my parents know she had any connection with COFO, so the deal was easily made.

Drumming the steering wheel with nervous guilt, I

drove us out of town in the black-and-white, seven-year-old '57 Chevy that my daddy had bought me for $500. Personifying the car as I did most of my possessions, it became "Booby Hooby" named for a silly greeting I used at the W my second year there, which was like my junior year. I would be graduating in three years; Sue Ann Taylor, ever the impatient one, took overloads each semester and went to summer school one summer in order to accomplish this.

My parents thought I was visiting one of my Rosette Social Club sisters in Paxton and was going to look the town over as a possible site for my student teaching. They trusted me completely. Besides, both my sisters would be home for the weekend, and they needed my bedroom.

As we headed down Highway 51, I let Tate drive and made myself content trying to find a good station on the radio. A news bulletin had just interrupted the broadcast on a station that I hit:

"The bodies of three slain civil rights workers were discovered in an earthen dam in Neshoba County this morning. Michael Schwerner, Andrew Goodman, and James Chaney had all been shot in the head. The FBI and local law enforcement agencies are investigating the murders. More information will be broadcast as we receive it."

"Law enforcement agencies, my ass! Damn them!" Tate shouted as he beat the steering wheel. Pulling over on the shoulder of the highway, he wept as I hugged him to me.

It was then that I found out he had known the three workers personally. He had been in training with two of them in Ohio and had been originally assigned to

Meridian, the COFO office managed by Michael Schwerner and his wife. At the last minute, he was moved to the Bartonville area. He had really hit it off with Andrew Goodman, who was also from New York, and was looking forward to working with him. Cold chills covered my body when I realized Tate could have easily been with the three when they were murdered.

When we reached the safe house at Paxton, there was no sign of life from the outside. It was a rundown but fairly large house with white asbestos shingles, and sat off the main highway, at least two miles down a dirt road. Unplanted fields grew wild on either side. Tate told me the house had been donated by an anonymous donor for COFO use during the Summer Project. Voices could be heard inside the house as we stepped onto the screened-in porch.

Tate knocked a signal knock before opening the door to expose a group of ten college-age students, both blacks and whites, huddled around a small television set. On the screen was a special broadcast out of Memphis, reporting the finding of the bodies of the three civil rights workers.

The room overflowed with tears and emotion, and I felt alone, an outsider, embarrassed because I was unable to weep for these three young men with whom I had no connection other than vicarious living through stories of their bravery. The deeds of the three would be recounted over and over by their COFO coworkers in the hours ahead.

In the back of the group, two young women embraced, sobbing aloud for their fallen comrades. One of them had shoulder-length black hair that glistened like black velvet as she rocked back and forth with emotion. I was reminded of a time, a very long time ago, when I had witnessed a similar scene, but in that sad time a young girl was rocked in the arms of her grandparents and was weeping over the death of her mother.

As I stared sympathetically at the girl, she looked up at me. I dove into magnetizing cat eyes, light green, the color of a summer fern. The girl stood and her tear-drenched face transformed into a smile.

"Liz Bess!" I ran to her outstretched embrace.

Chapter Twenty
The Homecoming

"What are you doing here, Sue Ann?"

"I'm with Tate Douglas. We've been dating all summer. What about you? I heard from Leonia that you were in university up north somewhere, majoring in pre-law."

"I just couldn't stay there. As unkind as it has been to my people and to me, Mississippi is still my home. I had to come back and try to convince as many people as possible to vote and fight for change in our state. I wanted to write you so many times but figured you had outgrown me by now. How about you? I know you're in college. You were always so smart. Are you majoring in journalism?"

"No, I'm in education. I want to be a history teacher, Liz Bess. Maybe I'll get to teach in the new Mississippi some day, where black and white children go to school together and eat ice cream sitting in the same booth at Nellie's Ice Cream Shack. The old racism and Jim Crow will be just that, history."

"I hope you're right. Introduce me to Tate. I'm taking his place at Bartonville. I'm coming home, Saca. What do you think of that?" Liz Bess squeezed my hand as her smile lit up her whole face.

"That's awesome, Liz Bess. Will you live with Leonia?"

"No, Leonia and I never got along very well. Besides, she'd be scared to death. Another house has been donated in Barton County for COFO to use, but I'm not sure where it is. Is our gully still there?"

Her smile faded, and I sensed she was changing the subject, not wanting to tell me where she would be living. I had learned from Tate this was information they were not to share with anyone.

"I'm not sure. A new interstate highway is coming through. Daddy has negotiated with them and sold most of our property, all but the old house and the pecan grove. The right-of-way is taking your old house and our gully."

"I guess I can assume you two know each other." Tate walked up and acted like he was hurt at being ignored.

"Oh, Tate, this is Liz Bess, my best friend ever. She's the one I told you about. She was also the one I was protecting that day I tried to beat up Booger Melton." I reached for Tate's hand.

"Nice to finally meet you, Liz Bess. I heard someone named Elizabeth was taking my place at Bartonville. Would that be you?"

"I go by Elizabeth now, Sue Ann. Those days of Liz Bess are gone, I'm afraid, along with Saca and Honta, but I still have my necklace." Elizabeth smiled as she gave me the forward fist of our old days. I returned the fist sign and hugged her again.

"We have so much to talk about, Sue Ann, but I don't know if I'll be able to see you much when I get to Bartonville. I hear it's pretty dangerous. What will your folks think when they hear I work for COFO? And you know Bartonville; they will hear."

"I don't know. They're both pretty adamant in thinking COFO is just a bunch of outsiders stirring up hostilities. They have no idea I've been dating Tate." Taking Tate's hand in mine, I smiled at him. "I guess they won't have to know, now that he's leaving."

"I'm not leaving you, Sue Ann." Tate seemed a little agitated that he had to repeat this, and he dropped my hand and placed his in his pocket.

"I don't care how dangerous it is, Liz Bess—I mean, Elizabeth. We will have to get together while you're home." I persisted, promising myself I would not give my friend up again.

"Sue Ann, you make it sound like I'm home from college for the summer. I'll be there for a cause, one that stirs up a lot of negative emotion and hatred, and yes, violent retribution. You see what happened in Philadelphia. You've always been a defender, but you've never been a joiner. I wouldn't think of asking you to join COFO. Besides, you've had no training in dealing with these madmen." Elizabeth looked to Tate for confirmation of what she was saying. Tate shook his head in agreement.

"I'll always be close if you need me, Elizabeth. I promise." I crossed my heart.

****

The weekend went fast. Elizabeth and Tate were busy talking and planning COFO activities left unfinished in Bartonville, and I was left on my own. I attempted to talk to the other students, but they were not very friendly. All of the white students were from the North and didn't seem to trust a southern white girl. I learned a little about what prejudice feels like that weekend, and I didn't like it.

The black students were much friendlier, most of them being from the South, but they treated me like a royal novelty. I had to beg to help cook and wash dishes. By the time I left on Sunday afternoon, I was becoming more accepted for who I was by both groups, but Tate and Elizabeth were constantly reassuring them all that I could be trusted.

During one of our conversations, one of the unfriendly northern white girls asked me why southerners called black people "colored." I became somewhat defensive and replied that the term "colored" was certainly more respectful than the "n" word, although the more educated and respectful, including myself, used the term "Negro." I then questioned her use of the term "black."

Quincy was quick to explain.

"I'm black, Sue Ann, and proud of it. It's part of the new movement, to teach our race to be proud of who we are. I'm not colored." Quincy held out his arm to me. "Here, rub it." I smiled and rubbed Quincy's arm, thinking I knew what he was demonstrating.

"See, Sue Ann? It don't rub off." Quincy smiled.

"So I should be using the term 'black' rather than 'Negro'?"

" 'Black' is preferred, but I'm not sure southern blacks are aware of it yet."

****

Tate and I never made the movie that weekend, nor did we get a chance to make love again. With the finding of the three civil rights workers' bodies, there were constant phone calls and meetings. I was not included in most of the discussion and found myself walking around in the yard quite a bit or sitting on the porch.

It was on one of the porch-sitting occasions on Sunday morning that I saw a reflection in the woods to the side of the house. Moving to the edge of the porch where I could get a better look, I partially hid behind a herd of giant elephant ears, plants like my mother always kept on the porch of the old house. The reflection vanished, but a few minutes later, I saw a familiar brown Buick pull from one of the fields and take off fast down the dirt road, kicking up dust like a Delta tornado.

I debated about telling Tate but knew I had no choice. This could very well be the same car that had chased him for thirty miles a couple of nights earlier. The group moaned in disbelief when they heard that someone was watching the house.

"I thought no one knew about this place but COFO." Tate became uneasy, with haunting recollections of what had happened at Sadie's.

"I'm sure no one knows." The leader of the group, Quincy tried to reassure him. "There's nothing we can do about it now. We have no other place to go. Maybe it was a hunter or something."

"There is no hunting season in August, Quincy," I corrected him hesitantly. "Maybe somebody just out for a hike in the woods."

When I left Tate that afternoon, I made him promise to be careful and alert. I had been hoping he would be in a safer location, but now I didn't know, with that Buick on the prowl again.

My emotions as I drove north on Highway 51 were a shambles, tossed around like a fruit salad mixed with vinegar, with a sour, sweet, sour, sweet connotation. I was devastated at losing Tate but felt he was safer. My best friend, Elizabeth, would be home, but would she be safe? Would I even get to acknowledge that Elizabeth was home?

Tate called two mornings later. Things were going well, and the Buick had not shown its ugly hood since I left. He told me Elizabeth was somewhere in the Bartonville area but could not tell me where. No plans were made, but he promised he would see me soon.

That afternoon, I saw Elizabeth on the square, giving out COFO leaflets. She was surrounded by black high school students, mostly males, who seemed more interested in being loud and silly trying to get this gorgeous girl's attention than in righting any social wrongs. Elizabeth played to the crowd, but took the opportunity to remind her young audience that they were important to their people and, even though they were too young to vote, needed to come to the Freedom School and learn about their constitutional rights and duties.

Seeing the enamored faces of her audience, both girls and boys, I knew the freedom classes would be full at River Road Missionary Baptist. As I proudly watched my friend in action, she looked across the street at me and gave me the forward fist against her forehead as if knocking the afternoon sun out of her eyes. I returned the sign and smiled as I got into Booby Hooby and drove away from town.

I was wrong about classes at River Road M.B. Church. The Klan struck again in mid August, and the Freedom School had to be moved. Even though the damage was less this time, the minister and church leaders just could not risk another attack that might finish it off.

The new Freedom School would be located down Harvey Road at Rock Church, a beautiful old church, one of the first Negro churches built in north Mississippi after the Civil War. It was made out of rock, Arkansas fieldstone, and had a tall steeple atop a bell tower that encased a huge iron bell. We could hear the bell ringing from Parrish Oaks on the Sundays when they had services, even though the church was three miles away.

I loved the old church and had always wanted to see what it looked like on the inside. Maybe now I'd get the chance. I hoped the Klan would be gracious enough to preserve this historical building and would not deface it as they had the newer one on River Road. The Klan gracious? Who did I think I was fooling?

The strange thing about the location of the new Freedom School was that it was directly across the road from the Harvey cotton gin, a huge, mostly tin monstrosity surrounded by old, weathered, rotting bales of cotton never hauled off and probably fifty empty cotton trailers and old wagons belonging to different farmers in the area.

The gin was pretty deserted in August, but come fall, it would be booming. Harvey Road would look like a melted trail through snow in the middle of winter as loose clumps of raw cotton, ugly and dirty with their seedy pimples, would fly off the wagons and cling to the shoulders in an attempt to escape the giant teeth of the gin monster.

"I bet it'll really grate on Mr. Harvey's nerves," I thought to myself, "to have to look out of his gin office window and watch the COFO he hates so much in action."

One afternoon when I was feeling perky, rebellious, and just generally in an I-don't-give-a-care mood, I drove Booby Hooby down to the church. Parking him under the big shade tree to the side of the church, not quite as obvious as parking in the front, I climbed the steep stairs to the side entrance.

Two classes were going on inside. An older white lady, obviously a nurse and not from around Bartonville by the nasally northern accent she used, talked to a group of young mothers about proper care and nutrition for their babies. I noticed Roweena among them. Quincy, one of the students I had met at Paxton, conducted a class on the Constitution to a group of about ten high-school-age students. He waved at me as I entered the sanctuary and pointed to the rear of the huge open room, obviously where Elizabeth was.

I absorbed the details of the church as I walked down the aisle toward the door at the back. Beautiful, but not elegant, the stone walls were covered with wide pine boards never painted. Their natural patina gave a simple, warm glow to the room that made me want to stop, drop to my knees, look up at the huge portrait of the dark-skinned Jesus, and pray, mostly for the safety of my friends who were fighting a crusade of their own. The pews, too, were simple, each one with a long, soft cushion of scarlet velvet symbolic of the blood shed by Christ.

The pulpit looked new, a shiny oak one with a white lace scarf that hung, at the front, in teardrops shaped like miniature stars. The pulpit was mismatched with the rustic pine that adorned the rest of the church's walls, ceiling and floors. The *Bartonville Weekly* had published an article on the church not long before, stating that the building might be placed on the National Register of Historic Places. If this transpired, the church would have to stay as near to its original condition as possible. I hoped this happened soon so the congregation could not change the rest of the sanctuary to match the modern pulpit.

I found Elizabeth in the back room, sitting in a circle of small children. She started a sentence saying, "I'm beautiful because..." and then spun a bottle. Whoever the bottle pointed to had to complete the sentence. The children said things like: "I have good hair; I have big muscles like my daddy; I can read good." The group would clap and cheer each time a child bragged on him or herself.

When the game was finished, Elizabeth introduced me to the children as her friend Sue Ann. Little shrieks of disbelief emanated from the semicircle.

"It's true," I reiterated, and began telling the children about the games Liz Bess and I played as children. They would not let me stop but wanted to hear more stories from our childhood. Elizabeth and I told about our Saca and Honta adventures and of our endless hours in the gully hideout.

One bright-eyed little boy of about eight reminded me of Ben Jr. and caught me completely off guard when he perceptively remarked, "Ya'll like each utha 'cause you both be white. You won't play wi' no nappy head like my sista, I bet."

Elizabeth's second sense when it came to me, even after all these years, got me off the hook by suggesting the children sing for me. Forming a circle around the wall and holding out their arms to make sure they had enough room to do all the actions, the children began swinging their hips and rhythmically chanting the words to their favorite action song:

Little Sally Walker
Settin' in a saucer
Rise, Sally, Rise!
Wipe yo' sleepy eyes
You put yo' hands on yo' hips
You let yo' backbone shake
Ah, shake it to da east
Ah, shake it to da west
Ah, shake it to da boy dat you like best!
Yo' mama say so
Yo' daddy say so
And da's de way yo' shake it
If yo' wanta catch a boy
If yo' wanta catch a boy!

I clapped enthusiastically at the black equal to the "London Bridges" of my upbringing, though Little Sally Walker had much more animation and fun, not to mention some amazing hip action. Elizabeth led the children out into the sanctuary after the performance and introduced them to the nurse, who was going to talk to them about the importance of good hygiene, proper tooth brushing, and healthy eating. She had a box filled with surprises for the children, everything from toothbrushes to apples and hand puppets.

As the children took turns picking their prizes, Elizabeth walked me to Booby Hooby.

"COFO does a lot more than voter registration, it seems. I wonder if the Klan realizes that," I remarked sarcastically while opening the door.

"Probably not. Why don't you see if you can get an

audience with the Imperial Wizard and clue him in?" We both laughed at the unlikely prospect.

As I got into the car, I noticed the brown Buick coming around the curve, starting its usual crawl, stare, and scare tactic.

"You need to watch out for that car, Elizabeth. It seems that every time it starts coming around, the Klan pulls a nasty. Be careful. Can you come with me for a few minutes? I want to show you my cabin in the woods. It isn't far from here and would be a great escape for you if you need it." I was thinking of escape from violence but made it sound like R & R.

Elizabeth told Quincy she would be gone for a few minutes and crawled in the passenger side of Booby Hooby.

"Booby Hooby, huh? Sounds just like something you'd name a car, Saca." Elizabeth rubbed her hand across the red dash of the black-and-white beauty whose only flaw was a small hole in the floorboard on the passenger side. I told her it was to let the water out after crossing gully streams. She looked like she believed me for an instant, and then started laughing.

"Gotcha!" I pointed my finger at my friend and laughed.

Booby Hooby made it down the dirt road to the woods where the cabin was hidden, but it was like trying to ride a bucking bronco in an eight-point earthquake. In the future, I'd come in the Jeep.

Elizabeth, like Tate and me, loved the cabin, with its potential for ghost stories or just good old historical fiction.

"Too bad you didn't have this when we were kids, Sue Ann. Can't you just see us playing mountain men, or women, here? Or Scarlett and Prissy! Oh, do it for me, Sue Ann. Please?" Liz Bess clasped her hands and put them under her chin, the begging pose I remembered from our childhood.

"I don't know nothin' bout birthin' babies," I screeched in my high-pitched Prissy voice, the one I always imitated as a kid when Liz Bess and I played scenes from *Gone with the Wind*, our most favorite book ever. We both fell back on the rope bed laughing.

We didn't stay long at the cabin. Elizabeth had to take over for Quincy in a few minutes. When I let her off at Rock Church, I made her promise she would remember where the cabin was and would use it if she needed to. I also made her promise to be careful and not try to be a martyr.

"I promise, Sue Ann," she said as she closed the door.

"Wait a minute." I threw up a hand to stop her. "You know the routine."

"Do I have to?" Liz Bess grimaced.

Without further adieu, we both spit in our hand and shook firmly.

"Ewww!" We both drawled disgustedly in synchronization.

Chapter Twenty-One
Ride 'Em, Cowgirl!

Elizabeth was happily teaching at her Freedom School, with no plans of going back to university this semester. Her aunt, Leonia, was not happy that her niece was in town, especially since she was working for COFO. Leonia, pleased with her own success as main hair stylist and manager of Mama's black salon in Bartonville, had even bought herself a small house, and vowed she was not about to lose it all because of Liz Bess, who had been "spoiled by her mama when she was alive and dead and didn't know what it was like to have to work to make somethin' of herself." She had no communication with Elizabeth for fear of Klan retaliation. Elizabeth did not blame Leonia, and honored her request to stay away from her.

One night, Mama came home from the salon late, and I was surprised to see Leonia trailing behind her with a suitcase in her hand. They both looked like they had been hit by an eighteen-wheeler. Mama's hair was disheveled, her dress seam was torn on one side, and her stockings were covered in wide runs. Leonia's mascara had run, which made her look like a raccoon, and the usual tight waves in her hair looked like they had been stretched out and tousled by a tornado. She was visibly shaken. Daddy followed the two into the house, and I could tell by the look on his face that he was concerned. Mama flopped down on the couch and began explaining what had happened.

It was ten o'clock at night, quitting time, as Leonia had swept the last vestiges of nap and curl from the marbled floor of the salon in Plessy Lane. The door was still unlocked—not that it would have mattered—when the two hooded men burst through it, grabbed Leonia, and pushed her to the floor, burying her face in the pile of hair and dirt.

"Lawd help me, Lawd help me!" she screamed, spitting hair and struggling to release herself from the sheet-clad, strong-armed men.

"Where's that white nigga sista of yours?" one of them demanded as he twisted her arm behind her.

"I ain't got no sista...she be dead a long time...Please don't hurt me! Money in da cash register. Jes' take it and leave!" Leonia begged, and yelled again as the man twisted harder.

"She may not be yo sista, but she's kin. You know who I mean, that white nigga relative of yours. Where's she at?" The second man stood over Leonia and kicked her in the side.

Leonia cried as pain rippled through her body. "I don't know nothin' 'bout her. Don't want to. I ain't done nothin' to nobody."

"You nigga families stick together. You know where she's at. Tell us or you'll be a dead nigga." He pretended he was going to kick her again but stopped as Leonia started crying and begging.

"I swear I don't know. Please don't kill me, missuh!" Leonia's survival instincts kicked in and she became the docile Uncle Tom she had hated so much as a teenager.

One of the men twisted her arm more as Leonia wailed.

Intent on their dastardly act, the two were not aware that the back door to the salon had opened and someone, a presence to be feared, was coming up behind them ready to swing a weapon more deadly than either of them could ever imagine, the metal wand to a vacuum cleaner that had stood out of sight until just then.

"Get your hands off her, you sorry bastard!" Mama swung the wand like a billy club, knocking the one straddling Leonia unconscious with her first deadly blow.

"Who do you think you are, coming in my business and attacking my employee?" Mama swung again, causing the other ghostly figure of what was a moment before a man to trip over the base of the hairdryer as he tried in vain to escape the wrath of the madwoman. She didn't stop, once she had him cowering on the floor, but proceeded to hit him again and again until he, like his victim only a few minutes before, was bleeding and begging for mercy.

"Stop, Miz Taylor. We don't have no fight with you, just the nigga. Let us go!" He held his hands up to escape the next blow.

"I'll let you go all right, but you'll be carried out on a stretcher by the sheriff!" Screaming at him like a wild panther, she flailed the wand again.

Leonia, still crying, huddled behind Mama The Protector, who never ceased from her torrential flogging of the masked assailant. She didn't stop until both of her victims lay unconscious and bleeding profusely.

"Bring me that plastic shampoo cape, Leonia, and stop that crying! Ain't nobody gonna hurt you now!"

Mama flopped the mighty Klansman nearest the door over on his stomach and straddled him, hiking up her stylish red silk dress and disclosing her garter belt. She never flinched, looking like a perverted 145-pound cowboy wrestling a 700-pound steer as she ripped the cape into long pieces with her teeth and tied the man's hands tight behind his back.

Once finished with that one, she turned her attention to the first man knocked unconscious and repeated the steer roping and wrestling tactics like a veteran rodeo hand. All she needed to complete the Wild West show were spurs attached to the red high-heeled shoes she still wore, having just come from a hair show in Memphis.

"Whew!" she blew as she stood admiring her handiwork. "Now let's see who these two overgrown trick-or-treaters really are." Mama grabbed the hood from each man's head, jerking hard enough that the head was sure to bounce back and hit the floor hard.

"Well, Clinton Blaylock, the redneck who runs the beer joint on the county line. What a surprise. He dudn't look so fierce now, does he, Leonia?"

Mama proceeded to the next Klansman, repeating the hood-jerking action.

"I do believe this one is Murray Hinds. Was the song director at Liberty Creek Baptist Church once upon a time, before he left his wife for some whore in Tallahatchie County. You watch 'em, Leonia. I'm gonna call Zeke and get him to come help me hold these big, strong men 'til the sheriff can get here."

"No, ma'am, Miz Taylor, don't leave me here with

'em! These mean men!" Leonia started crying again.

"Leonia, the phone is over yonder. It's not like I'm leaving the county. Besides, they don't look so mean right now."

Ten minutes later, Daddy and the sheriff arrived at the salon at the same time and carted off the two Klansmen. Leonia was too scared to go home that night, so Mama let her come to our house and stay.

Leonia got married the next day to a man she had only known for a month, a big, muscle-bound guy who had once been a bouncer in a bar on Beale Street. Leonia insisted that Rufus, her husband, be at the salon when it was closing time every night after that so she would never be alone there again.

Mama was the talk of Bartonville for a long time. Her picture appeared on the front page of the *Bartonville Weekly* along with the story of her rescue of her employee. The two Klansmen went to jail for thirty days each and had to pay damages to Mama in the amount of five hundred dollars. No damages were awarded to Leonia, but Mama gave her the money she was awarded.

"What happened to the justice in this world?" Mama asked the question a while later during one of the few nights we sat down together to share a meal as a family.

"It's the same as it's always been, Mama," I answered. "You're just getting where you finally recognize it for what it is or isn't."

Chapter Twenty-Two
The Long, Hot, Summer Night

It was late August, the hottest month of the summer, with temperatures at or over one hundred degrees for over a week. The only thing hotter was the activities of the White Knights of the Ku Klux Klan, who continued to burn crosses all over the state, many in Barton County. Anyone, black or white, suspected of sympathizing with the "Negro Movement" as the media called it, was fair game for cross burnings or worse.

Tear-gas exploded behind one home in our county where the black owners were suspected of harboring COFO workers. Deputies investigating the scene "accidentally" picked up the empty canisters, destroying any fingerprints that could have been used by the FBI to identify the culprits.

More black churches were burned across the state, and two in Barton County were vandalized, along with the homes of blacks who attempted to register to vote or who supported the civil rights efforts of COFO, SNCC, or the NAACP. Bodies of three black men who had been lynched some time ago were discovered but not identified. They were barely mentioned with the Philadelphia murders taking center stage in the media.

I talked to Tate on the phone at least twice a week but had not seen him since I took him to Paxton. He said he was not afraid, but I sensed by the tone of his voice he was lying. His parents were calling often, begging him to come home before he ended up like the three from the Meridian office, and had even promised him a new car of his choosing if he would just leave Mississippi. Tate declined the offer, determined to finish what he had started.

I kept myself busy packing suitcases, getting ready to head back to the W, and hoped I would be able to see Tate once I got to Columbus, hoped he wanted to see me as much as I did him. There was little time for conversation with Mama and Daddy these days, with both working from daylight to dark, but this was fine with me. It gave me less occasion to have to lie or tell half-truths and feel guilty.

All Mama wanted to know was when Dailey and I would get back together. Daddy told me in private one night that he knew Liz Bess was working for COFO and hoped I would use good judgment where she was concerned. Daddy never mentioned Tate to me, assuming or hoping that I had taken his advice and had never seen him after his near arrest that day. Daddy reminded me that he and Mama had worked hard for what we all had and would hate to see it go up in smoke. No mention was made of Leonia's ordeal, but I knew what he was talking about.

Rita Jean was home from summer school but was never really at home. She had a new boyfriend from Memphis, who kept her busy and away. I had a letter from Jew Baby, who had decided she liked New Jersey and was transferring to a college there. A new boyfriend helped her make this decision. Her parents had not made up their minds to move as yet but vowed that one more episode from the Klan and they would be finding a Presbyterian Church farther north...a lot farther north.

The tension in the air at Bartonville hung like thick swamp fog; it was nothing I could put my finger on, but something was different. The cliques of old farmers who sat around the square spittin' and talkin' of the good old days sensed it, talking in hushed tones. The loud laughs followed by the slapping of calloused hands on overalls and work khakis seemed buried inside their souls waiting for an appropriate time to reappear.

On the opposite side of the square were other cliques: younger men in blue jeans and T-shirts—some with an Elvis hairstyle, others with G.I. crew cuts or flattops; all were topped with dirty, misshapen tractor and gas company caps; all looked angry and smoked obsessively while watching and talking in whispers and jeers.

Other signs of tension were evident. The three civil rights workers were no longer the conversation of choice now that the speculations were over as to where they were hiding out trying to make it look bad for the people of central Mississippi. The old trust had vanished between many blacks and their white employers, the trust honored by the older generation. This trust had been discounted by young black revolutionaries who redefined it as "submission" and "Uncle Tomism."

Even minor mixing of the races had disappeared as the atmosphere choked even the most trivial socialization or contact. The Palace Theatre closed its balcony and no longer allowed Negroes the privilege of movie-going.

The investigation into the murders of Schwerner,

Chaney, and Goodman escalated, and media attention and speculation of guilt were aimed at the sheriff's office in Neshoba County, especially at a deputy who had arrested the three and brought them in to the jail on charges of speeding the night they disappeared. Most whites, the ones who chose to talk about the case, did not believe anyone would stand trial for the murders, knowing how well the Klan covered their tracks. The murder of Emmett Till and the trial that freed his murderers resurfaced in everyone's minds and conversation and were used as a basis for comparison in the trials sure to follow.

Such was the background and setting to what proved to be the longest, hottest night on record for Bartonville, Mississippi. It was the 26th of August and 102 degrees in the shade, with a virtual inferno in the minds of the Klansmen whose plot would engulf this small Mississippi town in violence never imagined possible until this fateful night.

It was 8:30 at night, and I was alone. Mama and Daddy were in Memphis visiting my aunt, who had just been released from the hospital. The phone rang. Elizabeth was crying on the other end.

"Sue Ann, is the cabin offer still good?"

"Of course, Liz Bess. What's wrong?" Nervously, I wrapped the curly phone cord around my hand.

"Do you remember the little boy at the school who reminded you of Ben, Jr.?"

"Yes. Why?"

"His daddy was just shot down in cold blood in front of his house. He spent the day delivering voter registration packets and had just come from the church, his last stop. Willy Paul saw his daddy fall, covered in blood. It was just like you said, Sue Ann. The brown Buick passed so many times today we stopped counting. Who is that man? Why would he want to kill an innocent man like Mr. Jones?"

"I'll come get you, Liz Bess. Where are you? I know I can convince Daddy to let you stay with us."

"No, Sue Ann. I don't want your family involved. Even using the cabin is risky. If anything happens, you pretend you didn't know I was there. Promise?"

"A promise wouldn't be any good without spit, and you can't spit over the phone. Tell me where you are."

"No. We thought the house was safe, but I got a call this afternoon right after Mr. Jones was murdered, telling me to stay away from the school and away from the house or I'd be next. No one should know about this safe house but COFO. There has to be an informant in our organization." Elizabeth paused. "Quincy might be with me at the cabin, if I can convince him to go. Is that all right, Sue Ann?"

"Of course, but what will you do long-term? I think you better go back up North, Liz Bess. It's too dangerous in Mississippi. Even if you left COFO, you're attached as far as the Klan is concerned, and you'll always be a target."

"I'm not a quitter; at least I don't think I am. But I've never seen so much blood as I did this afternoon. I need time to think. Maybe a night in the cabin will give me time to figure out exactly who I am and how far I'm willing to go to fight for what I believe."

"Do you want me to stay with you? I'm not afraid, Liz Bess."

"No. You stay as far away from me as you can. Look what happened to Leonia. You won't know when

222

I go to the cabin. I better go now and see if I can help the Jones family. Thanks, Sue Ann."

The phone went dead, leaving me to despair over my friend's predicament. I needed to do something, but what? The phone rang again, and I was sure it was Liz Bess calling me back to tell me to come and get her.

"Liz Bess?" I answered anxiously before thinking. The phone clicked dead on the other end. More worries. Is someone calling to see if I'm here? My mind began racing with what-ifs. I had to stop thinking and do something, but what? One thing was sure—I couldn't stay here in the safety of Parrish Oaks while my friend was in danger.

As I neared the end of the dark driveway in Booby Hooby, I saw a sight that shook me to the core. The brown Buick turned into the driveway of the Harvey Plantation. As my headlights shone on the Buick, I could see there were two men in it. Now I knew for sure that J.T. Harvey was involved with the Klan and probably with the murder that had transpired that very afternoon.

I needed to get word to Liz Bess that the Buick was too close for her to stay in the cabin. Somehow, I had to convince her to stay with me. Turning Booby, I headed for the church, but when I got there, I found the parking lot empty and the building dark.

"I know. I'll go to Sadie's. She'll know where the Jones family lives. That's where Liz Bess said she was going." I headed Booby in the opposite direction.

It was getting late, close to 9:30. If Liz Bess was going to the cabin, she would be making a move pretty soon. I watched for the old blue station wagon that she and Quincy drove; it was another anonymous donation from someone who believed in COFO but didn't want anyone else to know it.

I knocked on the door until Roweena answered.

"Roweena, I need to find Elizabeth or Quincy. Do you know where they are? They should be with the Jones family."

Roweena gave me directions to the Jones home, only a couple of miles away. The yard was packed with cars, most with out-of-state license plates, probably FBI. I walked far around the yellow ribbon that surrounded the crime scene where Mr. Jones had been shot down and headed for the door, but before I could knock, the door opened and Willy Paul came out.

How do children do it? He looked like nothing had happened as he stood licking a popsicle, staring at the crowd of strangers in his yard. The nightmares would come later, when the hullabaloo was over and the silence settled in.

"Willy Paul, remember me? I'm Sue Ann, Elizabeth's friend. Is she here?"

Willy Paul never took his eyes off the strangers, took another big suck on the popsicle and shook his head.

"Do you know where she is?" I hoped to get more information with this query, something other than a head shake.

The boy repeated the negative shake of his head. I thought about knocking on the door but could hear the wailing of what was obviously his mother inside and decided it would be too disrespectful.

"Now what?" I thought aloud.

As I pulled out of the driveway, headlights came on as a car left the shoulder of the road and pulled out a distance behind me.

"There goes my mind again," I said aloud, trying to convince my heart to stop palpitating. Deciding to conduct a test to see if the car was following me, I turned onto a gravel road that connected with another paved county road. The car turned, too. When I reached the paved road, I turned away from Bartonville, another test. Once again, the vehicle behind me followed suit. My heart was doing double time now, and there was no convincing it that its peer, my brain, was causing the problem.

Speeding up, I reached sixty miles per hour, too fast for an unlined county road. The car sped up also, but remained the same distance behind me. Quickly, I made a sharp turn left onto a gravel road that connected to the road to my house, and I breathed with relief as I looked in my mirror and saw no lights glaring back at me.

I decided to make another loop by Rock Church before going back to Parrish Oaks and discovered a dim light in the back room of the church. Even though I didn't see the blue station wagon, I decided to check and see if it might be Quincy or Liz Bess.

Not sure why but for some reason, I parked down the road from the church and walked back so no one could see me. The moon was bright, the stars were out by the billions, and all looked right in God's world. But my intuitions told me otherwise.

As I trod gingerly up the steps to the quaint old piece of history, I glanced over at the Harvey gin. There was a light burning in the upper level, probably the office where J.T. Harvey laid out his gruesome plots for his Klan operations. As I approached the door, my

225

instincts kicked in again and something told me not to open it. Obeying, I tiptoed across the porch to a window where I could see into the dark sanctuary.

Cupping my hands around my face as if shading my eyes would somehow help my night vision, I peered inside. It seemed quiet, still—too still—and ominous. Again I had a foreboding of something dreadful and wished I were at home entrenched in my featherbed even though it was close to a hundred degrees.

As I continued to let my eyes adjust to the dark interior of the church, I began to decipher faint shadows moving about behind the front door. Even though I wanted to move away, some unexplainable magnetic force held me to my position against the window.

I could see a faint light in the back room of the church, the room where children had laughed and sung "Little Sally Walker" only a short time previous. Forcing my body to leave its watchful position, I stole back down the steps to make my way to the back of the church where the light source was.

Like Nancy Drew, my hero from my childhood, I melted my body against the rock walls of the church and slithered my way to the back. The dim-lit window was too high for me to see into, so I looked around for something to stand on.

A rusty metal drum stood only a few feet away. Fortunately, it was empty, so I was able to walk it to a spot under the window. Holding onto the protruding edges of the rocks, I climbed up. I could barely see into the room, but I could see enough to make my legs shake so badly I almost lost my balance on the drum.

Quincy lay on the floor with his hands tied behind him and his feet bound with rope. His face was covered in blood that had dripped on to his shirt and pants and his mouth was sealed shut with duct tape.

Two men ducked into the room, whispering as if they thought the FBI had them surrounded. They both wore the cotton costumes of their derelict organization, but only one wore the hood. I quickly pulled my head out of sight but tried to stay close enough to the slightly raised window that I could hear what they were saying.

"She'll come. No way would she leave her nigga playmate here. He said she was coming at ten. We'll be waiting for her."

"You better put that hood back on, Booger. He might come to and see you. You know we're not s'posed to ever be on a mission without it."

"It's too damn hot for it. I'll put it on when I hear her drive up. Let's go back up front. She oughta be here any minute."

"What time is the big party?"

"Don't know fer shore. I heard eleven and twelve. One thang fer shore, Joe. Ever'body'll know when it happens." Both men laughed as they left the room, obviously going back to become shadows at the front door to wait for the only "she" that it could be—Elizabeth.

Booger Melton! I should have known the vile redneck would be part of something this horrific. I needed to go for help but couldn't risk leaving in case Elizabeth came. Somehow I had to warn her.

There was no time to make a plan. Lights shone against the ancient rocks as a blue station wagon pulled into the churchyard. Elizabeth didn't give me time to dismount from my drum watchtower before bolting up the steps and rushing into the church.

"Quincy, let's go! We have to leave town now!" Elizabeth ran down the dark aisle of the sanctuary, obviously heading for the light in the back room. The next sound I heard was a scuffle and Elizabeth's scream. Then silence once again.

Squatting down on the drum, I shook as tears, hot tears caused by witnessing violent abuse of someone I loved, flowed down my cheeks, which were becoming hotter with rage. I thought about Mama and how she was able to rescue Leonia, and I left the drum headed for the side door ready to do I-didn't-know-what but something to try to save my friend. Before I could reach the door, more lights shone on the rock walls, and I ducked under the stairs to the side entrance.

It looked like a ghost convention as the hooded Klansmen left their pickups, motors running, and leapt up the steps two and three at a time. Inside I could hear laughter. I was choking from the sobs I was forcing myself to swallow, but I could do nothing but sit hunkered under the dark, musty stairs and listen while my friend was inside being terrified and probably tortured.

Ashamed of myself, I almost forced my body to crawl from the hole where I crouched like a cowardly rat when two of the men came around the side of the church. They stood beside the steps with their sheets almost touching their shoes, and I could hear something like water sloshing around in a can. Then I smelled it, the undeniable smell of kerosene being sprinkled around the building. They planned to burn the church with Liz Bess and Quincy inside.

After the men left my side of the church, I forced myself to crawl from my position under the stairs, not sure what I would do but knowing I had to take action, and fast. No way could I fight off the mob of bed linens that had congregated at this historical sight, but I could run for Booby and try to get help.

I looked across at the Harvey gin and, before my mind could stop me, began running toward the light, staying at the edge of the woods that surrounded the church. Probably no one was there, since the Klan seemed to be congregated across the road, and I could get to the phone and call the sheriff or Daddy, anyone who might help Elizabeth and Quincy.

As I rounded the corner, making my way behind the gin to look for an entrance, terror seized me. There sat the brown Buick. I could only hope the phantom riders were across the street with their brood of murderers. Just as I got to the back door, I heard the pickups at the church start up. One of them tore from the scene, with the KKK crazies, as Mama referred to them, whooping like a bunch of school boys out vandalizing mailboxes or tipping cows. I had to hurry!

The blast that came next took the life right out of my body, and I fell to my knees. Flames shot so high in the air I could see them over the tall cotton gin as I jumped to my feet to run back toward the church.

"Liz Bess!" I screamed as I charged in the direction of the flames.

The blue station wagon had been used as the fuse for the fire and was engulfed in flames. It wasn't long before the church, too, was blazing. The only thing that was preventing it from becoming a gigantic fireball was the rock walls that were acting as a barrier between the flames and the interior of the church. The old, dry, wood trim was ablaze, outlining the walls and marking a trail to the wood steeple on the church roof that was now also burning.

My sides were aching, but I continued to run as fast as my legs would take me, my adrenaline pushing me way beyond my normal limits of endurance. I did not notice the brown Buick fast approaching from behind until it was on me. As it pulled alongside, not completely stopping, a deep voice yelled from the back door that had been swung wide open.

"Get in!"

As if knowing I would refuse, a big hand—a big black hand—reached out, grabbed my arm, and pulled me into the back seat. For some reason, I did not scream. The Buick screeched to a stop and slid sideways, blocking the exit of one of the pickups.

The driver of the Buick jumped out holding a handgun and shot into the front window of the pickup, hitting the hoodless driver square in the face. Blood splattered the shattered window of the truck as it careened into a ditch, hitting a tree and propelling two Klansmen from their stance in the back of the truck into the same clump of trees. One staggered to his feet and ran down the road trying to escape. The driver tore out after him, determined that none would be allowed to escape their dirty deeds.

The man on the passenger side had been first to disembark from the Buick and was running up the stairs of the burning church.

The black man looked at me and ordered, "Stay here." As if the scene could get anymore shocking, my mouth flew open. I was looking into the face of Silas Metcalf. Silas charged after the other man, a white man, into the Hades that had once been a house of God.

I jumped from the car, needing to get as close to where my friend was as I could. None of this made sense, but I knew now that the men in the Buick were there to try to save Elizabeth and Quincy. The "whys" would have to come later.

It seemed hours before either man appeared through the flames as I waited anxiously and prayed. It was the white man who carried Quincy, his feet and hands still bound, over his shoulder, dropping him to the ground at my feet, knowing that I would do my best to help him.

"Liz Bess is in there! Please help her!" I screamed.

The man turned toward me. "I'll get her, Sue Ann. Don't worry!" It was J.T. Harvey. He wasted no time, not hesitating for even a second before diving back into hell.

I held Quincy's head in my lap, helpless to do more. Silas was next out and ran in my direction.

"Where is she? Where's Liz Bess?"

"The back of the church, I think!" I answered knowing that was where they had held Quincy captive. Silas disappeared around the side of the church.

Moments later, Mr. Harvey exited, carrying the limp body of Elizabeth. His clothes were on fire as he raced to me and dropped her on the ground. He screamed, falling to the ground and rolling in an effort to put out the flames. From the shadows of the woods, the driver ran to his side, beating the various blazes with his shirt, pulled off while running. Mr. Harvey lay smoldering, motionless.

"Silas is still in there!" I cried, hoping the man might be able to save him from the building that was now totally engulfed in flames. As the man ran toward the building, he was stopped by a tremendous blast from inside the church.

Fiery fingers reached out, pushing him back to where Mr. Harvey lay. He pulled the big man away from the flames and nearer to where I sat with the other two innocent victims, both unconscious but alive, and squatted down beside me.

In the fiery light of the night, I recognized black-and-white snake boots, python, like on *Nyoka the Jungle Girl*. The roof of Rock Church collapsed and the steeple catapulted into the ocean of flames below it. Somewhere within its holy walls lay the body of Silas Metcalf.

Sirens wailed above the roar of the fire and the thunder of falling timbers. The road filled with local spectators, most of whom stood silent as if transposed from their noble heritage into the harsh reality of its cruelties.

The sheriff and his deputies carted off the criminals to jail, or at least the ones who did not need ambulances for their ride to justice. Two deputies directed traffic away from the scene as the ambulances arrived to take away the innocent and their heroes, as well as the Klansmen who had got some of what they deserved.

Later I sat beside Elizabeth's bed in the hospital. She had a concussion and minor burns but would be all right, though she was still unconscious. Quincy's wounds were more serious, but he would survive. His parents had been called in Ohio and were on their way to Bartonville.

Rock Church was not the only target of the Klan on that long, hot, summer night. Steiner's store had been set on fire, but the fire department arrived in time to save it from being completely destroyed.

Sadie and Roweena lost their home to the Klan's torch of hatred, but luckily no one was hurt. Sadie came by the hospital and told me they were moving into our old house in the pecan grove. Daddy had told her they could stay there as long as she was working for Mama. Daddy had never really liked renting it anyway. He knew Sadie would take good care of the old home place just like Nagalee had the board-and-batten house.

I dozed off for a few minutes, exhausted from the night of horror, and awoke to find the man with the snake boots leaning over me.

"I'm sorry, Sue Ann. I hate to wake you, but Mr. Harvey is asking for you."

As we walked down the hall of the hospital toward Intensive Care where Mr. Harvey had been placed, the man introduced himself.

"By the way, I'm Andy Smithers. I'm an attorney. I work for Mr. Harvey and have ever since that summer I pulled that Melton kid off your back. Remember?"

"That's where I saw those snake boots before." I looked perplexed at the identity of Andy Smithers and at the whole Harvey/Hero scenario. "If you're a lawyer, why haven't I seen you around town?"

"I don't practice law, only work for Mr. Harvey personally. It's a long story, several years long, as a matter of fact. I promise it will all make sense to you eventually. Before you see Mr. Harvey, I need to warn you. He's in bad shape. The doctors don't think he'll make it. He was burned over sixty percent of his body, first degree burns, for the most part. He's heavily sedated but requested to speak to you before he receives his next shot."

Mr. Harvey had a private nurse by his side, as I knew he would. He lay with only his head exposed, his body under a tent-like covering because of the severity of his burns, his head wrapped in gauze bandages.

The nurse directed me to his side. I was very uncomfortable in the presence of this man whom I had made jokes about during my young adulthood, not to mention hating his only child, Lady Victoria. I couldn't imagine why he wanted to see me. We had nothing in common other than this horrifying night, and I still didn't know why he had changed sides, assuming he ever had a side.

I looked down at Mr. Harvey and began to speak. Andy motioned for me to move closer and lean over so he could hear me.

"Mr. Harvey, it's Sue Ann Taylor. You wanted to see me?" I spoke just above a whisper, not wanting to startle the sleeping man.

Slowly he opened his eyes. I was not sure anyone else in Bartonville had ever seen Mr. Harvey's eyes, since he never went anywhere without his dark sunglasses. In fact, speculating on the color of his eyes was a favorite game to play in Bartonville. Most thought they were probably light blue, knowing that light-colored eyes are supposed to be more sensitive to sunlight. He was often jokingly referred to as the local movie star, both because of his wealth and because of his sunglasses.

His hand moved from under the tent as he reached over and placed it on top of mine. It was the hand of a wealthy businessman, soft, never having known hard labor. Yet these delicate hands were the hands of a hero who had carried two people out of a flaming building, saving them from the most horrible death imaginable.

His mouth jerked slightly as he began to speak in a muffled whisper. He looked up at me with eyes light green, the color of a summer fern, and said, "Thank you for being Elizabeth's friend. Tell her I'm sorry." He closed his eyes, but not before moisture formed deep puddles in the corners. My tears fell on his cheek as I patted his hand and left his side.

As I rounded the corner, leaving Mr. Harvey's room, my heart was full, my emotions on the verge of exploding, and there he stood as if knowing I needed comfort and security. Tate smiled, reaching out his arms to me, and I fell into his embrace and cried for several minutes, not able to speak.

"What are you doing here? How did you know?"

Tate kept his arm around me and led me to the corner of the waiting room. "I didn't know, not for sure, until I got to the church. Someone called me late this afternoon, warning me that something big was going to happen here and I needed to warn my friends before it was too late. I kept calling but couldn't get anyone to answer at the church, so I hit the road. Drove ninety all the way, scared to death you'd be in the middle of it, since I was warned Elizabeth's life in particular was in jeopardy."

I noticed Andy Smithers at the nurses' station and had an idea he knew who had made the call.

"Come on, Tate. There's someone I want you to meet."

Before I could make the introduction, Andy turned and smiled at us.

"Hello, Tate. I figured I'd see you before this night was over."

"I'm sorry. Am I supposed to know you?" Tate cocked his head and stared at Andy.

"Tate, this is Andy Smithers. He's an attorney who works for J.T. Harvey, the man who saved Elizabeth and Quincy from the fire."

"I don't understand. I thought the Harvey man was Klan."

"And you had every right to think so, Tate, but he was always on whatever side Elizabeth was on. I hate to keep you guessing, but I promise you'll understand more later. Right now, I need to get back to Mr. Harvey. His doctors don't think he'll make it through the night."

Holding Tate's hand, we started toward Elizabeth's room. Intent on holding onto Tate, I did not see Daddy until we were right on him. We stared at each other without saying anything, but our looks spoke volumes.

"Well...at least I know you're all right. How's Liz Bess?" Daddy crossed his arms and leaned back against the wall.

"She'll be fine. Just a concussion and some minor burns. I'm staying here tonight, Daddy, until she regains consciousness."

"Guess you're old enough to make up your own mind. I don't guess there's nothin' I could say to make you come home with me right now?" Daddy looked from me to Tate, giving his most concerned daddy look.

"No, Daddy. There isn't."

"Then I'll see you tomorrow. Tell Liz Bess I checked on her." With these words, Daddy turned and left the hospital.

"He hates me, Sue Ann. Thinks I'm some kind of monster who's going to do his little girl harm."

"He doesn't know you, Tate."

"Maybe he's right. I got here too late to protect you. If something had happened to you, I would never forgive myself." Tate faced me and pulled me to him, holding me tight.

"But it didn't. I'm safe, and you're here now. That's all that matters." I looked into Tate's face and gave him my most reassuring smile.

"I'll be glad when you're back at the W so I can be with you more. I've missed you so much, Sue Ann."

"Where are you staying tonight?" I asked.

"I don't know. Didn't take time to make plans."

"Then I think I know where that'll be." I smiled squeezing Tate's hand. "Let's go see if Elizabeth is awake yet. After I talk to her, we'll go to our cabin."

****

Cars stretched for miles—the longest funeral procession ever remembered in the county—behind two black hearses carrying the earthly remains of two unlikely heroes, one black, the other white.

J.T. Harvey, the wealthiest man in Barton County, was buried at Liberty Creek Cemetery, in the family plot where other heroes, ancestors from his family, fallen officers in the Confederacy, were also buried. The other hearse carried the remains of hero Silas Metcalf, who was buried across the fence beside his sister, Nagalee Donnelly, and his niece, Lucille.

There was no racially designated order for the procession of mourners that followed the hearses. Cars carrying blacks and cars carrying whites—and at least one vehicle, my '57 Chevy, carrying both—proceeded to the same church, the same cemetery, the same eulogy. Centuries of hatred were buried for a day while mourners, like the fallen heroes, embraced each other, though some from a distance, not in the forever act of caring but in the temporary, guilt-driven moment of compassion and forgiving.

Chapter Twenty-Three
Last Will and Testament

Elizabeth and I were directed to be at the reading of the last will and testament of Mr. J.T. Harvey the week after Elizabeth was released from the hospital. It was no secret now why Elizabeth had to be there, but my necessity for being there was a mystery. Andy Smithers had promised a full explanation that night at the hospital, but he had been so busy trying to get Mr. Harvey's affairs in order that the question-answering session had to be put on hold.

It was a strange scene in the big conference room in the Harvey Building. Many people were present, some strangers I did not know. Lady Victoria and her second husband were seated on one side of the massive table with their entourage of lawyers. She refused to make eye contact with either of us.

Daddy accompanied Elizabeth and me, not wanting us to go by ourselves with no support, and he was curious about the reason I was asked to attend. As it turned out, Elizabeth had plenty of support. Several lawyers had been hired out of a big firm in Memphis to represent her, paid for by the estate of the late Lucille Donnelly. This really added to the suspense and perplexity where Elizabeth was concerned.

Andy Smithers sat on our side of the table but did not take the role of executor. Another big-time attorney, from a firm in Jackson, was in charge of the final execution of the will. J.T. Harvey had made sure that all legal dots and crosses were in order so there would be no room for haggling or appeals.

After an hour of disclosure, Elizabeth Donnelly became a millionaire many times over and also became my new neighbor, heir to Five Oaks, the plantation home of J.T. Harvey, her father. The bulk of the Harvey estate had been left to Elizabeth, with Andy Smithers retained to serve as her main assistant, aiding her in her transition to Chief Executive Officer of Harvey Enterprises, which consisted of three cotton gins, two factories, and a new catfish-farming business in the Delta.

Lady Victoria inherited a million dollars from her father's estate and all of the properties formerly owned by her mother, Annette Holden Harvey, which included the plantation in Beeville.

When the reading of the will was finished, everyone left except for Elizabeth, Andy, and me. Lady Victoria glared at Elizabeth as she left the room.

"Now for that question-answering session I promised." Andy pushed back from the big table and crossed his legs as if getting comfortable for a long haul. "Shoot."

The first question Elizabeth wanted answered was, "Why me and not Lady Victoria as main heir to the Harvey empire?" The answer he gave stunned both of us.

"Lady Victoria was not J.T.'s daughter. Annette was pregnant when the two married, victim of a thwarted romance with a would-be movie star that went sour and went the way of the wind before he went

240

Hollywood. It was a marriage of financial convenience arranged by Annette's father. J.T. was having some financial problems at the time and needed big bucks to prevent losing the bulk of his business interests. Annette's father, who had been a close friend of J.T.'s father, paid him to marry Annette and give the baby his name. J.T. promised to include Lady Victoria in his will as well as to leave her all properties left to Annette Holden when her parents died."

Elizabeth's next question was about the relationship of J.T. and her mother, Lucille. Andy took a deep breath before starting. Elizabeth and I had talked for hours previous to the meeting, trying to decipher how this whole affair had transpired, but all we had was several chapters of fiction when we finished.

"Your father had loved your mother for many years, ever since Nagalee and Bay moved to Annette's family plantation in Beeville. Lucille was a teenager, a beauty who caught J.T.'s eye right off. He was already married to Annette, but their marriage was very unhappy, rarely consummated. The truth was, J.T. and Annette could hardly stand each other, and their daughter was a brat, spoiled to death by her mother and grandparents."

"Annette knew about Lucille and made J.T. promise to keep his relationship with her secretive, especially after he was elected to the state Senate, the dream of his father-in-law and Annette, not J.T. He hated being a senator, always afraid Lucille would be hurt if the press got wind of her, knowing how the yellow journalists of Mississippi—and of the Delta especially—love political scandals. He refused to run for reelection after serving two terms, much to the disappointment and anger of his father-in-law and wife. J.T. escaped his unhappiness in marriage through Lucille. Annette escaped through alcohol."

"Lucille left home when she was nineteen, upset because J.T. would not acknowledge her publicly, and moved to Memphis, where she became a high-priced call girl. Sorry to have to disclose this to you, Elizabeth, but I promised J.T. Finally, he convinced Celia, as he called her, to set up her own business and backed her financially with the promise that she would take herself off any clients' list and reserve her passion for him alone. He visited her as often as possible, usually every week. I believe you saw him once, Sue Ann."

"Madame Celia's Boarding House for Young Ladies, off Beale Street in Memphis!" I thought back to the daring escapade of Tommy, Glenn, and myself, that day so long ago. "You mean J.T. recognized me that day my cousin and I were there? Celia…short for Lucille. I should have figured that out after seeing J.T. there, especially with all my Nancy Drew training, but since I had no idea what the boarding house really was at that age, I guess it was understandable and forgivable."

"He didn't recognize you, but Silas did. Silas drove J.T.'s limousine after he got out of Parchman and always drove J.T. when he visited Memphis, so he could slip in and out incognito. He saw you and the two boys that day and told J.T. about it."

"Who murdered my mother, Andy?" Elizabeth asked the question with sadness and bitterness in her eyes as she leaned forward, her hands clasped tightly.

"I don't know, Elizabeth, but J.T. suspected it was the family of one of the girls that worked for Celia.

Even with the care and protection she gave the young girls, it was not exactly a profession a father, or perhaps brothers or a boyfriend, would be proud of. Celia had left a will and had given a copy to J.T. a few weeks before she was killed. J.T. figured she must have had threats that she didn't tell him about. She requested burial in a white cemetery, the one where he would most likely be buried, vowing to make him 'acknowledge her in death even if he wouldn't in life.' He paid Liberty Creek Baptist thousands of dollars, anonymously of course, in order to honor this request, but could only get them to agree to the plot across the fence."

"She also had arranged for J.T. to finance boarding school up north as soon as you were old enough, Elizabeth, where you could pass for white if you so chose and could be educated with peers deserving of you. She loved her parents but did not want you raised by them once you reached twelve years of age. She felt she had no choice but to allow you to live with them as a young child, especially since she did not want you to learn what her real profession was but wanted you close enough that she could see you. After you were sent up north, Silas was sent to oversee your well-being while there, although you never saw him. He found a family to befriend you and care for you on weekends."

"My father didn't miss a trick, did he, except for letting me know who he was and loving me like a real daughter. I would gladly trade the millions for a real father who cared about me like Sue Ann's father does her."

"Oh, he cared, Elizabeth. He kept up with every detail and with your every movement throughout your whole life. Remember the fight with Booger, Sue Ann, outside Nellie's Ice Cream Shack?"

"Yeah! He passed right by and never gave us a glance when Booger was bullying Elizabeth and little Ben and beating me up. Some father!"

"Why do you think I came out to save the day? I was a young lawyer fresh out of Ole Miss, had just started working for J.T. He came into the office that day mad as hell and directed me to get out there and get that redneck kid away from Elizabeth. That was also when he started keeping up with you, Sue Ann. He appreciated your friendship with Elizabeth. Lucille did, too. That's why the money for your education was included in his will. He always said, 'That girl will be somebody some day.' "

"He sure surprised me. I had him pegged for the assistant to the Imperial Wizard of the KKK. I'm glad I was wrong."

"That's another story. Once Elizabeth decided to come back to Mississippi, J.T. had me hire informants in both organizations, COFO and the Klan, so he would know what his daughter was up against all the time. Even though she wasn't in Barton County, he knew it would just be a matter of time before she'd return, so he wanted to know everything possible in both places, here and Paxton."

"J.T. anonymously donated houses and cars to COFO just for your benefit, Elizabeth. He also wanted to make sure Rock Church was used for the Freedom School once you came back, so he could watch the school from his office in the gin. I hate to say it, but the second time River Road M. B. Church was vandalized, Silas was the culprit. J.T. told him to do just enough damage to make the church insist that the Freedom School be moved. J.T. donated money to cover the damages and more and also paid, anonymously, to help Rock Church decide to allow the Freedom School to be located there."

"Before he died, J.T. had me deliver a check to Rock Church to have the church rebuilt. All those warning calls to you, Elizabeth, and even to the Steiner home, I made at J.T.'s direction. I was also the one who followed your friend, Sue Ann, to keep him from going back to Sadie's house that night the Klan tried to set it on fire. My informant told me the Klan planned to burn a cross there that night, and J.T. didn't want to take a chance on it becoming more than just a cross-burning, knowing the hotheads involved in the terrorist group of 'bad old boys.' Tate drove so fast I was afraid I had made a mistake that night, that maybe he would have been safer dealing with the Klan than with me.

"Once he entered Quitman County, I let him lose me, knowing the Klan had already completed their dirty work by that time of night. Silas made sure Sadie and Roweena were out of the house, too."

"About Silas. Did he rob that gas station? Why was he shot? I actually thought he had died until he pulled me into the brown Buick the other night." I asked hoping to find out if my daddy had any part in this great scheme.

"No, he was no thief. Joe Johnson was the one who stole the money Silas went to prison for in the first place. Silas went to confront him about it, and Joe Johnson shot him, afraid he'd tell the sheriff the truth. Joe claimed Silas was trying to rob him."

"Nagalee didn't know Silas was back until you

girls found him in the gully. Your daddy had no idea he was Nagalee's brother until she told him while she was patching Silas up. Silas was raised by his grandfather, and Zeke knew he had a sister but knew nothing about her. Nagalee asked Zeke to take Silas to St. Louis, where Ben was. When Silas got well, he came back to work for J.T. He's been living across the road on the Harvey plantation the whole time Elizabeth has been back in Mississippi. Silas was kind of a paid guardian angel for you, Elizabeth, a job he took very personally since you were his niece."

"I know he died trying to save me, like Mr. Harvey—uh, my father—did, but I wish I could have known him as an uncle. I've missed out on having a real family. Now my whole family is gone except for Leonia and Ben. Maybe Leonia won't be afraid to be around me now that I have such a big house and can afford some bodyguards. Heck, I can afford a bodyguard for her, too, so Mrs. Taylor won't have to protect her with her trusty vacuum cleaner anymore."

We all laughed, although Elizabeth's longing for family was not funny. Family was not something that could be bought, something J.T. and Annette Harvey had both learned the hard way. I was even more grateful for my family after hearing how badly Elizabeth's family had been screwed up.

I left the room with Elizabeth still trying to sort out all the details of her life, details so complex that it would take a while for comprehension to occur. Acceptance would take even longer, if it was ever to be accomplished at all.

Booby Hooby and I took the long way to Parrish Oaks by way of the old house, back to my roots, my wonderful, simple, deep, uncomplicated, unchanging roots, Taylor roots that could not be bought or sold.

Chapter Twenty-Four
The Legacy

Nagalee's Quilt
A two-room shanty, a cotton field
A life simple, never fast
On a small front porch,
'Neath a big shade tree
I hear echoes of the past.

.

"Cum set on de po'ch, Nagalee
De sun nere off de lan'
Leev yo' quilt in de shanty
And res' yo' cripple han's.

.

De Gud Lawd go'n' let ya'll finish dat quilt
Why ya look sa worry?
Put it down now an' set a spell
Ain't no need to hurry.

.

Bay, see dat sun, how fas' it go?
Dis ol' soul mite be da same
A few mo' sews an' I'll leave dis quilt
So folks'ul 'memba ma name.

.

Ain't no pertier, I'll agree
But what do it all mean?
All dem flow'rs, leafs and sech

Ain't no finer quilt no man seen.
.
Dis quilt ma life, Bay
Dez flow'rs our chillun
De cott'n bolls is de ha'd work
Dat made dis body mo' willin.
.
Dis leaf minds me o' da joys o' ma life
Like dat cool breez unda de shade tree
Dis red bird in de ko'ner
Minds me dat ma chillun be free.
.
Dis big sun in de middle
Jes' where it always stay
I's de bes' pa't o' ma life
Das you, Bay.
.
Ever li'l ol' patch a mem'ry
Dat pink cott'n wuz ma weddin' dress
Dis white wuz Leonia's baptizin'
An de choir singin' robe of ma Bess.
.
Dat blue dot patch wuz Baby Ben's gown
Wuz jes' 'bout too rotten
Dat red plad went on ma strong man's back
It pick a lotta bale o' cotton.
.
Dis black patch wuz ma moanin' dress
Fus fa Mama, den ma pre'chus li'l Burt
To ol' Fanny's and John Kuykendahl's
I figa one mo time ain't gon' hurt.
.
Bay, cum hep dis ol' woman

Dez ol han's so stiff and so'
Stitch in ma name in de ko'ner
Spell it lik ya did once befo.

.

Ni 75 and still can't write yo name
De' now, Nagalee, i's dun
Cum set on de po'ch wif me a spell
No matta now if i's no mo' suns.

.

The shade tree dying,
The front porch fallen
Soybeans but no cotton
Noisy machines and days unending
A simple life forgotten.

.

No headstones, no epitaphs
No one left to mourn her
Only a ragged patchwork quilt
With "Nagalee" in the corner.
                            (August 30, 1964)

.

My pecan trees waved a warm "hello" as I rounded the curve to my home place. "Home place," what a wonderful sound! I loved Parrish Oaks, but it was someone else's home place long before it was mine.

I brushed away the tears as I realized work had started on the new interstate highway, a sign of progress, a sign of passing. My gully was gone. Its crimson banks had disappeared, making way for inhospitable pavement for traffic to speed everywhere and nowhere. Reverberations of Tarzan yelps swinging through muscadine vine jungles and mountain climbers' shrieks of excitement as they raised the flag of success on distant red clay summits had been obscured by mounds of impersonal dirt moved from some place of insignificance, reminiscent of the burial grounds of ancient Indian tribes suffocated by concrete shopping centers.

Then I saw it. The board-and-batten house stood on the hill scraped naked of its tickly green grass and bloomless jonquils; the hill was devoid of shade trees, human emotions, and the sounds of children playing hide-and-seek or beating on washtub African drums. It had fallen to the ground on one end, knocked off its foundation by a bulldozer that stood silent, resting, preparing for its final attack.

I climbed up into my friend's home, my birthplace, and imagined again that night twenty years earlier. My mother had told the story over and over of ordering old Dr. Martin to "sit down…you're not going anywhere, 'cause I'm getting this job over with tonight!"

The next morning I was born, entering the world on the cotton-filled mattress of my parents' bed, protected from the could-have-been grime of a poor family's environment by boiled cistern water and the everyday scrubbing by an immaculate mother driven by a vision of bettering.

I held onto the wall to keep from sliding back down the whop-sided house and climbed my way into the second room. Something caught my eye in the corner, among boxes and trash left from Bay's quick move after Nagalee's death. It was bright yellow: a sun, someone's sun, beamed a reminder of something forgotten but worth saving. I pulled out the remnants of Nagalee's quilt. It had lain neglected a long time. Moths and mice had done their handiwork, but a name could still be deciphered in the bottom corner.

I remembered what Nagalee had said about the Sunday quilt. It was a "story" of her family, memories sewed together with love so her family would never forget. Yet here it was, Nagalee's autobiography as only she could write it, overlooked in the rush of moving, or perhaps left intentionally as if the sight of it was too painful to endure.

I held the quilt to my heart and felt the tears come again. Materially, there was nothing left worth saving, but as a reflection of a dear old woman, an important part of my childhood, it was priceless. It would be placed in the trunk, my chest that was no longer hopeless.

But the quilt was not needed for Nagalee to be remembered. And it didn't matter that my birthplace would be torn down in a few days, leaving not even so much as one small piece of board as a shrine to my ever "being" in the first place. Bricksiding, tarpaper, board and batten, painted wood, marble, velvet, cotton; they were all just materials. What mattered was not the materials but the people, the families who used them to live life as God intended, in peace, harmony, and love.

Elizabeth and I and the generations of children to come would be the legacies of our parents and also of our home place, Mississippi. We would rise above the absinthe of racial hatred and the bigotry of our parents and ancestors and prove that our two races could live together in brotherly or sisterly love, in the forever act of caring and compassion, for we had learned from those special few like Nagalee who knew it first: "Love ain't black and love ain't white, it just is."

Chapter Twenty-Five
The Promise

COFO disbanded and Tate finally gave in to the demands of his parents, leaving Mississippi and me in the spring of 1965. This was incomprehensible to me, ever the optimist, believing forever was actually attainable.

We spent several wonderful months together from that turbulent August in 1964 until he left. The last four months, we hid from our families and Mississippi on a lake, in a small isolated cabin that I rented out near Paxton while I did my student teaching.

But it was more than just a shabby cabin. It was a haven, our utopia, a place where Tate and I could play house and pretend our lives and loves would go on for eternity in our world filled only with brotherly love, void of racial hatred, violence, and misunderstanding. We lived and loved each day like it was our last, with no thought of a reality-based tomorrow.

Tate taught me to fly fish that spring, and when we weren't making love and playing like an old married couple, we were fishing for brim in the lake, listening for the magical explosion as the fish hit our popping bugs, followed by the dance across the glassy water.

At night, we cuddled before the wood-burning stove, our only source of heat, but we needed little warmth, being capable of producing quite enough on our own. Our passion never waned, and to make the cabin reminiscent of the one where we first made love, Tate carved "T.P. Decimbur 1862" on the baseboard beside our bed. It was in this cabin on the lake, with Tobi casting shadows beside us, where we loved unabated and often carelessly.

On one evening in particular, we sat wrapped in a blanket before the wood stove, mesmerized by the amber glow and the red hot crackles and pops created by the green wood we were forced to burn, being at the end of our winter supply. As usual, Tate had his arm around me, playing with my hair, twisting my curls around his fingers, his main entertainment other than when we fondled each other's bodies.

"Can you imagine the hair our kids will have, Sue Ann, both of us with these blonde curly mops? They'll hate us for it."

"Is that a prospective proposal, Mr. Douglas?"

"Just thinking, wishing, ahead a few years. We both have to finish college first."

"Well, I'm ahead of you there. I graduate in a few weeks. Remember?"

"Yeah! But I've got some catching up to do."

Tate became quiet and reflective, making me think he was just enjoying the atmosphere created by the fire.

"There's something I need to tell you, Sue Ann. It's not something we've wanted to think about, but it's happening."

I left his arms and looked into his face, noticing for the first time his serious expression.

"You're scaring me, Tate. What is it?"

"COFO is disbanding. I'll be leaving at the end of the month. Going back to New York, back to my parents and college."

"Oh, I see."

But I didn't see. I had assumed we would stay like this forever and would eventually get married and live happily, somewhere other than Mississippi where "ever after" was possible.

"I can't take you with me right away, Sue Ann, but I promise I'll come back for you. Will you wait for me?"

"Why do I have to wait? I could go with you, get a job teaching, and support us while you go to college."

"No. I want everything perfect for us. No wife of mine is going to be the breadwinner. You didn't answer my question. Will you wait for me?"

"How long are we talking here? Years? Decades? Have you been just stringing me along, Tate? Maybe I should have listened to Daddy the first time he told me to stay away from you."

Furious and hurt, I left the blanket and stormed to the door. As I opened it, Tate reached around, slammed it, and turned me to face him.

"Don't say that, Sue Ann. I love you. I'll always love you, and you know it. I just want things to be right for us when we make that move. Two years, max, and I'll see you every chance I get. Don't be upset. Please tell me you'll wait for me."

As always, I gave in to Tate's affections and promises of love. We vowed to each other to make every moment we had left unforgettable, and sealed it with our usual passion.

Tate left at the end of March assuring me he loved me and would come back to me soon. I never heard from him again.

When I found out I was pregnant, two months later, I called his parents' house and was told Tate was at a going-away party at the home of his fiancée. Tate had been drafted and would, no doubt, be sent to Vietnam to fight in the war he hated. I did not leave my name or number but only told his mother I was an old friend from COFO and that I wished him well.

As I paraded in the Chain of Magnolias procession to receive my college degree, I looked down at my parents' adoring faces, looked hard into my mother's pride and knew she was engraving this moment in her mind forever as she witnessed the accomplishment of the first Taylor to graduate from college. The flutter I felt in my newly protruding belly secretly warned her to savor the moment, for it would be short-lived, to be overshadowed by a mother's worst nightmare, an unwed mother for a daughter.

My secret remained with me until I was unable to hide the inevitable any longer. When I confessed my sin to stunned parents, my daddy sat silent, as if in trauma, with eyes full of fear and pity. Mama reacted just as I knew she would, with rantings and sermons and "How could you do this to me?" The more she demanded I tell her who the "s.o.b." was who was responsible, the more determined I was to remain silent.

After all, I had kept Tate a secret from my parents, at least from my mother, and from my community during those volatile months in the summer of 1964. I vowed to keep him a secret all the way to the delivery room and even to the grave, if necessary.

Mama, furious with my silence, took matters into her own hands. Regardless of what I wanted to do, or not do, she found a doctor who performed illegal abortions in Tennessee. Within the week we were heading north up Highway 51.

"Sue Ann, it's going to be just like normal. You'll see. I'm going home and bake us a chocolate pie. You want fried chicken? We'll have a good supper and all this will be behind us. I bet church will be packed tomorrow. It's fifth Sunday, you know. I better think about what I'm carrying to the church for dinner. Maybe I'll make two chocolate pies. You know there's never a piece of my pie or any of my cooking left over after our fifth-Sunday dinners."

Mama rambled on and on as if this were just any day rather than the end of my life. Daddy drove in silence, but I felt him looking in the mirror at me as I sat frozen in time.

"Watch where you're going, Zeke! You almost ran off the road."

Mama had obviously noticed Daddy's constant gaze in his rearview mirror and intended to put a stop to it, probably afraid we would start some of our silent talking to each other and he might turn around and head back to Parrish Oaks where they both knew I wanted to go.

"Speed up, Zeke! My lord, you drive like you're sixty. The speed limit is 55, not 40."

"You all right back there, Sudi?" Daddy asked into the mirror, letting Mama know he was ignoring her orders.

"Of course she's all right. You just concentrate on driving."

I sat motionless, stoned by guilt and trepidation, indifferent to the conversation from the front seat. My emerald green eyes, Mama's eyes, stared at the trees passing too fast on the side of the two-lane highway.

Why wouldn't she let me make the decision I wanted to? After all, I was almost twenty-one. But in 1965, parents had a large measure of control over their children, and a person couldn't get an abortion just anywhere. Mama was determined this would not ruin my, or rather our, life, and had found a doctor who would "rid the Taylor family of this blight."

We pulled up to a rundown, faded green concrete building in Dyersburg, Tennessee, four hours from home, but the nearest place Mama could find that committed such atrocities. The clinic fit well into the shabby section of town, and my stomach, our stomach, curled into a knot in anticipation of the horror that awaited me.

Minutes later, I lay on a cold metal table in a plain room that, though clean, reeked of disease and crime. The only décor was a calendar, a gift from a propane company probably owned by a deacon in the First Baptist Church.

It had two angelic children on top, a boy and a girl dressed in their Sunday finest, each holding the hand of a parent, a mother and father also dressed for church. Over the picture was written, "Don't send your children to church, take them." I tried to concentrate on the picture and pretend I was somewhere other than on this slab about to commit murder.

The doctor, a thin man with graying hair, did not look like a murderer as he examined me for ten day-long minutes. My body trembled with cold terror.

"Be still, please," the doctor demanded sharply.

"Be still, Sue Ann," Mama repeated, "It will be over soon."

The doctor looked up from the table and said, "She's too far along. It will be more complicated than I thought."

"You mean it will cost more than you said," interpreted Daddy from across the room with a frown on his face.

"At least a hundred more." The doctor directed his statement to Mama, perhaps sensing she was the one in control and the one who would not hesitate to pay the extra money to end her nightmare.

"We'll pay it," assured Mama, "Just get this over with."

Daddy looked at Mama with anger as he approached and looked down at my sweat-soaked, pale face, all that was showing from under the tent sheet the doctor had draped over me and the stirrups to protect the abominable transgression he was about to perform from the watchful gaze of my distraught parents; this was obviously a scene he had become accustomed to, a scene for which he had developed emotional immunity.

"It ain't our decision!" Daddy said it emphatically, more to Mama with a look that told her to be quiet than to the doctor.

"Sue Ann, do you want to go through with this?"

"No, Daddy, I don't," came my tearful reply.

"Then let's get the hell out of here."

I was whisked away to wait out my pregnancy with an uncle in Arkansas. Mama told the lie that I had run off and got married, moving away with my fantasy husband. I went along with the story to pacify Mama and took it one step further, changing my last name to Parish so my baby could grow up in dishonest acceptance in a South that shunned bastards.

Elizabeth had Andy do the legal papers to make the change and helped me decide on Parish as a name, much to Mama's disagreement, sure that this would make the story unbelievable to the locals since our house was named Parrish Oaks. I would not budge on the issue but dropped one "r" to appease her.

Endless days were spent in Arkansas as I holed up away from outsiders. The only exception was the graduate classes I took at the small college nearby. I had only occasional visits from Mama and Daddy.

Mama further embellished the story in the House of Style by telling how I had to divorce my husband soon after our marriage because he had a "bad problem with alcohol and was even abusive when drinking." Her clients all sympathized with my plight of being the young expectant mother without the support of a husband.

I passed my time reading and looking at the children's section of the Sears and Roebuck Catalog, trying to envision what my child, who I was sure would be a boy, would look like. But I was not to have the satisfaction of knowing how close my imagination was. There would be no woods colt, an old southern name which my grandmother, being gentle and unlike most southern women notorious for gossip, preferred to the usual "bastard." There would be no little curly-haired, towheaded boy who walked on his tiptoes for this degenerate daughter of Mississippi.

I buried my son, Tobias Ezekiel Parish, next to Old Ma, 'neath the biggest, most beautiful cedar tree in Liberty Creek Cemetery. Daddy cried more than I did. I guess for the one short day of Tobi's life Daddy felt God had finally given him a boy, only to snatch the precious gift back before he could even feel his little boy's heart beat as he held him in his arms for the first and last time.

My grief was overshadowed by my guilt, and I was sure Tobi's death was a punishment from God for my having strayed from what I knew was right, for allowing passion and love of a man to supersede my Christian values and strength.

But in that last instant before God carried out this great retribution, He had a change of heart and decided perhaps the penalty was too harsh, especially for one who had been so faithful for twenty years of life in practicing virtue and, in the last few years of growing in maturation, keeping virginity intact. In that last moment of predetermination, he relinquished his pride, and gave me a healthy baby girl, a living part of twins. I named her Elizabeth Ann Taylor Parish after Liz Bess and me, but from her first day of life, she was my Betsy.

As I held her in my arms in the back seat of my parents' car on our way home from the hospital, I made a vow to myself, one that I would never break.

"I am Sue Ann Taylor Parish, daughter of a new Mississippi. Nothing can prevent me from being what I want to be. I will not tolerate condemnation and will not stop until I have made a name for myself, a name Betsy can be proud of. With God's help, all is possible.

"Tomorrow will be a brilliant forever, Baby Girl. No regrets."

Epilogue

The Ghost

"Earth to Sue Ann!"

Elizabeth's voice brought me out of my reverie. Once again, as had happened way too much lately, my mind had wandered back to Tate Douglas. With each stage of Betsy's growth, and especially as she became a teenager, the more of her father I could see in her, and the more I was reminded of my love and his betrayal.

"Methinks you're on a ghost chase in your mind, dear friend. Am I right?"

"Yes. You're right as usual. I think about Tate a lot as I look at Betsy."

"Sue Ann, you need to stop waiting for ghosts and get on with your life. Tate was not your knight in shining armor, and he's not off on a crusade dreaming of the day he can return to you. And you have to stop punishing yourself. God forgave you the first time you asked. Now you have to do the same and allow yourself to love again, and I don't mean the odd dinner date every two months, like you've done for fourteen years. If you don't do it for yourself, then do it for Betsy. She deserves a chance to have a real family with a mama and a daddy. Believe me, I know what it's like to grow up without parents."

We were sitting on the porch of Parrish Oaks, the

house I had become caretaker of once my parents moved to south Mississippi to expand their businesses. Elizabeth and I watched as our daughters practiced cheerleading under the giant oaks.

Though our girls were two years apart in age, they were inseparable, just as their moms had been at that age. Much had happened since our childhood, but the one thing that remained constant was our friendship.

Liz Bess had grown up to be Elizabeth, wife of prominent lawyer Andy Smithers who, though several years her senior, had made her extremely happy. She and Andy lived in Five Oaks.

But even though Elizabeth had married her own knight and finished a law degree at Ole Miss, she would never be completely accepted as a prominent member of Bartonville society. Elizabeth was the product of a racially mixed relationship and had married a white man, something still taboo in Mississippi in the 1980s. She claimed she didn't have time for bridge with the little old blue-hairs anyway, since she was CEO of Harvey Enterprises, the vast business interests left to her by her father, J.T. Harvey.

Elizabeth and I were more alike than she cared to admit. Each of us pretended we did not need acceptance from our community, but the truth was we both were overachievers because of it, always trying to convince someone, perhaps ourselves, that we were worthy. This was a contradiction to the "don't-give-a-care" attitude we both sported to the public and to each other.

I had done a good job of convincing myself that the reason I pretended to have been married to Betsy's father was for Betsy's sake. The truth was it was more from my own sense of denial. Perhaps Elizabeth was right. I was waiting for ghosts, for Tate to ride up one day and say he had never loved anyone but me.

Of course, if this fantasy ever became a reality, I'd have a lot of explaining to do to Betsy and everyone in the closed society of Bartonville, Mississippi, beginning with my fictitious married name of Parish. I had lived this life for fifteen years, so long that in my mind the story was true.

Being referred to as Mrs. Parish always made me feel like a traitor and a liar and was the main reason I had been determined to get my doctorate. After several years of hard work, I earned the right to be Dr. Sue Ann Parish, a successful principal, never having to explain titles and phantom husbands again.

"You're right, Elizabeth. I do need to get on with my life. It's time I did something about that dream of mine. When school is out, Betsy and I are moving to Alaska. That is, if I can get a job there. There's a job fair coming up in June in Fairbanks. I'll be there with resume in hand."

"Wait a minute! I only meant you should start mingling, maybe date someone. Think this through, Sue Ann. What about Betsy? Do you think she'll be willing to give up Annie and Parrish Oaks? And all she and Annie have talked about is trying out for cheerleader in high school. To think, Sue Ann, they have always been able to go to school together even though they were in different classes, something history did not allow us to do. Annie will be devastated to lose her best friend. I don't want you to chase ghosts, but I don't want you to run away from them, either, especially not to the end of the world—the frozen end, at that."

"Betsy has always wanted to go to Alaska. We've

been reading about it since she was just a toddler. She's up for a challenge. Besides, I told her if we ever move there, she can have a sled dog. I promise we'll come home every summer. Maybe you and Annie can visit us there."

"Don't count on it. Remember, I'm the one who likes the Mississippi heat. If you're really serious about this, I know you'll do it. Just don't forget where your roots are, Sue Ann, and don't forget your best friend, who will always love you unconditionally."

Betsy and I left for Alaska in August, headed to a small village in the interior where I would be principal/teacher in a two-teacher school. Here, Betsy and I could be ourselves without pretending, part of a community of dog mushers, trappers, gold miners, writers, artists, shady characters running from the law, and rugged individualists in general, each one with a story, whether told or secret.

My daughter would grow to maturity in the "frozen end of the world" and so would I, carving my place and my identity at last.

A word about the author...

Dr. Sue Clifton is a traveler, fly fisher, retired educator, present-day ghost hunter, lover of all things vintage, and author of seven novels. Dr. Sue, as she is known, can't remember a time when she did not write, beginning with two plays published at sixteen.

Her writing career was put on hold while she traveled the world with her husband Woody in his work and with her own career as a teacher and school administrator in Mississippi, Alaska, New Zealand, and on the Northern Cheyenne Reservation in Montana. The places she has lived provide rich background for the novels she creates.

Dr. Sue now divides her time among Montana, Arkansas, and Mississippi. *The Gully Path* is the first novel in the Daughters of Parrish Oaks series, with three novels to follow.

For more information about Dr. Sue, go to:
www.drsueclifton.com.

Thank you for purchasing
this publication of The Wild Rose Press, Inc.

If you enjoyed the story, we would appreciate
your letting others know by leaving a review.

For other wonderful stories,
please visit our on-line bookstore at
www.thewildrosepress.com.

For questions or more information
contact us at
info@thewildrosepress.com.

The Wild Rose Press, Inc.
www.thewildrosepress.com

Stay current with The Wild Rose Press, Inc.

Like us on Facebook
https://www.facebook.com/TheWildRosePress

And Follow us on Twitter

https://twitter.com/WildRosePress